Fate Howled

Fated Huntress

Tiffani Skye

To my husband, Dan. Once again, thank you for your endless support.

Chapter One

Life was an egg, and Fate liked to cook. Fate cracked your life wide open, then scrambled it all up. Have you ever had an unwanted houseguest that force-fed you breakfast? That's Fate. She stuffed it down your throat even though it may be hard to swallow.

I crouched behind a boulder in the pitch-black. Listening. I closed my eyes and focused on the sounds. My breathing slowed. *Thump...thump...thump.* The small squeak of shoes alerted me that someone was behind me, but I remained in my low position and bluffed that I hadn't heard my assailant.

Whoosh. Metal rose in the air. Without a second guess, I rolled and barely escaped. The sword crashed down onto the giant rock. I hopped to my feet and sprinted.

That was close. Too close.

I leaped over a log. I touched down like a ballerina and glanced over my shoulder. I couldn't let them capture me—if they did, then it was all over. I kept running. I didn't have another option. In my peripheral vision, a copper wolf

1

flanked me to my right. To my left, a strapping man. He was either a Hunter or a Vampire. In each scenario, I was doomed.

I ran harder, faster. Only a bit further and I'd be in the clear. The copper wolf barked, and two more wolves appeared at its side. I groaned. A girl just couldn't catch a break.

I didn't see the line of intimidating beefcakes till I was closer. I tried to come to a stop. My beat-up black Adidas slid against the gravel. It would have been so cool if I hadn't lost my balance, landed on my forearm, and ate dirt. The bitter taste lingered on my tongue. I spat and sputtered, trying to eliminate the powder from my mouth.

I twisted back to the way I'd come in hopes of making a retreat. Fear surged in my chest, and my heart pounded. There were too many of them. They were closing in too fast. I was surrounded.

Uh-oh.

I didn't stand a chance going through them. My odds weren't great. I knew that. They knew that. If I couldn't go through them, then I would have to take a detour.

I searched for any weakness in their formation. There was a tiny opening between the beefcakes and the wolves. It was like they would contract cooties if they stood too close to each other. I decided to use the oldest trick in the book.

"Ow!" I dropped to the ground. I wrapped my hands around my knee and pretended to wince in pain. "Ow," I cried again, only this time more theatrical.

The three groups of assailants closed in. Triumphant faces stared at me. I mustered up my courage and sprang from my spot. I made a mad dash between the wolves and the beefcakes. The four-legged predators chased after me, snapping at my heels. Sounds of heavy panting lingered behind me as I stepped closer to safety.

There it was. My key to victory.

It was on a square platform, hovering off the ground. There was no ladder for me to use. How was I going to reach it?

Howls and laughter reverberated in my wake. My breathing quickened and my chest pinched with panic. I was so close. So close, but so far away.

Blue orbs flew past me. "Sorcerers," I hissed. "Crap."

I was a goner. No one was coming to save me. With trembling fingers, I fiddled with the necklace my father gave me. If I could somehow get up there, then all of this would end.

There was a tree a short—but sizeable—distance from the white floating target. If I fell, I'd be injured and captured. If I succeeded, I'd be safe.

"Go big or go home," I muttered.

With a running leap, I grabbed a branch. I hoisted myself onto it, and the dark bark scraped across the palms. Not wasting time, I began to ascend. Halfway up, I glanced down. Wolves circled the tree, waiting for me to fall. Beyond them, I didn't find any Hunters, Vampires, or Sorcerers. I climbed faster.

I took another glance at the wolves. They had disappeared. Something was up, but I couldn't spare a second to figure out why they'd changed their tactic.

I reached a branch that extended the furthest to the platform. Luckily, it was wide and sturdy enough that I could walk out on it.

"This is stupid. I'm stupid. This entire situation is stupid." I puffed out my cheeks and exhaled. "I can't turn into a pansy now."

I pushed off the trunk, took two gigantic steps, and jumped. For a moment, the air brushed over me, and I savored it. This was the closest I would ever get to flying. I reveled in the joy that this would all be over in a matter of seconds.

Only, I saw it too late—a Vampire was waiting.

I flailed my arms. I tried to think of something. Anything. I caught the edges of the platform and held on for dear life. Literally.

Death by jumping. Or rather, death by stupidity. I could imagine the headlines.

"You are making this too easy," the Vampire said.

I strained my neck up and studied him. He had chin-length black wavy hair and donned a completely black outfit. Someone needed to introduce him to the rainbow.

"Bite me," I shot back. My legs dangled, and my grip threatened to loosen.

"Promises, promises." He moved closer. He knew what he was doing. With one small step, he would crush my bones.

Snickers echoed from below. I peered down, and the beefcakes were underneath me. It was creepy that a collective group of hotties would have the same facial expression.

I swung my legs and built momentum. I put my forearm on the platform and swung over. My leg hit my opponent, and his knees buckled. He dropped, and I scrambled to stand.

The Vampire up-righted himself and faced me. Victory was almost in my grasp, but so was falling to my demise. He looked at me, then at the item.

It was going to be a fight till the end.

We stared at each. Waiting for the other to make a

move. His eyes lit up with the thrill of the hunt. While I narrowed mine.

"You won't win," he boasted.

Challenge accepted!

The Vampire launched himself in my direction. But I was faster. I darted toward the object and swiped at it. I gripped the red cotton fabric in my fingers. I landed on my stomach. I smirked back at the Vampire and stifled a laugh. The Vampire's face contorted in anger, and he pounded his fists against the white surface.

I stood and did the Cabbage-Patch—my go-to choice for a celebratory dance.

"In your face!" I yelled at the Vampire, dropping the octave of my voice.

The lights in the auditorium came on, and the simulation terminated. The platform disappeared, sending me straight to the floor. I touched down in a pair of strong arms.

"Blayde," I said, my tone light and happy.

"Princess." He beamed at me.

My heart melted at the sight of him.

I swear Fate sculpted him out of clay; six feet two inches, chiseled biceps, a shapely butt in jeans, scruffy beard, dark-brown hair, and blue eyes with flakes of amber. Mister Tall, Dark, and Handsome was a beautiful salt-'n'-pepper wolf Shifter whose dad was the Alpha King of North America. He was also my *mate*.

I'd been at the Eastland Hunter Academy for a few weeks now. I thought it would be similar to high school. Basic information with basic classes. Boy, was I wrong. It was like MIT or Caltech. For the first few weeks, I had to have the teachers explain things to me at an elementary level. I didn't expect being a Hunter to be so complicated.

Being a Huntress was even worse; higher expectations were placed upon me than the other Hunters. It was exasperating.

Blayde placed me on my feet and stood next to me. Our arms grazed each other, sending a tingle through my body. No matter how many times it happened, it still surprised me. In the past few weeks, he hasn't once pushed me out of my comfort zone. He was a real gentleman. Annoying, but a gentleman. He hoped I'd use this time to see why we belonged together. I was using this time to show him my more amiable qualities...like being a pain in the butt. If he could truly care for me, then we might have a chance.

I waved the red triangle of fabric in the air. "What is the score now? Sixteen to zero?"

Ricardo and Agrona walked toward me.

"I owe you some double fudge brownie ice cream." Ricardo shook his head. "When will you stop being on the defensive and participate in a fight?"

Ricardo was a Spanish Adonis. A model specimen and his accent only made him dreamier.

"Why should I change my game plan when it obviously works? I don't die, no one gets hurt, and I win. It is the perfect tactic." I moved the flag back and forth in front of my mentor.

In the beginning, Ricardo forced me to play "capture the flag"—his goal was for me to practice battle strategy and how to survive an attack.

"We should make her protect the flag instead. She would have to engage in combat that way," Agrona said with a hint of teasing.

I shot her an icy glare.

The hot, dark-haired, medium-complexioned goddess

was my best friend and as such was supposed to be on my side.

"That's not a bad idea. You must preserve the flag. If someone takes it, you lose. You defend your position until everyone has been defeated or time runs out." Ricardo beamed at his new scheme.

His arm had to be getting sore from patting his own back. Since coming to the Eastland Hunter Academy and being in charge of my training, he kept finding inventive ways to torture me.

"Nah, that sounds like too much work," I declared, smoothing out my blonde hair. I tended to leave these games looking like I'd wrestled a hippopotamus.

"If you win, I'll give you a brownie with your ice cream," Ricardo spurred.

I tapped my index finger to my lips and took a second to think about it. It had been twenty-two days since I'd eaten a gooey pastry, and I missed them. *Dearly*. Ricardo learned early on that I would almost do anything containing cocoa, so he'd wiped the school of anything chocolate. He used it as an incentive to get me to try harder.

"No deal." I stared at their stunned faces. Even Blayde was taken aback. "I'll do it if you let me go into town."

A growl slipped from Blayde. I arched a brow at him, and I beheld his clenched fists at his sides. Another rumble escaped him, and without a second thought, I flicked him on the nose. Blayde's face went from furious to shocked to annoyed. I rolled my eyes and faced Ricardo again.

"Do we have a deal?" I asked.

Ricardo's mouth formed a tight line, and his gaze flitted in Blayde's direction.

"No, Bonita. No deal. There is no neighboring town for you to explore, and it wouldn't be irresponsible for me to let you leave the safety of the academy," Ricardo said, his Spanish accent thick.

I pursed my lips. No one had told me what city we were in. Everyone had kept our location a secret for "my own protection." Blah. Blah. Blah. And here I was thinking we were done with all the secrets.

"Is that so? Answer me this, if there are no towns nearby, then why does the academy receive almost daily deliveries?" I asked.

From my own curiosity, I noticed the same four delivery drivers. They came close to every day, if not every other day. If the Dean paid these companies to drive to the middle of nowhere, their shipment fees must be astronomical.

One by one, I made eye contact with each of them. A smirk from Agrona reassured me that I was right. Ricardo tried to seem disapproving, but a hint of amusement danced around the corners of his mouth.

Blayde. Oh, Blay Blay. His arms crossed his broad chest and his eyes narrowed. This wasn't the first time we'd had this argument. He assumed I'd sneak out and never return. Well, I'd definitely sneak out, but I'd always return.

"Ha! She figured it out. Ten points to Cedar!" Chantel yelled, sashaying toward us.

I'd recently introduced her to the Harry Potter movies, and she was way too obsessed. How she had gone her whole life without hearing about them was beyond me.

Chantel received a collective glare from them. Her shoulder-length brown curls bounced as she slowed her steps. She lifted her hands in the air, surrendering to the potential onslaught from my babysitters.

With their backs to me, I decided to make my escape.

My stomach grumbled. There were bound to be some snacks in the mess hall.

"This isn't over, Bonita!" Ricardo's voice echoed across the simulation room.

I didn't give pause. I didn't acknowledge what he said. I didn't even give him a shake of my head. I jogged to the doors to go see the one man who knew my heart inside and out.

Chapter Two

Whistling, I walked through the off-white hallways to visit the person who would never let me down. I struggled to focus on anything else besides the stench of dirty gym socks and mothballs.

I entered, and the scent of peach cobbler hit me. The mess hall was empty, and it reminded me of high school—different tables were claimed by different cliques. One half for all the high and mighty. You know, the ones who wore a sweater tied around their neck and wanted to date a senator's daughter. The other half thought they were bad to the bone with their ripped jeans and biker jackets. I was still waiting for them to carry motorcycle helmets like a girl carried a purse.

In the middle were the teachers. The teachers ate with their respective species. On the first day, my so-called friends sat in the middle. Other Hunters, for both segregated groups, offered me a spot. The pressure got to me. I ended up hiding in the kitchen. That was how I'd met the most wonderful man.

I skipped to the door. I tried to open it but instead, my

face mashed into it. Annoyed, I pushed off, and I rubbed my cheek. In the three weeks I'd been here, this door has never been locked.

I pressed my ear to my blockade, and a muffled melody filtered through. My nostrils flared, and I released a long breath. If music was playing, then he was in there. His harmonious voice carried through the walls. He was going to get an earful for locking me out.

The roll-up coiled serving door was open with just a gap. It gave me an idea. Hopping my butt onto the counter, I swiveled, swinging my legs up and through the slot. That was the easy part. Hands pressed against the counter, I shimmied my way under it. It was a tight squeeze, but I managed.

Without being able to see into the area, I didn't know what waited on the other side. My feet crashed into a pot, sending it to the floor. *Clang.* My shoulders bunched and cringed at the reverberation.

"I told you to stay out of my kitchen!" he yelled, his dulcet tone turned furious. "You stupid Hunters think you are Angel's gift."

I caught a glimpse of him coming around the corner. He shook a ladle in the air, flinging soup onto the muted-yellow walls. He stopped as soon as he spotted me. The tension in his body melted, and the ladle came to his side.

He was wearing a chef's hat and jacket. Even under his uniform, you could see the shape of his gut. He wasn't built like the others at this school. You could tell he enjoyed the fruit of his labor. He reminded me of a surfer who'd let himself go—dark-blond dreads and a light-brown beard. Since meeting him, I hadn't been able to discern his age. He appeared similar to a Human washed-out thirty-year-old, but he acted like a grumpy grandpa. Every time I asked him, he evaded.

"Quin." I glared, pointing my index finger at him. "You locked me out. I thought our love was stronger than that." My tone softened, and I allowed some teasing to shine through. I added a sniffle for dramatic effect.

"Cedar, I assumed you were someone else." He walked over to me and pinched my cheek. "Our love is strong as a raging fire. Just don't let Blayde hear us. I enjoy having my limbs attached to my body."

I scoffed despite the fact there was a hint of truth to it. Blayde has been patient with me, but it didn't mean he liked seeing me with other men.

I bent down and picked up the pot, and Quin snatched a rag to wipe up the trail of soup he'd left behind.

I studied him, making mental notes about his movements. I'd yet to figure out what magical species he belonged to. I deduced he wasn't a Vampire. I'd ruled out Hunter because he fostered disdain for them. And, well, I'd never seen one with a gut before—didn't mean there wasn't one. At some point, I'd asked Blayde if Quin was a Shifter. He shrugged. I'd asked Chantel if he was a Sorcerer. She'd laughed and said, "He wishes."

"What do I owe this pleasure to?" Quin asked after he finished cleaning up.

"I'm hurt. I can't come here to relish in your company." I batted my eyes.

The small hitch of his eyebrows let me know he didn't believe what I'd said.

"Fine," I conceded. "I'm hiding from my babysitters."

"You mean friends." He led me to where he was working.

I raised my right shoulder to signify he wasn't wrong. I

was just annoyed with them. I grabbed a spoon from a drawer and edged closer to the liquid meal.

"Don't. You. Dare." He slapped my hand.

I jutted my bottom lip out and crossed my arms against my chest. I laid on my pout thick, only because whatever he made was divine. His cooking was the best thing about the academy. I hopped up and sat on the counter next to him, earning me a frigid glare.

"It is either I sit here, or I dip my spoon into your pretty little pot." I lifted the utensil in the air, ready to strike.

He grabbed a wooden ladle and shoved it at me. "Here. Make yourself useful."

I set my utensil next to me and took it from his fingers. I dipped it into the broth and moved it clockwise.

After making sure I wouldn't ruin his precious creation, he turned from me and focused on chopping vegetables. Quin engrossed himself in his carrots, never glancing in my direction.

Now was the perfect time.

I pulled the spoon out and swiped my index finger along it. I brought it to my lips and licked the soup off. *Mmm.* My taste buds sang rounds of Hallelujah.

"I saw that," he said.

I froze. How did he know? You think by now I would've figured it out—I'd only done this five hundred and twenty-three times before. Give or take. He came over and dropped the carrots into the silver pot. I tried to look ashamed regardless of it being a lie.

"Have you heard about a dagger or magic crystals?" I asked casually.

I hadn't learned anything about the dagger the Dark Master wanted. Even spending what little free time I had in the library at the academy, I still wasn't well-informed.

"How was capture the flag?" he asked, not taking his gaze off the vegetables.

I narrowed my eyes into slits. He changed the subject. Avoided my question. Either he didn't want to seem ignorant or he was hiding something.

But going with the flow, I faked enthusiasm. "I kicked butt!"

He looked up, and a proud grin spread across his face. He got almost as much enjoyment as I did from beating them.

"Did you engage in one-on-one?" he asked.

Ugh.

"Why is everyone harping on me to switch to offensive? I'm Defensive Huntress of the Year."

"A day will come when you run yourself into a corner and your only way out will be by force. You'd be wise in practicing." His lips pressed tight into a line. He extracted the ladle from my hand and stirred.

He didn't have to say it out loud. The disappointment showed on his face. My throat constricted. I hated letting him down. Quin was the closest thing I had to a father.

Enough with my pity party. I'd hidden long enough. Time to get to class.

I jumped off the counter and took a few steps toward the door.

"I almost forgot. I have a special treat for you."

That stopped my feet in my worn Adidas shoes from taking another step. "Gimme, gimme, gimme," I pleaded and bounced up and down.

He went into the walk-in fridge for a moment before he reappeared. He held out a small box wrapped like a present, complete with a red bow on top.

I scrutinized Quin, and his expression lit up with excitement. A wide grin spread across my face, mirroring his. He nudged the box toward me. I didn't need to be told twice. Lifting the lid, I wanted to weep. It was the most beautiful thing I had ever seen. I flung my arms around him, giving him a quick embrace.

I removed the brownie from the container and bit into it. A stifled moan escaped. This was the best confection to pass my lips in three weeks.

"I love you," I sighed.

A thunderous growl interrupted my bliss. A loud crash followed, shaking the walls.

"Out! Out now before he destroys my kitchen!" Quin pushed me out the door and locked it before I could mutter a word.

I shoved the brownie in my mouth, trying to hide the evidence when I noticed a heap of tables next to the wall. Blayde stalked toward me, and he became furrier with every tick of the clock.

Oh gosh. He might have heard some things out of context.

He halted, not closing the gap that separated us, and fumed. His eyes glowed amber, signifying his wolf was close to the surface.

Even though he was patient and allowed me to lead our relationship, I could only imagine how he felt with me professing my love for Quin. Secretly, I loved seeing him get territorial. It helped me see that the attraction between us was real and mutual.

I stepped toward him slowly, as if approaching a frenzied chimpanzee. I didn't want to make the situation worse. I stopped when we were toe to toe. I tilted my head up to look at him, and I expected his attention to be on me. But it wasn't. His glare was on the kitchen. I placed my hand on his chest and created shushing sounds. I made circling motions with my finger and watched the tension in his shoulders relax.

"You're not that tough," I joked.

He dropped his gaze down, and I saw the emotion in his eyes. The rage extinguished, and a longing replaced it. My heart squeezed. I wished I could give him what he desired. I wished I could declare him mine, but the truth was, I didn't know if what I felt wasn't a byproduct of the mate bond.

Blayde's fists loosened, and he wrapped his arms around me, pulling me into a hug. I took a deep breath and smelled his earthy musk scent. Two weeks ago, his black leather jacket lost his aroma and gained mine. I gave it back to him and he wore it for a few days before I mentioned he looked like some of the Hunters. I haven't seen him wear it since.

I lace my hand in his and tugged him out of the mess hall. His thumb brushed my skin, and I led him through the halls and out the doors.

We stepped outside, and a blast of sunlight hit me. I plopped down on the grass and let the August sunshine warm me.

I closed my eyes and enjoyed the quiet. It was hard to find time alone. Blayde rustled beside me. I sensed he was still tense from my interaction with Quin.

"I don't love him. At least not in the way you are thinking," I said.

Blayde lolled next to me.

"He offered me a brownie. Before you get worked up about it, I deserved the chocolatey goodness. I have been working my butt off and doing my best."

Blayde released a throaty chuckle. "If I knew that's all it took for you to say I love you, then I would've given you one a while ago."

I slugged him on the arm, which only made him laugh harder. "Jerk," I mumbled.

"I'm sorry, Princess." He wiped his joyous tears away. He rolled to lie on his side, leaning on his forearm.

"You think you are so charming," I said sarcastically.

"Because I am." Blayde's mouth tipped up into one of his knee-weakening smiles.

My heart went into overdrive.

I gave him a once over. The summer sun had tanned his skin, and his hair was tousled by running his hand through it too many times. His amber-flaked blue eyes held slight amusement and warmth.

"Like what you see, Princess?" Blayde smirked.

Uh-oh. Busted. Heat flooded my cheeks, and I knew they were red.

"You wanna know what I love the most?" I asked, trying to place attention on anything else besides my embarrassment.

His body stilled, and his expression turned earnest.

"Your eyes. For when I stare into them, I see my reflection. And hot dang! I look good." I chuckled.

"You should learn about some of my finer qualities, like my lips." He winked.

Excitement filled me. "I just might do that," I whispered. My voice raspy; I moved closer. Only mere inches separated us.

Blayde froze. His gaze scoured my face, searching for any sign that I was serious. His lighthearted demeanor disappeared, and his pupils dilated. My pulse raced. It would be so easy to lean in and kiss him. But not yet.

"Maybe another time, though." I sprang up and ran from him.

A playful growl came from behind me, and I couldn't

help but snicker. Shifters loved the game of chase. I wondered how far I could get before he caught up. I smiled and remembered that once Blayde had told me that he had a feeling he would always be chasing me.

I racked my brain for any way to elude him. I couldn't maneuver past Blayde if I tried to exit where we had come through. I'd have to go to the doors connected to the training room.

I pumped my arms and raced across the open lawn. The entrance was in range. I was almost in the clear.

A hand enclosed on my ankle, and I fell, glancing at my captor, Blayde gave me a smug smile, and his grip tightened.

"Get off me, King Kong!" I shook my foot.

Blayde chuckled, and I kicked my other at his wrist. He released, and I scrambled to stand.

"One, two, Blayde's coming for you," Blayde called after me.

A Nightmare on Elm Street quote. Out of all the time to reference pop culture, he picked now.

I sprinted away and focused on getting to the building. It took me a second to realize I didn't hear Blayde behind me. I scanned my surroundings. He wasn't anywhere in sight. Maybe I'd left him in my dust. I returned my attention to the door, only to see Blayde positioned in front of it.

I skidded to a halt, and we eyed each other, waiting for the other to make a move. Just like an old Western movie.

"I could do this all day, Princess," Blayde said.

What would make this situation perfect would be if a tumbleweed blew between us.

"Bring it on, Blay Blay," I shot back.

Before I could overthink it, I pushed off the ground and charged toward him. At the exact moment, he did the same.

I dropped to my knees and slid against the grass, laughing as I outplayed him. Standing, I threw him a smirk over my shoulder. He quickly turned on his heel and did a one-eighty to face me. I was mere seconds from winning our little game of chase. I reached out and placed my palm on the doorknob. The safety of the training room beckoned.

Strong arms encircled my waist, pulling me from the threshold. Blayde swung me around, claiming victory. I thrashed, refusing to accept defeat. We tumbled down in a tangled heap. Laughter bubbled up in my throat, and Blayde joined me. It felt good to blow off some steam.

We lay there for a few minutes with me in his embrace. I wouldn't admit it to him, but I loved being in his arms. He made me feel safe, cared for.

"Princess," Blayde whispered.

His breath tickled my skin, sending a shiver down my spine.

"Blay Blay." I strained my neck to look at him.

Blayde scowled. He hated my nickname for him. But I enjoyed the rise I got out of him.

"I wanted to say goodbye before I left," he said.

That had my attention. My stomach knotted at the thought of him leaving. I turned in comforting hold to face him.

"Leave?" My voice squeaked. "Where to?"

My eyebrows cinched together, and he lazily drew circles down my spine.

"I like it when you are concerned about me."

I snorted. "More like I'm relieved," I lied.

"We both know that isn't true." He sighed. "I'm going on a run with some of the other Shifters for the full moon. It's only for a few days." He sounded like he was trying to reassure both of us.

The back of his hand brushed against my cheek. I leaned into it, enjoying his gentle touch.

I lingered in his arms without saying a word. I'd learned that around a full moon, Shifters spent the majority of their time in their animal form. That big rock in the sky called to their animal half—think the way lunar phases affected tidal waves. Wolves would run and hunt deer. The only instance I remembered Blayde being gone for a run was back at my stepmom's house. That was weeks ago.

"You haven't been on a pack outing in weeks. Have you not gone because of me?" Guilt burned in my throat. I hate being the reason he remained behind.

Silence stretched between us, and he didn't speak for a long minute.

"I stayed because you're my top priority. You mean everything to me." He rested his forehead against mine, and for a moment, the world stood still. "I won't be too far away, Princess. I promise I'll return."

His promise resonated in my soul. I wanted so badly to utter the words he craved to hear, but something held me back. I couldn't. Not yet.

With an exaggerated exhale, he withdrew. He lightly kissed my hand, and before I knew it, he disappeared. My heart squeezed. I hated myself for being sappy. He was only going to be gone for a few days. Gosh, I hadn't known him for very long. I lay in the grass for a few minutes longer. But the ache in my heart became too much. This was silly.

I got up and headed toward my room. I needed the distraction of girls' night.

Chapter Three

My knees bounced, and my fingers tapped my thighs. I'd been waiting for Chantel and Agrona to arrive for girls' night. Patience had never been a virtue of mine. I didn't know what was keeping them. They both had rooms next to mine, even though they could've had teachers' apartments. Blayde was forbidden to be on the same floor as me—it was designated for Huntresses. Since the lack thereof, the living quarters never got used.

My room was almost a complete apartment in itself. All it was missing was a kitchen, which there was plenty of space for. When you walked in, you were greeted by a sofa and two armchairs. Accompanied by a fuzzy blue rug. Off to the left was a full bathroom. It had a shower and a separate white farmhouse tub. It was glorious. My bed was to the right of my lounge area. I had a plain white comforter with pillows galore. Nearly every girls' night ended up in a pillow fight. For the first get-together, we utilized the academy's credit card and bought all the furnishings. We wanted to see how far I could push before backlash—I still hadn't gotten there.

I jumped at the knock on my door. I threw it open and launched myself into their arms. Admittedly, it would've been embarrassing if it hadn't been them. Chantel waltzed in and flopped on the couch. Agrona froze just past the threshold.

"What are you wearing?" Agrona's voice was inquisitive. Her gaze roamed me from head to toe.

"What? These old rags?" I gestured to my outfit.

I had changed into dark jeans that made me look bootylicious and paired it with a deep-red sequin top. To top it off, black kitten boots. I was ready to party.

Chantel perked up. "Are we going out?" She was practically bouncing in glee.

"No, no, no. We promised that Cedar would stay inside the academy grounds." Agrona crossed her arms.

"Oh, come on! We deserve some fun. It has been forever since we've had a real girls' night. Let's go to the nearest town and let our hair down," I coaxed.

"No," Agrona said firmly, yet I knew she was itching to.

Chantel stood and pointed her wand at herself, mumbling a spell. In an instant, her brown curls were long dread braids. She fashioned a halter top that showed off her light-brown skin and bell bottoms. Tubular.

"Come on. Blayde is gone for a few days. Prisoners are allowed more freedom than me," I argued.

Agrona relaxed her shoulders, releasing some of the tension she was holding.

"Besides, when we come back, you can brag to Blayde that you are a better protector than he is. It would kill him."

Agrona chewed on the corner of her mouth. I could see the proverbial thought wheels turning in her head. Chantel decided to lay it on thick—she dropped to her knees, widened her eyes, and jutted her trembling bottom lip. She put puppies to shame. Agrona released a defeated sigh.

"If, and I mean *if* we go, then you have to follow what I say. I don't want you taking any unnecessary risks or getting hurt," Agrona said.

Chantel got up, and we bounced beside Agrona.

Time to party.

Agrona quickly went to her room to change. She returned before I was done brushing my teeth.

"How are we getting out of here?" I asked.

"Easy peasy, lemon squeezy," Chantel said.

She placed her hand on my shoulder, and Agrona touched Chantel's arm.

"Hold on tight." She raised her wand in the air. "*Effugium,*" she said, and we were gone.

Within a blink, we were in my room, and the next we were standing in a dimly lit area. One that smelled. Atrociously. Like garbage and vomit. I let go of Chantel and stumbled into the swaying alley. I planted my palm on the rough brick of one of the buildings, steadying myself. And I made sure the world didn't go topsy-turvy.

"Oh, sorry. I should've mentioned the aftereffects of this spell if it is your first time. Sorry, Cedar." Chantel laced my arm through hers and helped me balance until the reaction subsided.

Chantel led us down the alleyway, and we stood on the sidewalk facing a nightclub. The last time I was in a club, Mrs. Rose cornered me in the bathroom. That night forced the rest of the events to fall with cascading speed. Without that night, I wouldn't be here today. Without that night, the magical world would still be hidden from me. Without that night, I wouldn't have met Blayde. My epiphany slammed into me. And for a moment—a small moment—I was glad for Mrs. Rose's intervention. Even if Jordan was the puppet master.

A dull ache filled my chest. Jordan was my best friend. A Hunter. We grew up together. It stung to have all of that thrown away. Thrown away by his betrayal.

We crossed the road, and I shook Jordan from my thoughts. Buildings were close together and palm trees lined the street like sentinels. A light fog gave the city an ominous feeling, while a slight cool breeze made me think we were near the ocean.

"Are we in California?" I asked as we marched up to the club entrance.

"Umm, maybe." Chantel bit the inside of her cheek.

The bouncer ushered us in, and we were immediately surrounded by a sea of people. I watched them cavort and sway to the music. Strobe lights crossed the room in shades of blue, purple, and pink. Bass thumped in my eardrums. Voices faded away. The sensations became too much. Shutting my eyes tight, I covered my ears. I repeated "la la la la" over and over to drown out the deafening noise.

Hands on my shoulders shook me. I peeked at Agrona. Her lips moved in an inaudible cadence. I couldn't hear her over the loud buzzing sound. She motioned for me to draw in a deep breath. I filled my lungs and held it. One. Two. Three. Four. Five. And release. I duplicated the action until the high-pitched hum disappeared. It took a couple more times before the lights dulled. My senses were once again normal. Chantel stood on the other side of Agrona, appearing equally concerned.

"Are you okay?" Agrona asked.

"Yeah, I think so. What happened?" I took another look around me. Nobody else seemed to be affected.

"You opened your senses, and you permitted it to overwhelm you. The academy has a controlled environment, so this was the first unimpeded situation you have been in. Luckily, you reined it in," Agrona answered with a soft smile.

"Now it is time to par-tay!" Chantel grabbed our wrists and pulled us to the dance floor.

The EDM tune washed over me and rocked my hips to the beat. The song picked up the tempo, and we jumped on the balls of our feet. I thrust my hand into the air above my head and let the rhythm melt my stress.

We danced for several songs, all the while declining partner invitations. I couldn't stomach the idea of a stranger holding me close. Agrona had her protector face on, and I had a suspicion that Chantel only had eyes for Ricardo. After the fifth song, we decided to take a break.

Pushing through the crowd, we headed to the bar. Chantel waved, and her silver bracelet jingled as she tried to get the attention of one of the bartenders. I stared at the back of one of their heads. It was familiar. The dark-brown hair and sculpted shoulders. I couldn't place where I knew him. I was about to ask Agrona when he turned around.

Desmond.

Desmond was the bartender at Agrona and I's preferred club in Virginia. The same Desmond who was there the night Mrs. Rose attacked me. This couldn't be a coincidence. Could it?

Desmond made eye contact with me and smiled.

"Well, well, well. My favorite girls," Desmond said as he approached.

"Yummy. I like what I see." Chantel leaned over to me.

"But...what...how?" I stammered. I wanted to high-five my forehead at my lack of articulation.

"It appears I owe Quin twenty bucks." He wiped up the droplets of leftover drinks.

My eyes bugged. How did he know Quin? I peered over at Agrona, but she didn't seem fazed.

"Quin and Desmond are two of a kind." Agrona shrugged.

Before I could inquire what they exactly were, Desmond spoke, "Quin and I go way, way, *way* back." A small chuckle escaped him.

I was missing a clue about my favorite chef. I'd have to ask him when I returned to the academy. We would have a lengthy chat where I would finally obtain some information.

"How about I get you ladies something to drink?" he asked.

I held up my hand. "I don't—"

"Drink. I remember." He winked.

Desmond placed three sodas in front of us. I studied him, wishing to discover answers without asking questions. Why did he leave Virginia? Did he follow me out here? Was it possible he was in cahoots with Jordan?

I ignored the last thought. If Desmond was evil, then it would mean Quin could be too, and I refused to believe that. Anyone who could make desserts so divine was heaven-sent.

I observed the evasive barkeep as he served other customers. He had always been nice and watched out for Agrona and me. There was no way he was working against us. No way at all. That left the more stalkerish option. But why would he follow?

Drumming my fingers, I waited for Desmond to come back. My attention turned to Chantel. She giggled and moved to the dance floor, holding on to a random guy's hand. He was shorter than Ricardo and had a body of a model. His face was sharp and angular—perfect for a cover of a magazine.

"Come on, let's dance before you attract a weirdo." Agrona tugged me out of my spot and after our Sorceress.

We hovered close to Chantel. I could tell Agrona didn't want us to be divided for too long. After the third guy asked me to dance, I gave in. Maybe if I danced with one guy, they would bug off. I made sure there was enough space between us that a nun would squeal with glee. A few times, his arm brushed mine, and it repulsed me. Almost like I had rubbed fish guts and pickle juice on my skin.

I couldn't help but compare him to Blayde. I wouldn't say the guy was ugly, but he didn't have Blayde's rugged handsomeness. He was about the same height as my Shifter but had a smaller build. Compared to Blayde, he wasn't that impressive.

Sometime during the song, I got separated from my friends. The number ended, and I bolted. I wasn't sticking around for another.

I dashed through the crowd, working to lose him. My heart raced, and a tightness settled in. I searched for Agrona and Chantel without success. I went to ask Desmond if he had seen them, but he wasn't there. I leaned against the bar, trying to decide what I should do. My bladder had an idea.

I weaved through the mass of people, and I headed to the bathroom, all the while keeping an eye out for my friends. But no luck. I stopped a small distance away in surprise that there was no line. Déjà vu washed over me. Images of Mrs. Rose ambushing me flashed through my mind.

My brow wrinkled, and I bit my bottom lip. Disquietude convinced me that I didn't want to go in, but alas, my bladder forced my hand.

Two girls exited as I entered. Even though I couldn't see anyone, the ripping of toilet paper alerted me that someone was in the stalls. My pulse pounded, and my palms became damp.

I was being irrational. Mrs. Rose was dead. I had nothing to fear.

After relieving myself and washing my hands, I stared at myself in the mirror. A lot had changed in the past few weeks. I was a completely different person.

The stall door banged open, and I spun in the direction of the noise. Out stepped Jordan. My stomach turned sour. I wanted to scream, but no sound left my vocal cords. Every crevice of my body was full of panic.

"Out of all the bathrooms, you walked into this one. You know, I never did take you clubbing." Jordan stalked toward me. He was a tiger, and I a dodo bird.

These past weeks had changed him. His face was harder, more prominent, like he had lost weight. His dark-blond hair was longer and covered parts of his eyebrows. His deep-blue eyes didn't hold any spark of light.

I backed up into the sink and gripped the porcelain. I had nowhere to flee. What was with evil villains cornering me in places with toilets? There were better locations to confront a person like a dessert-tasting café. It would be short and to the point since you couldn't stay mad when your mouth was full of chocolate.

"You are in the wrong bathroom. The sign clearly said women." I pushed my trepidation down.

This was just Jordan. The Jordan I'd grown up with wouldn't let my obituary say I had died next to a ceramic throne. But he wasn't the Jordan I knew, I reminded myself.

Jordan threw his head back and laughed. "Cedar, I have missed you." There was no malice in his voice. He sounded happy. At ease.

"What are you doing here?"

"I came to talk. We never finished our conversation." He strode toward me.

"We ended it. I remember it very clearly. You sent zombies to kill me because I wouldn't be your mistress of the night." I raised my chin. I refused to back down.

Jordan moved closer to me so only a small step separated us. "I will always give you the option to be with me. We belong together." He stroked my cheek.

"What happened to you? Who made you into this?" I turned my face away from his.

He huffed at my rejection. "What happened to me? What happened to me! I went to learn to be a Hunter." He spat on the black-and-white checkered tiled floor. "I was introduced to a world that is ruled by the oldest of their species, and they didn't care about making room for us pawns. It is our turn to rise. To make a new order!" he shouted.

"Jordan, this isn't the real you. What did the Dark Master do to you?" My gaze met his. I saw no light, no hope. Only darkness.

"The Dark Master showed me a better way. The only way."

Fear bubbled to the surface. My best friend, my childhood confidant, wasn't the person standing in front of me.

"Give me the dagger and your necklace. Join me, Cedar." He ran his fingers through my blonde locks.

I stiffened at his touch.

"What dagger?" I asked, purposely not mentioning the

white crystal hanging around my neck. I had a suspicion, and I hoped I was wrong.

"I know you have the book that tells you where the dagger is. Bennett found it, and you're the current owner."

How did he know about the journal? What else did he have information about?

"I don't have it," I said honestly.

He put his finger under my chin and stared into my eyes, trying to decide if I was telling the truth. We stood there in silence—him brooding, and me petrified in terror.

He could reach down right this instant and yank the dainty chain off me, and I'd be powerless to stop him. After a minute, the tension left him, and his stance relaxed. A glimmer of warmth shone through his eyes. He leaned down, and his lips were inches from mine. I recoiled.

His grip on my hair tightened, yanking me backward. He let go and smashed his fist into the mirror behind me. I covered my head with my arms to protect myself from the airborne shards.

I ducked under his arm and sprinted to the door.

"Cedar, this isn't over!" Jordan yelled.

I ran into the throng of people.

Chapter Four

I was *never* going into a nightclub bathroom by myself
ever again. Only bad things happened there.

I ran into the middle of the crowd and spun in a
circle, searching for Agrona and Chantel.

"Agrona!" I yelled over and over and over. A Human
wouldn't be able to hear me, but with Vampire hearing, she
would. It only took a second for Agrona to appear with
Chantel.

"We need to go! Quickly!" I waved my hands in panic.

Without a question, my friends placed their palms on
my shoulders.

"*Effugium.*" Chantel flicked her wrist.

In a blink, we were in my bedroom, and the pressure in
my chest eased.

"Let's not tell anyone about this," I said. Bile threatened
to rise and make an appearance. I was starting to despise the
aftereffects of this incantation.

"I would love to learn what you three have been up to,
Bonita." Ricardo flipped on the light.

Still dizzy from the transportation spell, I stumbled into

the bathroom, making it to the sink before I got personal with the toilet. I washed my face and brushed my teeth before I came back out. Ricardo leaned against the door, and Agrona and Chantel were situated on the couch. All eyes were on me. I plopped down on the armchair and waited for someone to speak.

"Explain to me what transpired tonight." Ricardo bit out. His jaw was clenched, and his arms crossed. His normal light-heartedness was nowhere in sight.

"I take full responsibility." Agrona sat up straighter. Always the martyr.

"No, I'm responsible. It was my magic that got us out of the academy," Chantel argued.

"But it was my idea," I declared.

The three of us bickered. We all felt culpable. Guilt swam within me. I was the reason for us getting reprimanded.

"Quiet!" Ricardo yelled and effectively shut us up. "Now, someone please tell me where you guys went this evening?"

I gnawed on my lip. I was ready to come clean, only to be beaten by Chantel's rambling.

"We had some fun. Cedar had a brilliant idea that we needed to get out and let our hair down. It isn't healthy for a vibrant young woman to be cooped up for so long. Prisoners see the sun more than Cedar does. We just wanted to give her some type of normalcy. That is what best frien—" Chantel stopped when Ricardo put his hand up.

He pointed at Agrona.

"No excuses. We left. No one was harmed. We were all safe," she said.

Ricardo then gestured to me.

"We went to a club."

I didn't know how much I should add. Did I mention Jordan? Did I mention Desmond knowing Quin?

The Hunter pinched the bridge of his nose. I was familiar with this expression. Usually, it meant he was counting to ten before he said anything.

"She could've been found." Ricardo's voice was low. Even though it was above a whisper, it was full of rage.

"No one found her. No one knows that she is here," Chantel said.

"Well," I drawled out in a high-pitched tone.

Three heads snapped in my direction.

"What. Do. You. Mean?" Ricardo stepped closer to me. Under the scrutiny of his glare, I squirmed in my chair.

"Um...see...well...Someone did find me," I began. "That someone was Jordan," I mumbled against my palm and hoped they wouldn't hear it.

Agrona sprang upright. "Is that why you were in such a rush to leave?" Her timbre rose.

I did not like being the object of their rage.

"Yep," I said, putting emphasis on the p. I told them what happened in the bathroom, and that Jordan wanted the dagger and my necklace. When I finished, they stared at me with a mix of anger, shock, and frustration.

Ricardo slumped in the armchair opposite mine and laughed. I peered at Chantel and Agrona, but they shrugged. They were in a cloud of confusion as much as I was.

"I am so glad I'm not you. I can't wait to watch Blayde's reaction." He wiped a tear away.

Dread filled me, and I groaned, swiping my hand down my face. "Kill me now. You would be putting me out of my misery." I rolled my head back and closed my eyes.

Once Blayde caught wind of this, it would be hard to

convince him to leave my side. I knew his wolf got restless and going for a run with other Shifters was a good thing, and I'd just made it harder for him.

After a few rounds of laughs and jokes at my expense, they left with a promise that we would talk about this later. A promise of more than stern talking lingered in Ricardo's voice. Despite things ending on a light note, I hadn't escaped the consequences of my actions. I took a shower, trying to push Jordan out of my thoughts. It was only when I fell headfirst onto my bed that I finally succeeded.

* * *

I ended up skipping breakfast when I woke up the next morning. I hadn't set my alarm last night and now I was paying for it. The sunlight through my window had awoken me just in time to not be outrageously behind schedule for today's lectures.

I walked into the classroom, and the professor had already started. With his right arm up, he wrote on the whiteboard.

"You're late, Huntress Hastings," Professor Morris said.

He must have eyes on the back of his head. Sliding into my seat, I glanced around. When I arrived three weeks ago, I was surprised to discover that most of the classrooms looked like they belonged in an old high school—it even had the same smell, gym socks. Each room had ten to twenty desks, depending on the type of subject.

Potions looked like a chemistry lab—with cauldrons instead of beakers. Spells was in a gym with Vectors on the floor. PE was separated into various classes; hand-to-hand combat, sword fighting, shooting guns, defense against the Big Three, and simulation training.

Professor Morris continued to write, and the high-pitched squeak of dry-erase markers grated on my nerves. The ten other Hunters in the class scribbled notes. Having left my notebook and pen in the simulation room, I picked at my nails and pretended to be busy.

"Shifters have a unique advantage. Through their pack link, they share hundreds of decades' worth of battle and hunting methodology. Each species has a different view on the tactic. A hawk wouldn't approach the situation the same way a bear would," Professor Morris said.

I snapped my head up. Shifters had a collective knowledge of maneuvers within their pack. Was that the reason I fought better against Blayde? Was I somehow tapping into it?

"So as Hunters during an attack, we have access to Shifter strategy?" I asked, not bothering to raise my hand. I'd learned early on I could get away with things that other Hunters couldn't. I'd been testing those boundaries ever since.

Professor Morris let out a sigh, and he pinched the bridge of his nose. I bet he was struggling against the urge to bang his skull against the wall.

"No, Cedar. It is a particular quality of the pack bond. And before you ask, no, being a mate to a Shifter doesn't grant you the ability to utilize said attribute. It is a Shifter-specific characteristic."

I frowned. Professor Morris perceived my submissive act as having nailed what I was thinking. He couldn't have been further from the truth. I didn't understand how my body moved smarter, stronger when I was around Blayde or other Shifters. I was hoping bond magic would've been the explanation.

I didn't comprehend why I could do a lot of things.

How could I use spells without being in the Vector? How could I use the Shadow Creature magic? How could I use any of the Big Three powers without being engaged in a brawl?

The other Hunters here had years of expertise on me. When you hit puberty, your magic emerged. Another thing I couldn't decipher. Why didn't I start to experience my abilities until my twenty-first birthday? When I'd asked Agrona about this, she shrugged and told me it was a question only Caroline—my stepmom—could answer.

Up until a few months ago, I thought my stepmom was my birth mom. It had shattered me when I'd found out. Agrona didn't step in to start helping Caroline until I reached college. While I was growing up, she never spoke of her parents. Or any family for that matter. I figured they were all dead. It wasn't until recently I discovered she had been disowned for forsaking her responsibilities and marrying my father. I also learned she was the Siren Princess. When I tried to press for more details, she effortlessly changed the subject. There was still a lot I didn't know about her—like how she was rumored to be a brilliant fighter.

Professor Morris continued with his lesson. We were expected to memorize battle strategies and techniques of the various species of Shifters. We were required to be familiar, so if we were ever fighting a Shifter, we could anticipate their actions. We would have a test on it in two weeks. Just another reason to visit the library.

Class ended, and I dropped by the simulation room to grab my bag, and then I stopped to get the journal from underneath my mattress.

I headed for the library, and my stomach grumbled, reminding me I had questions only Quin could answer.

Unfortunately, he would have to wait. I had a date with a stack of books. Irrationally paranoid, I kept looking over my shoulder.

I pushed the library doors wide, and the motion-activated lights flickered on. My anxiety eased knowing I was the only one here. I sat at a table and laid everything out.

It had been a few days since I'd last opened the journal. Prior to my coming to the academy, Chantel had given it to me. Bennett had gone to great lengths to retrieve it before he'd died. He instructed me to keep it safe and only share it with those I trusted. Once I'd arrived here, I told the rest of the gang about it. I read it in my spare time–which wasn't often between training, classes, and sleep. But alas, I needed to give the journal more of my attention. Jordan wanted the dagger and my necklace, and it was essential to know why.

I cracked open the brown leather-bound journal and brushed my fingers against the worn pages. Curly hand-written letters covered each page. I hated reading cursive. I'd learned how to read and write it in the third grade, but I'd always preferred to print when I wrote. Plus, everything online was in print, not cursive. I suddenly longed for a cell phone or a laptop or something to connect me to the outside world. With a sigh, I glanced down.

The first couple of pages talked about being around humans and their zest for life. Flipping forward, I skimmed for anything that would help us.

With a prick of my finger, adding a drop of blood into the cauldron, I increased their vitality.

I stopped and backtracked a few paragraphs. It mentioned the creation of the original Hunter. This journal belonged to an Angel.

I jotted it down, followed by a question mark after the word Angel. I ought to ask Ricardo who helped create the Hunter race. I thumbed the corners of the pages and perused them.

They formed a ruling body, a council, to help guide them when we cannot. I took the five crystals off my dagger, eliminating its power. I fashioned the crystals into ornaments they could wear. After they settled into their roles in the council, I visited them individually and gave them each one. I did not tell them what it was. Only to keep it safe for the day I would call upon them and require it.

I wrote down key phrases in my notebook. *Dagger. Removed crystals. Ornaments. First Council.* I stared at what I had written. I gnawed on the end of my pen cap.

I had to think through this. The dagger had five crystals, which had been extracted. So, if I put the crystals back on, what power would the dagger wield? The crystals were shaped into ornaments and given to the founding Council members. What kind of ornaments? Like ones you hung on a Christmas tree? Where did my necklace fall in all of this?

My knee bounced, and I tapped my pen against the table. I had pieces to a puzzle that I didn't know what the picture was yet. I needed to get the Scooby gang together in one place and see what could be made of all of this.

A hand touched my shoulder, startling me. I closed the journal and flipped my notebook over. I turned my attention to who had surprised me. It was a man. A gray-haired man. A gray-haired man in a navy business suit.

I squinted. I had never seen him here before. But, then again, I hadn't met everyone at the academy.

"Shouldn't you be in class?" he asked. His presence loomed over me, caging me in.

"Yes. I was doing some research and lost track of time," I said, gathering up my belongings and placing them into my bag. I glanced around the library. Just me and the gray-haired man.

"What could be so important that you were truant from your classes for the afternoon?" He rocked on the balls of his feet, his hands clasped behind his back like he was waiting for me to screw up.

"A project for Battle Strategy," I lied. How did he know I'd skipped? Was he following me?

He emitted a noncommittal noise and eyed me. "Hurry now. You have a lot to learn. You can't afford to skip."

Taking the opening he offered me, I fled the library with my bag in tow. But before I exited, I squinted up at the wall clock. Fifteen minutes before class was over. I made my way downstairs, and my stomach growled. I might as well ditch and grab something to eat. My next class was magical training with Chantel. I wouldn't want to perform magic with an empty belly, I justified.

Walking into the vacant mess hall, I beelined for the kitchen. The clanks from pots and pans were a happy indication that my favorite cook was preparing lunch. I don't know how he did it, meal after meal, day after day, month after month. He fed a lot of mouths.

"Knock, knock." I pushed the door open.

"Cedar! You skipped breakfast." Quin scowled at me.

It was times like this when he seemed more like a father to me than a friend. The ache in my chest flared at the thought of my own dad. Instead of rubbing the twinge, I rolled my eyes and hopped onto the counter. He, in return, gave me a croissant. Which I accepted happily.

I bit into the buttery goodness. Heaven. I chewed in silence, and my thoughts drifted back to the journal. Who was the Angel? Would Quin know?

Well, only one way to find out.

"In Mythical Origins, we were learning about how every species was created by a specific Angel. What do you know about the Angel who formed Hunters? I couldn't find anything in my textbook." I took another bite out of the pastry.

Quin got a glossy, distant look in his eyes. "She was beautiful. Everything an Angel should be."

"What was her name?" I prodded.

His mouth flattened, and he focused on peeling the potatoes. I studied him, watching for any hint that he would continue. But he never did. He knew more than he was letting on, that's for sure. Did I press him on the subject and potentially get tossed out, or did I try to obtain some other answers? To be on the safe side, I decided to switch topics.

"So, Desmond tells me that you owe him twenty bucks. Care to explain?" I stuffed the rest of the croissant in my piehole.

Quin laughed and chopped the potatoes into cubes. I hoped that was a good sign. But, again, he didn't utter a single word.

I stared at him. Waiting. I narrowed my eyes.

"That is all I'm going to get? How about you tell me how you know Desmond? Or better yet, what species you are because no one seems to have a clue." I folded my arms and added a dramatic pout to my lips. I might be laying it on thick like too much chunky peanut butter. But every unanswered question grew my annoyance.

"Some things are better to wonder about and not know.

Knowing can be dangerous." He stared at me, his gaze unreadable, then returned his focus to the starchy vegetable.

"That wasn't cryptic at all, Obi Wan," I said.

"One day, Cedar, all will be revealed."

I hopped off the counter and snagged a second buttered croissant. "One day, I'll force you to tell me your secrets."

He didn't say another word or even acknowledge my words. I took that as my clue to leave. I shuffled out of the mess hall and down the hallway to the Vector room. I swore the academy had more training areas than actual classrooms.

I pushed the doors open and found Chantel talking to Ricardo. Well, more like flirting. There was a lot of hair twirling and causal arm grazing. Those two needed to admit to each other how they felt already. It was obvious to everyone but them.

I walked to them, watching their easy banter and listening to their light giggles. My heart squeezed. Seeing them reminded me of Blayde. I ignored the pang. I wouldn't confess how much I missed him.

"Bonita, how wonderful for you to join us," Ricardo greeted.

"We have a surprise for you." Chantel bounced up and down.

I arched my eyebrow at her, expecting her to blurt it out.

Ricardo slid his hand into his back pocket and presented a wand.

"Tada!" Chantel clapped.

Her enthusiasm was contagious. I'd been impatiently waiting to get my own. I reached for it, but before I could take it, Ricardo pulled it away.

"Hey!" I protested. "Not nice! That's not how you give gifts."

"Bonita, it will be yours in a moment. There is something that we must do first," Ricardo said.

Chantel grabbed my hand and lifted a knife in the air with the other. She had a mad scientist expression on her face, and she let out an evil witch cackle. I tested her strength and tried to withdraw from her grip. But I didn't prevail.

"Who gave her a knife?" I asked Ricardo with a look of horror. I fully expected lightning to flash behind her.

Ricardo shot Chantel a hard glare, and she lowered the sharp instrument. "You guys are no fun." She jutted her lower lip out.

"Chantel is going to bind you to your wand," Ricardo explained.

Chantel pricked my finger. A drop of blood formed, and she finger-painted it across the wand.

"This will bind the wand to you. It will learn your style and listen to you. It will help feed and direct your magic," Chantel said.

"You talk as if it is alive," I said.

Chantel's head snapped up. "Have I taught you nothing? Everything has magic. It isn't alive like you or me, but living magic courses through it, giving it the ability to adapt and to learn. Even Humans have a small amount of magic. They tend to interpret it as déjà vu or intuition."

"Okay. Let's do this," I said.

Chantel placed it in my hand. It looked like an ordinary stick you would find outside. Brown. Nothing special.

"*Ut magicis vinculo ligare, ut sicut unum,*" Chantel repeated three times.

Gold and black circled the wand and my hand in a

figure eight formation. The stick transformed into a rose-gold wand with two twisted strands encircling the grip. For it being rose gold, it was as light as the piece of wood had been. It was stunning.

I clasped the end and twirled it, flowing it like a conductor's baton. It was as if it was an extension of my limb.

"It's perfect." My gaze never left my wand.

"Of course it is. It is bound to you. It is a reflection of you," Chantel said. "Now let's get on to our lesson."

Chantel shooed Ricardo out, then directed me to a Vector. I sat in the center of it. It was a circle in the middle with a triangle around it. Followed by an inverted triangle overlapping the first one. Then, to top it off, a square encompassed it all. The Vector was a safe place for magic. When you were learning a new spell, you practiced it in the Vector. It was a controlled space that, if a spell went awry, it wouldn't harm anyone or anything.

Chantel led me through her version of a warm-up. Flicking my wrist in different fashions and repeating different incantations. *Dearmo* for disarm, *obsepio* for block, *contego* for shield, *tardo* for stop, and *flagro* to send up a flare. It felt like a weird Harry Potter workout.

After the warm-up, I wondered what she would teach me—I hoped it would be how to disappear.

"Today, let's do something different."

Chapter Five

Chantel was crazy. A complete nutzo.

With a deep breath, I focused my thoughts on Blayde. It was uncomfortable, to say the least. You know, since I spent an obscene amount of energy avoiding anything about him.

"Since you and Blayde are fated mates, it's imperative for you to explore the boundaries of your bond," Chantel said. "Fated mates have magical bonds. And you haven't yet discovered what unique qualities it has given you both. Now focus on Blayde. The way he looks, smells, the tone of his voice. Visualize being with him."

I tried to mentally picture him. Our first conversation popped into my mind. I had just met the Council, and we were in the kitchen. His pompous smirk had gotten under my skin. I chuckled, remembering the muffin I'd thrown at him.

I conjured up an image of how I saw him now. There were times I still wanted to wipe that smug smile from his face, but I knew when I needed him, he would be there. Alone, he was sweet and thoughtful to me...well, most of the time. I would never admit it to him, but my favorite shirt to sleep in was the Barbie T-shirt he'd given me from our shopping trip before we got to the academy. He challenged me. He made me better.

The wall around my heart came crumbling down, and I saw him. I saw him as if he were right in front of me.

Blayde was talking to another Shifter; one I'd never seen before. Two guys standing there, shooting the breeze.

Blayde's brown hair was windblown and wild. His scruff was getting thicker and longer. He wore gray sweatpants and a matching jacket. His feet were bare, even though he was in the middle of a forest.

"Blayde," I whispered.

His head turned in my direction, and his eyebrows knitted together. He stared for a moment before turning back to his companion. Had he heard me, or had someone else called him?

"Blayde," I repeated louder.

He spun and scanned the area where my words had come from.

"Blayde!" I waved my arms, hoping he would spot me.

He took a few steps toward the sound of my voice. He rubbed his eyes and continued to search.

"Blayde, this is bananas. Say something if you can hear —" I started, only to be jerked by a force, pulling me away.

Chantel shook my shoulders and yelled my name. I blink rapidly. The Sorceress towered over me with her hand raised, poised to slap me. I was back in the Vector training room.

"Wait!" I caught her wrist.

She released my shoulder and squinted. Without giving me pause, she slapped me with her free palm.

"What was that for?" I let her hand go to rub my cheek.

45

"That was for scaring the crap out of me! I couldn't get you to come out of the trance for ten minutes! Ten! Minutes! What happened?" Chantel exhaled her frustrations. She sat across from me. Her expression was lined with distress.

"I saw him. I saw Blayde, and he heard me," I said, amazed at my own words.

I scrambled to the exit. Within a few steps, I tripped over my own feet, and I ate the mat. Hard. Groaning, I stood back up. Chantel stopped me by grabbing my hand.

"Where are you going?" she asked.

"I need a phone. Blayde looked really concerned and confused. He needs to know that I'm all right." I ran out of the training room while Chantel shouted my name.

I dashed down the off-white hallway and ended up at Headmaster Hunter Grant's office. I burst through the door, forgoing my manners. Headmaster Grant and the gray-haired man were in a heated conversation—and I had interrupted.

Whoops. Talk about awkward.

"Manners, young lady!" the gray-haired man spat.

"In any other situation, I'd be happy to oblige, but not this one." I turned to Grant. "I need to use your phone."

"Why would you ever need to do that?" the gray-haired man interjected.

I scrunched up my face before relinquishing a breath. "Because it's important I speak with Blayde. There is a good chance that he is worried about me right now." I silently pleaded with Grant.

"Why would he be worried about you?"

I threw my hands in the air. Enough with the questions. "Ugh! I don't have time for this! Headmaster Grant, please tell Blayde I'm fine."

Grant nodded. "I'll make sure he gets the message."

The gray-haired man's eyes bore into Grant. I exited before I created more trouble.

I closed the door, and the gray-haired man's lecture seeped through the walls. Apparently, helping me wasn't what he wanted.

I blew out my frustration and trudged toward class. For once, I wouldn't be late for Battle Strategy. I was the first to arrive, and I took my regular chair. I wasn't alone for much longer. Students filed in, and soon every seat was filled.

I watched Professor Morris walk in, and his gaze landed on me. His head recoiled, and his mouth gaped open. What a glorious moment. A moment I would replay in my mind for days. A moment that made me feel triumphant.

"Cedar, how lovely for you to join us on time. But one time doesn't erase the many, and I do mean many, tardies." With one sentence, he took away my victory.

Shoulders caving, I slumped and wondered what I did to make Professor Morris despise me. There seemed to be a lot of that going around the academy. Either they loved me, or they loathed me, and I couldn't discern why. I drummed my fingers on my desk.

Professor Morris continued where he'd left off yesterday —the topic of Wolf hunting strategy and then progressed onto bears. Bears bit their prey on their neck or their back. They often struck with their paws with ample force to break a person's spine.

My mind wandered. Why was it so hard for me to focus on this class? In any other, I had no issue. I wished I could blame it on Professor Morris' voice, but it was like chocolate pudding. He was passionate and brought his lessons to life. The problem must be with me.

"Cedar," Professor Morris commanded. "You are needed in the hallway."

"Jeez," I muttered and inched out of my seat. Maybe Professor Morris didn't like me, since I seemed to tune him out.

In the hallway stood Headmaster Grant, the gray-haired man, and a Hunter I'd seen around school. Anger burned in my throat.

Another set-up.

When would they get it through their inflatable brains that I didn't want them to play matchmaker?

"No, no, no, no." I shook my head.

Grant advanced and pulled me to the side. "The Council wants me to introduce you to this Hunter."

I rolled my eyes and let Grant direct me toward the Hunter. A wide victorious smile spread across the gray-haired man's mouth.

That was the last straw. I was done.

"No! I've had enough!" I bellowed. "The Council doesn't get to decide who I date. I have a..." I paused and chose my words wisely. "I have Blayde. I'm finished meeting other potential suitors." I poked my finger into Grant's chest.

The gray-haired man's face blazed red. I was too angry to try to figure out what part he played in all of this.

I spun away from them and stomped down the hall.

"We aren't done here!" the gray-haired man barked.

I whirled and stuck out my tongue before continuing down the hall. I was being childish, but I didn't care.

I ended up in the training room I used with Ricardo. Not bothering to change my clothes, I punched the bag. Repeatedly. I imagined the Council members' faces on the bag, fueling my fire. The gray-haired man's sentence rang in my ears. *We aren't done here.* How many more Hunters did I need to turn down before they got it through their dense skulls that my answer was no. N. O.

I focused all my rage into my fist. I punched the bag, knocking it to the floor. Huffing and puffing, I stared at the broken equipment.

"Remind me to not get on your bad side, Bonita," Ricardo said from behind me. "Let's try something else to calm you down."

He sauntered over to an iPod that was connected to the room's sound system. He strolled for a moment before pressing play. "Conga" by Gloria Estefan blasted through the speakers.

Ricardo started to salsa, moving his hips from side to side. With a flirty grin, he wiggled his eyebrows. He danced his way over to me and snagged my hand. He guided my arms back and forth until my legs copied.

A piece of my anger disappeared as I let the song lead me. I swayed to the beat. Ricardo twirled me in a circle and dipped me. Happiness tugged at the corners of my lips.

By the time the chorus came around again, we were dancing like professionals–if professionals stepped on their dance partner's toes.

A smile was plastered on my face, and with every shake of my booty, my irritation melted. Ricardo spun me out and in as the song ended. Even though some of my temper still lingered, I felt better. Loads better.

"Thank you," I said.

"Anytime, Bonita. Now that you are amiable, I have a surprise for you." He went over to the bleachers and grabbed something. With his arms behind his back, he walked back to me.

When he reached me, he brought his hands forward

and showed me two circular discs. They weren't complete circles, more like two half-circles with a handle.

"What's with the protractors?" I asked.

Ricardo placed one in each of my hands. The discs glowed. The light grew into a blue fire. I glanced up at Ricardo in panic. Ricardo looked at me without a worry in the world.

Gripping the brown leather-wrapped handles, I rotated my wrists and studied the discs. The flame didn't burn my skin. It didn't feel hot or cold. But the discs hummed. The blue fire didn't extinguish, no matter how fast I moved them. I touched them together, and the flames grew. I quickly pulled them apart and watched the flame shrivel.

"They are called Chakrams of Tacienne. Traditionally, they are the Huntress' weapon, since Huntresses are more agile than Hunters. The chakrams are embedded with magic. They will only have their flame for a Huntress. Only you can make the fire start or stop." Ricardo motioned for me to place the weapon in his grasp. The instant they left my fingertips and were in his, the flames died.

"What else can they do?" I took the chakrams, and they glowed.

Ricardo shrugged. "Dunno, Bonita. There hasn't been a Huntress in four hundred and twenty-three years."

I stared at my new toys, enthralled by their flames. Out of the corner of my eye, I spotted the bullseye. And it gave me an idea. Without a second thought, I acted. I threw one of the chakrams, and the fiery disc sailed through the air. It was breathtaking. Mesmerizing. It hit the target only a few inches off from dead center.

Ricardo laughed. "I think we should have a fire extinguisher handy when you use those."

I gestured to the target, and the chakram flew into my hand. It arrived with such force that I stumbled.

"It's like Thor's Hammer!" I screamed, jumping up and down. I was a bona fide superhero. "What else can it do?" I poised to throw both of them, but Ricardo stopped me.

"How about we first learn how to turn off and on the fire at will? That way, you can practice without destroying the academy." He pointed to the scorching bullseye.

I parked my butt on the mat with the chakrams in my hands and watched Ricardo use the extinguisher to douse the now black target.

I decided now was as good as any to practice. I closed my eyes and inhaled through my nose. I visualized the chakram's flame terminating. I opened my eyes and nothing. Absolutely nothing had changed. Nada.

After my fifth time, I was ready to throw the weapons against the wall. I huffed. What was I doing wrong?

"Close your eyes," Ricardo finally spoke and sat across from me.

I eyed him. Why? It hadn't helped the other times. He arched his eyebrow at me, but instead of challenging him, I did what he'd asked.

"Now envision a light switch. Imagine the light burning so bright, and the only way to get rid of it is by flipping the switch."

I took a large breath and held it. I pictured turning off a light switch. I peeked through one eye. I exhaled with a laugh.

"I did it!" I lunged and threw my arms around my mentor.

A growl emitted through the training room door, and I pulled back.

I knew that growl.

51

I whirled to see Blayde marching to me. He wore blue sweatpants, and his chest was bare. My gaze roamed, ogling every inch of him. Every well-sculpted muscle. Every visible piece of tan skin. Did it get hotter in here or was it just me? I licked my lips and waited for Blayde to reach me.

Ricardo stood and trod carefully toward the Shifter. I had almost forgotten Ricardo was present.

"You must have heard about the little trip the girls took." Ricardo took another step.

Blayde fumed. "What trip?" His words dripped with anger. Fur began to cover his hands, and he bristled.

"The trip to San Francisco..." Ricardo clamped his mouth shut.

Blayde's hands formed a fist, and his body shook. His eyes darkened, and his mouth curled, showing his canines. Muscles and veins strained against his skin.

"Bonita, take a few steps back."

I shot Ricardo a confused look. Blayde needed to get his anger in check, and I knew dancing wouldn't be the cure.

"You can go," I told Ricardo.

"I don't think that is a wise idea," Ricardo replied.

Blayde growled and snapped his teeth.

"Go," I whispered.

His eyes darted between Blayde and me, then finally he nodded. Ricardo slowly backed out and closed the door without a sound.

Blayde stood a few feet from me, and I took one small step at a time. With each movement, the air became electric, wild, more intense. Or maybe that was happening inside me. I didn't know for sure if I could settle the wolf within, but that wasn't going to stop me. Wrapping my arms around his waist, I ignored the tingles shooting up my muscles and lay my head against his chest. And prayed for the best.

Chapter Six

Having my arms around him calmed me instantly. Everything inside me went from erratic to serene. I had yet to notice if I had the same effect on Blayde. But after a few seconds, my bravery was rewarded.

My head moved with the rhythmic rise and fall of his lungs. His body ceased to shake, and I knew that was a good sign. I drew tiny swirls on his back, and the tension in his muscles melted away. His hands encircled me, and he lay his head on mine.

"See, you aren't so tough," I said against his broad chest.

He released a chuckle that rumbled through him, and he tightened his hold on me. "We need to talk about a few things."

I tried to break his embrace—admittedly, I didn't try that hard—but he held on for a bit longer before unwrapping. He intertwined our fingers, not wanting to let me go just yet, and he led me to the bleachers. My hand in his felt right, and rather than analyzing my feelings, I enjoyed the moment. I sat, expecting him to sit next to me. Instead, he paced back and forth, running his fingers through his hair.

"I don't even know where to begin. I heard your voice, and it worried me I couldn't see you. I came back to find out that you'd left the academy." Frown lines around his mouth deepened.

I chose the lesser of the two evils. "Chantel was having me explore the magical qualities of our bond. I imagined you and then I was with you. I asked Grant to give you a message that I was all right, but I guess you didn't receive it." I chewed my lip, hoping that mentioning our bond would distract him from my girls' night out.

He stopped pacing. A wide smile spread across his face that met the happy glint in his eyes. "Our bond?"

I rolled my eyes at what he was hinting at. I avoided this subject. Shoot, I avoided saying he was my mate out loud in fear I'd accidentally claim him.

"Yeah, you know that magical thing that has linked us together? That thing."

Blayde laughed, and for a minute he looked the happiest I'd ever seen him. He leaned down, and his hand brushed my cheek, sending small tingles through me. His hand lingered for a second before he twirled the ends of my blonde locks. My heart picked up the pace, and I fought the urge to close the distance between us.

"Have you given any thought to this bond thing of ours?" he asked, not breaking eye contact with me. Making me feel like he could see into my soul.

"Do you mean our bond or about you?"

"Both. I'd be lying if I didn't admit to that." His eyes shined with hope.

"I have," I started to say as his breath hitched. "And I

don't have answers." My gaze left his, and I studied the gray flakes on the floor.

I don't know how to be sure that my feelings weren't fabricated by a magical bond. Would I even like Blayde if we weren't mates? We were silent, and I was afraid to ask what his thoughts were.

Blayde sat next to me and pulled me into his arms. "What can I do to help you come to a conclusion in my favor?"

A tingle ran through my body. It was hard to think of reasons why I was fighting us in the comfort of his embrace. I sank into him and rested my head at the base of his neck. And his head nuzzled mine. It should bother me that he was marking me with his scent. Instead, it sent a thrill through me.

His familiar scent of earthy tones—that reminded me of a forest—and musk filled me. It comforted me in a way I couldn't explain.

I exhaled. He needed to understand what was holding me back.

"I don't trust my feelings for you. Are my feelings a byproduct of the bond or vice versa?" I paused. "Besides, we haven't even been on a real date." I nibbled on my bottom lip. The last part was more than I wanted to admit—that I cared that we hadn't had a date...that I wanted one.

His breathing was steady. He didn't release me at my admission.

"Since the moment I left for the run, my thoughts were consumed by you. The first time I heard your voice, I thought I'd imagined it. No one else could hear you." Blayde let out a long breath. "It scared me that I would find you hurt or taken."

Tears welled up. No one had ever said words like that to

me. No one had cared so deeply about me. Maybe I needed to take a leap of faith and trust he would catch me.

I opened my mouth, but Blayde spoke once more. "How about I take you on that date?"

I moved so I could see his eyes. Briefly, love peeked through, but in a blink, it vanished.

"I'd really like that."

We smiled at each other. His with a hint of mischievous and mine flirty. What would happen if I allowed myself to completely fall for him?

Somber erased his smile. "Now tell me about leaving the academy."

Cold dread replaced the comfortable warmth. I shifted in my spot and looked away, avoiding eye contact. I spat it out like an auctioneer in hopes if I spoke fast enough, he wouldn't catch the tidbit about Jordan.

But it wasn't fast enough.

I peeked up at Blayde through my eyelashes. His nostrils flared, and his teeth ground together. He dropped his arms and stepped away from me, moving across the training room. Staying rooted on the bleachers, I watched him pace. His hands clenched and released, clenched and released. The veins in his muscles popped as he flexed. I couldn't tell the thoughts storming through his head, but I knew they were dripping in anger.

Descending to the floor, he pounded his fist against the vinyl. He punched it again. And again. And again. With each impact, the floor tremored. What were they putting in his food? Blayde had so much unbridled strength.

I sat there with wide eyes, not knowing if I should stop him or not. How long was he going to continue until he realized he couldn't win against a solid surface? In the time I'd known him, he had never reacted this way before. Reacted with unconstrained fury.

This wasn't normal.

Even though I observed him pound the floor over and over again, I wasn't afraid of him.

The door burst open, and my three friends ran in. Weapons drawn and ready for battle. Confusion crossed their faces when they registered the source of the destruction.

"Is he all right?" Ricardo asked when they reached me.

"He is just having a tantrum," I said, attempting humor.

"Ha! It is more like an exorcism." Chantel laughed.

Blayde moved on from the floor to bashing metal chairs into the wall.

"You need to let it run its course." Ricardo grabbed my arm as I stood.

I gave him a questioning look.

"Before mates seal their bond, they can experience heightened emotions," he continued. "I'm guessing since you told him about Jordan, he is experiencing uncontrollable rage."

My mouth tumbled open. Blayde was undergoing this because of me. I walked up to him. Carefully. Not wanting to make the situation worse. I hoped uncontrolled rage wasn't the same as blind rage. I approached the side of him, and he had yet to notice me.

"Blayde!" I yelled in his ear.

He hesitated for a second.

I positioned myself between the wall and him. This was a stupid idea. I held my breath—the chair in Blayde's hand came toward me. It stopped mere inches from my face.

The chair clanked against the floor, echoing. His eyes

were more amber than blue and had a predatory gleam to them. His chest rose and fell rapidly with his eyes never leaving mine. Salt-'n'-pepper fur covered his body, and his muscles tripled in size. His sweatpants were torn and hanging on by threads. This must be what the Hulk felt like.

Fury engulfed his eyes. If I didn't know him, I would've peed my pants. But I knew deep down in my soul he wouldn't ever hurt me. He needed to snap out of it.

"Bad dog." I flicked his nose.

He jerked and shook his head, baring his teeth. A low growl escaped his lips—his luscious, kissable lips.

"What big teeth you have." I flicked his nose again. "Bad dog. If you want to get with this," I gestured to myself, "then you can't act like that." I went to repeat the motion, but his hand grabbed my wrist.

"Mine," he growled and pulled me closer.

His arms wrapped around me tightly, and I snuggled against his soft fur. It was like hugging a giant plush wolf.

Slowly, his fur disappeared, and his Hulkness shrank. I let his "mine" comment go for now since he was finally coming back to reality.

After a few minutes, he regained control over his rage. He leaned down to my ear and whispered, "Thank you, Princess."

I didn't have a clue as to how to respond. What I'd done was stupid, but I knew he would never hurt me. Secretly, it thrilled me to know he cared so deeply.

I stood on my tiptoes and gave his cheek a lingering kiss. One day we might be able to share more, but for now, that was what I could offer him.

Hand in hand, we cut across the mats to where my friends sat on the bleachers. Chantel gave me two thumbs-up while Agrona's mouth was in a half smile. She and Blayde didn't get along, but she wanted me to be happy.

When we reached them, Ricardo said, "We have many things to discuss. Chantel, if you'll give us some privacy, please."

The Sorceress pointed her wand at the ceiling. *"Secretum silentium."* A blue-tinted dome covered the room.

"Two items. First, Jordan knows where you are. Second, we need to figure out your magical abilities. I checked, and no Hunter—or Huntress—has been able to do what you do."

Dread swelled in my chest. If we hadn't gone to the club, then Jordan wouldn't know my location. But seeing the traitor enabled me to know he thought the dagger was in my possession.

"Jordan wants the dagger. We just have to find it before him," Chantel said.

"In the journal Bennett found, it mentions that crystals were taken off the dagger and fashioned into ornaments. So, it would be safe to say that not only does Jordan want the dagger but the crystals as well," I said.

"So, we just have to find them before Jordan. Easy," Chantel said, her voice a little too perky.

"Does the journal say where they are hidden?" Agrona asked. Her tone may be light, but the grim lines bracketing her mouth showed me her underlying feelings.

"I'm not sure. I haven't read all of it," I admitted sheepishly. "But I do know the Angel who created the OG Hunter gave each one of the original council members a crystal in some type of ornament. Maybe we start with learning more about her."

"Her?" Ricardo questioned.

"Yeah...the Angel. Quin told me she was beautiful."

"Nowhere in our records does the Angel have a name, not even a gender." Ricardo pursed his lips.

"Cedar, you should ask Quin more questions while we search for information about these ornaments and the first Council," Agrona suggested.

"We need to get Cedar somewhere safe," Blayde proclaimed. Although his voice didn't waver in his claim, hints of sadness broke through. Almost as if a part of him was defeated by not being able to keep me safe.

"She is protected here." Ricardo sat straight, puffing out his chest. He would never admit the Academy wasn't secure.

"Weeelll...I've been thinking about that," Chantel squeaked. "It was like Jordan was waiting for Cedar. Heck, he seemed to know we were going to the club before we did. I could've picked any place for all he knew. He must be aware of Cedar's location, and if he does...She isn't safe here."

An eerie quiet fell upon the room. She was right. How had I not seen it? Being a Hunter, Jordan had contacts, and of course, his evil master was helping him.

A growl vibrated from Blayde. His handsome features were pinched as if the thought of me being in danger caused him actual physical pain. I wanted to reassure him I was fine, that nothing would happen. But that would be a lie. I wouldn't be out of harm's way until the Dark Master was dead, and until then, I had to prepare for the worst.

I took his coarse—but strong—hand in mine and made soothing circles against his skin with my thumb.

"She's right," I admitted in a low voice.

His eyebrows knitted together, and sadness pierced his

eyes. "I know." After a breath, he added, "I can take her to pack land. She'll be free from danger there."

"We will still have the small issue of keeping Cedar's abnormal powers secret. We need to figure out why she can do things outside of the normal Hunter capabilities," Agrona reaffirmed.

"I've been trying to locate anything that could give us insight, but there are no instances like Cedar. But I did hear of a whispering of an object that can tell you magical origins. It might be a long shot, but if it works..." Ricardo allowed his words to trail off.

"So, we find this magical object, research the dagger and ornaments, and all the while evading Jordan and the Dark Master. Super." I let sarcasm roll over the last part. This was a lot to ask of my friends. Not only were they all protecting me, but they were risking their lives to do it.

A snarl next to me yanked me out of my thoughts.

"You are going to pack land where you will be safe. You will *not* put yourself into unnecessary danger," Blayde said.

A protectiveness shone in his eyes and some vulnerability I hadn't seen before. I didn't have time to dissect it, but I would make time to revisit it.

"I think it is better if we split up," Ricardo said reluctantly. "I'll search for the magical object while the rest of you go with Cedar. I'm not aware of what risk surrounds it, so it would be better to keep Cedar away from the search. You can look into the dagger and ornaments on pack land. Research only. You might be able to discover some information that we don't have at the academy."

"Maybe Agrona should go with you," Blayde suggested.

I snapped my head in his direction. It was bad enough to have Ricardo leave us and now he was recommending Agrona do the same?

Sensing my irritation, he bit out, "Shifters don't like Vampires. I can't guarantee she won't be met with hostility."

Sure, Agrona and Blayde didn't quite get along, but in a weird way, he was protecting her. My heart melted, and longing flooded my body. I craved to throw my arms around him and press my lips against his.

I bit my lip, and my gaze met my handsome Shifter's. He gave me a knowing grin. He knew how much I wanted him, even though I didn't say it out loud. Smug wolf.

"No, it's best if you all go together. While Cedar is still learning, she'll need extra protection." Ricardo's voice was firm with a hint of sadness.

I bet he didn't want to be away from Chantel.

Agrona nodded with her mouth pressed in a tight line. She wasn't thrilled to be going to pack land but would always stand by my side. Sisters before Shifters.

"Who will help me with my Chakrams of Tacienne?" I asked.

I secretly hoped Ricardo would change his mind about leaving. Not only was he my friend, but he was my mentor. My teacher. My guru for all things Hunter.

"These three are fully capable of taking over your training while I'm gone. Besides, the pack should have a weapons expert if you run into any problems," Ricardo said.

Blayde inclined his head, acknowledging that he could get their specialist to assist.

A weapons expert? I was unsure if I could trust someone else. I'd trusted Jordan, who was my childhood best friend, and where had that got me? Nowhere good, I'd tell you that. I trusted Caroline. Admittedly, her betrayal wasn't as severe—it just hurt to find out she wasn't my biological mother.

I stared at the floor, hiding the water that rimmed my vision. Darn emotions. I was supposed to be a hardcore Huntress! Now, look at me, wanting to blubber over our gang splitting up.

But if Ricardo thought this was the best course of action, then I would trust him. From the beginning, he had always been truthful. I filled my lungs and squished the tears in my eyes and glanced at Ricardo. I would miss my Spanish friend and his doltish jokes.

Ricardo's gaze found mine, and he gave me a dejected grin. This wasn't easy for him either.

"You know, this reminds me of a joke. A Shifter walks into a bar, and the bartender says—"

"Ricardo!" the four of us shouted at once with a smile on each of our faces.

I lied. I wouldn't miss his jokes. Not one bit.

The doors banged open, and I almost jumped out of my seat. I rested my palm over my racing heart. Blayde stood between the door and me, ready to pounce on any potential danger. His stance eased when the gray-haired man and Headmaster Grant came into view. A pop sound alerted me that Chantel had dismantled the privacy bubble. Hopefully, the gray-haired man hadn't noticed.

I wasn't sure the gray-haired man wasn't a threat, but nobody moved to harm him.

"Headmaster Grant, Councilman Hunter Ralph, what a surprise," Blayde said.

My lips parted, and I was able to stop my mouth from mimicking an opening of a cave. So, the gray-haired man was Bennett's replacement. From the moment Councilman Ralph had laid his cold eyes on me, I'd felt his disdain.

Ricardo pulled me into an embrace and whispered, "Go now. I'll distract him and Grant so that you and the others can leave. Don't dillydally." He let go and urged me toward the door in my confused state.

I was leaving the academy right now? This very instant?

Apparently, I wasn't moving fast enough for him. He swatted my butt and pushed me forward. Blayde growled, and Ricardo shot him a glare. A silent exchange passed between them and ended when Blayde nodded and grabbed my hand, propelling me to the exit. Agrona and Chantel were at my side without question.

"Councilman Ralph, how great to see you." Ricardo stepped to intercept the Hunter.

"Where is she going? I need to assess her training." Councilman Ralph frowned, and I tried to move past him.

"She is done for the day. Cedar needs to eat and rest," Blayde bit out.

"She is done when I say she is done."

Councilman Ralph threw Blayde a challenging stare, one that Blayde didn't flinch at. Instead, he gave the Councilman an equally scary glare.

I didn't know what to do. I didn't want to stir up more problems for Blayde. I didn't know what power the Councilman wielded. Bennett had been part of our team, so I had no idea what type of wrath or trouble a Councilman could create.

What could I do? I could pretend to faint. But that would lead Blayde to lose the staring contest and put more attention on me so I couldn't leave.

I could punch the councilman. But, once again, that would put the spotlight on me.

Settling on the least drama-filled option, I took a deep

breath. I flipped my hair over my shoulder and walked between them, heading toward the door.

"Get back here," Councilman Ralph yelled.

But that didn't stop me. I made my way through the door without looking back. Picking up my pace, I dashed through the halls to get to my room. I had packing to do.

Chapter Seven

P arting is such sweet sorrow. I never understood Shakespeare's line until this instant. I wasn't sad about leaving the academy. Far from it. I was sad about departing without Ricardo. I hadn't got a proper goodbye, and now I was fleeing like I stole the Queen of England's crown jewels.

I threw clothes on my bed only to realize I lacked a suitcase. How was I supposed to pack anything? I had a black bag and my backpack, but that was it.

A knock almost scared me out of my socks. I went to the door, wishing I had a peephole and cracked it a sliver.

Chantel.

I sighed in relief. I gripped her shirt and pulled her into my room.

"You ready, girl?" She moved toward the heap of fabric.

"I don't have a suitcase," I mumbled. Somehow, saying it out loud made me feel inferior. Like, what person didn't own a suitcase?

Chantel grabbed my black bag. "Girl, you don't need one when you have magic."

Muttering words, she tapped my bag with her wand. She set it next to the clothes. Scooping the outfits with both hands, she shoved them into my bag. It never changed size but seemed to swallow the garments like a tasty treat. I was half expecting the bag to burp—it didn't.

Magic was still relatively new to me, but every time I saw Chantel do something like this, it amazed me, as if I were seeing a spell for the first time. Chantel was like my own fairy godmother. Er Sorceress godmother? *Whatever*.

Another knock sounded. My eyes widened, and my legs rendered me motionless. I kept thinking Councilman Ralph was going to pop up at any second. Chantel chuckled, and she opened the door. Agrona stepped in, and I think I aged ten years from all this stress.

"You guys ready? Blayde is getting transportation together." Agrona carried her bag over her shoulder.

I wondered if it, too, was magically enchanted. It didn't look big enough to hold more than two outfits and a pair of shoes.

"Yes," Chantel squealed in glee. "I've always wanted to go on a road trip."

"Road trip? How do you know? We could be flying," I challenged.

"You have to bring your ID, and that can be flagged, and then anyone could find you. Duh." Chantel said it like it was common sense.

"Let's go," Agrona declared.

I fished the journal from under my mattress and slid it into my now magical bag. I'd rather eat an entire container of black licorice than give it up.

With my chakrams hanging from my belt, I followed my friends out of my room. Not giving it a second glance. I assumed we'd return sometime, but if we didn't, I was sure I could get Grant or Quin to send me the rest of my belongings.

I swallowed some spit and trailed behind them. Since the other Hunters were either in class or training, the only sound was our rubber soles against the vinyl. The silent hallways were eerie and sinister.

Agrona led us to the mess hall, which still gave me the creeps when it was empty. She stopped by the door that was the entrance to Quin's kitchen. She tilted her head, listening. Satisfied with the lack of noise, she went over the threshold.

The three of us walked silently. I spotted a chocolate dessert on the counter, and my mouth salivated. He wouldn't miss it, and if he did, he could bake another, I justified.

I made a slight detour and picked up the cupcake. There was a note sitting beside it.

Good Luck Cedar. Don't eat it all in one bite.

-Q

How did he know we were leaving? Had Blayde told him? I would have to mention it when we were on our way.

I took a bite and rushed to catch up. Agrona's eyebrow curled in question to the dessert in my hand, whereas Chantel used her finger to swipe some of the frosting. I bit back a growl.

Blayde stood next to his Jeep by the loading docks, where, I presumed, they received all of their deliveries. I felt a little foolish that I'd spent time in the kitchen and never bothered to check the back door. Rookie mistake.

Taking another bite, I climbed into the front seat of the

Jeep. I moaned. This was the best cupcake I'd ever had in my entire life—and I'd had some fancy cupcakes before.

Blayde's head snapped in my direction, and he watched me shove the last piece into my mouth. I darted my tongue out, swiping the frosting off my lips. His eyes fixated on the movement, and I fought the urge to do it again. Butterflies swarmed in my stomach. I wanted to look away, but I couldn't. Blayde's eyes were pools of amber desire, staring at me with a fierce intensity.

"Woo wee, it is getting hot in here! Just make out already," Chantel catcalled from the back seat.

My cheeks flushed, and an embarrassed laugh escaped me. Breaking his spell over me, I buckled my seatbelt.

At that moment, if he would've reached for me, I wouldn't have said no. Which only furthered my confusion. Until I figured out my feelings and what future we could have together, I had to stay on top of my game, so this didn't progress any further.

The engine roared to life, and we were off like we were escaping from prison. Blayde had a lead foot, and I gripped the door handle. In no time, the closed gate was in front of us. Blayde accelerated. The Jeep was going to ram it. Nerves bubbled in my throat, threatening a scream.

Chantel pointed her wand and muttered a spell. The gate opened similarly to an automatic door.

"Get back here! Close the gate! Close the gate!" Councilman Ralph shouted from the academy grounds.

Ricardo was behind him, smirking and waving. Hopefully, he wouldn't get into too much trouble.

We passed through the gate, and Blayde gunned it. I leaned over to see how fast we were going, but Blayde pushed me into my seat. His touch sent a warm tingle through me.

With the academy in our rearview mirror, I relaxed. Chantel stretched her arm over the middle console and fiddled with the radio. She reclined once she'd found a song she liked.

She pumped her fist several times, chanting, "Road trip, road trip, road trip."

I thought she would be sad and mopey that Ricardo wasn't with us, and yet here she was, singing along with the music. Had I misread what was between her and Ricardo?

"Where are we going?" I asked.

"Denver, Colorado. It will be a full day's drive if we don't stop. My father is currently there and can help us figure this out." Blayde's hands tightened around the steering wheel. He tensed up at the mention of his father. Was there bad blood between them?

Hopefully, when we arrived, I would get more answers and have fewer questions. My gut told me it would be the reverse.

"Can we pleeeease stop and see some sights?" Chantel gave Blayde a pleading pout accompanied by a lip tremor.

"I don't think that is a good idea. We need to get Cedar to a secure location as soon as possible," Agrona said.

Blayde nodded at her statement.

It was weirding me out that those two were on the same side instead of fighting. I guessed my safety was important enough for them not to bicker.

"No stopping," Blayde agreed.

A flash of horror crossed Chantel's face. "What about bathroom breaks? I'm not a dude, I can't pee in a bottle! What about food and water? I didn't bring enough snacks to last a full day," she wailed.

I chuckled. "Chantel, first off, you're a Sorceress. You can make food appear out of thin air. Second, Blayde didn't mean no stopping for bathroom breaks. He means no sightseeing."

"Oh. Okay then." Chantel sat back, relaxing.

We drove on a road that was literally a road less traveled. I had yet to spot another car. Heck, the only signs of life were a field full of cows. I knew we were somewhere in California. My guess was near San Francisco since that was where Chantel had taken us to go clubbing.

I itched to reach out and lace my fingers through Blayde's. Instead, I focused my attention out the window. The peaceful scenery calmed me.

It frustrated me that I couldn't distinguish my feelings. It was like the age-old question: which came first, the chicken or the egg? But in my case, it was the mate bond or my sentiments.

A decision had to be made soon. Either I claimed Blayde as my mate, or I gave him up. My stomach knotted. Could I give him up? Could I watch him date another woman? I didn't know if I could...

I needed to think of something other than Blayde and how close he was currently.

"Did you tell Quin we were leaving?" I asked Blayde.

Before he could answer, a blast hit the Jeep. The vehicle rolled, and my hair flew in every direction, blocking my sight. My body was frozen in shock, and gravity pulled me around like a rag doll. The Jeep rotated several times before it stopped, and the world was upended.

My vision was fuzzy and filled with black spots. Once it started to clear, I took a moment to assess myself and sighed to find I wasn't hurt—well, not hurt enough that a bone was broken. I had a ringing in my ears and an instant headache. I couldn't tell if I had any cuts, but I was sure I'd end up with some nasty bruises.

Strong hands undid my seatbelt and prevented me from smashing against the roof. I was cradled against Blayde, and his fingers roamed, searching for injuries. Blayde mumbled, but I couldn't understand him. It felt like I had cotton balls shoved in my ear canals.

He placed a hand on the sides of my face and forced me to make eye contact. He had a small gash above his brow, and it had begun to heal. I wondered what I looked like. Hopefully, my increased healing ability was already doing its job.

A tingle ran through me, and the resonant sound settled. Though I kept hearing was similar to someone throwing a ball against a wall. My ears must be damaged.

"Are you okay?" Blayde asked with worry in his eyes. It melted my heart to see how much he cared about me. I knew I'd always be safe with him. He wouldn't let me come to any harm.

"Are you okay? Answer me, Cedar." His voice cracked, his words laced with panic.

I lifted my palm to his cheek and offered him a small smile.

"I'll be okay as long as you're with me." I clamped my mouth shut. I hadn't meant to say that out loud.

His lazy grin sent butterflies to my abdomen. How could one facial expression have so much impact on me? He gave me a kiss on my forehead that delivered a shiver down my spine. Remembering the situation we were in, I turned to check on Agrona and Chantel, but they weren't there.

My chest pinched, and my throat tightened. Where had they gone?

Blayde nudged my chin and forced my gaze to meet his. "Chantel has crafted a temporary shield around us so I could make sure you were unharmed. She and Agrona are keeping our assailants at bay. But we need to move."

I stared out of the shattered windshield. Chantel flung purple orbs of energy at the attackers. Agrona had her own MMA match going on. The third attacker was stabbing the barrier protecting the Jeep.

Huh, that's where the ball-hitting-the-wall sound was coming from.

I scowled at the third goon.

Jordan.

I wasn't flattered by my new stalker. It only made me want to flee faster. I wasn't ready to confront the Dark Master.

With a smirk, Jordan beckoned me with a twitch of his fingers.

Like I'd be dumb enough to do what he wanted.

My anger flared. I narrowed my eyes. If only I could fry him with a glare. How had he known we were on this road? A pit in my stomach formed, filled with dread.

"We need to go before someone ends up in a body bag." I swallowed the lump lodged in my esophagus.

"Since our car is totaled, hijacking is the plan. Don't be a hero. Get Chantel and Agrona and get out of here." Blayde grabbed my hand, sending a tingle up my arm. "Prepare to run."

Don't be a hero.

I rolled my eyes. He didn't have to tell me twice. Though deep down in my heart, past the trust issues and confusion about love, I knew I would sacrifice myself for any of them. Hopefully, today wasn't the day I would need to.

We sprinted in the direction of Jordan and his goons,

and the barrier disappeared. Jordan sneered and charged at us. He was really enjoying this. That jerk.

I released Blayde's hand and pulled my chakrams from my belt. They hummed in response, and the blue fire glowed.

Let's put these bad boys to the test.

I threw one like a frisbee, and it sailed through the air. It cut across Jordan's shin and flopped on the ground. Jordan recoiled and hissed in pain.

A growl emitted from Blayde upon seeing Jordan shaking off the pain from his bleeding shin. He ran at me at full speed with another stupid grin on his face.

Blayde jumped in front of me and acted as a shield. I raised my arm, calling my chakram. It sailed through the air until it landed in my hand. *Coolest protractor boomerang EVER!*

I glanced at the blade, expecting to find it bloody, but the fire sparked, and no blood remained. Self-cleaning chakrams—how awesome was that?

Jordan charged at Blayde and pulled a knife from his belt. It was long enough that I almost considered it a short sword.

Blayde braced himself for Jordan's attack. He planted his feet with his hands poised to take Jordan's weapon.

I swooned. I couldn't help it. Here he was, looking fine, protecting me. I pushed my thoughts away, silently chastising myself. How naïve was I that I would be a damsel in distress and react to a guy in the middle of an ambush? I was better than this.

If I was to ever have a life with Blayde—or even a life of freedom—I had to fight my own battles. The problem was, I was afraid.

Jordan leaped with his knife out, angling it for a kill strike. Fear rose in my throat, threatening a scream.

"Go now," Blayde yelled.

He swatted Jordan's knife away, thinking fast. His right hand made a tight fist and connected with Jordan's nose. I cringed at the audible crack that rang out. *Ouch.*

The blow sent Jordan flying, and he skidded across the asphalt. Red liquid oozed from his nose.

This was my chance!

I sprinted past them and headed for the truck. It was black like their souls.

"Stop her," Jordan yelled.

I didn't look back. I knew Blayde could defend himself. Plus, I didn't have it in me to see him get hurt.

CRACK.

It came from Agrona's direction, and I spotted her hovering over the goon's limp body. I didn't even want to know what had made that sound. It would be filed under something to never ask. Ever.

"Duck," Agrona shouted.

I was unsure who it was for, but I wasn't going to take any chances. I dropped to the ground and covered my head with my arms. A blue energy orb zipped past me. My heart thumped faster, and the flight or fight sensation flooded my system. I had to get to the truck.

Agrona was beside me before I could move. She gripped my wrist and tugged me to standing. We raced to the pickup, and I climbed into the passenger side. Agrona got into the driver's seat. She fiddled under the steering wheel.

"We don't have keys," I shrieked. We needed to escape, like five minutes ago.

Agrona scoffed. "Hot-wire." The engine roared to life, and a victorious smile lit her face.

All we had left to do was get Chantel and Blayde in the car, and we could leave this behind.

Agrona's expression went from momentarily happy to sheer panic. "Get out of the truck!"

"Wh—" was what I was able to get out before she tore me from my seat, wrapped her arms around me, and sprang from the truck.

BOOM.

A wave of heat hit me. The crazy Sorcerer had blown up the truck! *Who blows up a truck? A freakin' psycho, that's who.* Now none of us, including the goons, would be leaving.

"Stay." Agrona set me down and rushed over to Chantel.

Bags under Chantel's eyes had formed, and the usual pep in her step was gone. I assumed she was close to using up her magical reserve. Without her magic, she would be defenseless.

Agrona jumped on the Sorcerer's back and placed her hands on his head. *CRACK.*

Welp, I now knew where that sound had come from. The Sorcerer's body slumped to the pavement. I ran over to Chantel, and a look of relief washed over her.

Jordan was the only one left.

Chapter Eight

Was there anything worse than watching someone you loved... err, liked... getting injured? Fighting for you. Protecting you.

My vision was glued to Blayde and Jordan. Their fight definitely wasn't suitable for TV.

There was so much blood.

Bile threatened to rise, but I shoved it down along with the thoughts that Blayde could be seriously hurt. He was a Shifter. A hunky Shifter. A Shifter who could defend himself. I didn't like thinking I could lose him, especially before I found out what was really between us.

I stepped toward them, but Agrona snatched my wrist. "Don't. He would kill me if I let you get between them. He can handle himself."

"But...but we need to do something," I cried.

I couldn't stand to witness anymore. With every blow Jordan landed, a tiny crack in my heart formed. Blayde was better than Jordan—Jordan had more blood and cuts than Blayde—but that didn't mean I liked seeing it.

"Fine," Agrona sighed. "Chantel, fire when you see the opening."

Agrona left in a blur, and Chantel and I remained behind. She approached Jordan from the rear and grabbed onto his tattered shirt. Jordan dropped low and performed a leg sweep. But like the fearless woman my best friend was, she jumped over his leg and moved past Jordan. She gave Blayde a hard shove, sending him onto the ground.

Whose side is she on?

Before I could throttle her, Chantel muttered a spell. A blast collided with Jordan, blowing him back in the air. Chantel snagged my arm, and we ran to Agrona and Blayde.

"Hold on. *Effugium,*" Chantel said.

We scrambled to place a hand on each other before she could finish saying the words. Blayde's arm encircled my waist, and a tingle shot down my legs.

Safety. Home.

I should be the one comforting Blayde, not the other way around.

In a blink, we were transported somewhere else. The contents of my stomach wanted to launch, but I willed it to stay down.

With my head spinning, I didn't scan my surroundings, instead, I asked, "Where are we?"

"Pack land," Agrona said next to me. "Why didn't we travel this way originally?"

Once I stopped feeling like a tilt-a-whirl, I focused on Chantel. Her bottom lip jutted out, and she folded her arms over her chest.

"I've never been on a road trip before and it sounded fun, okay? So, sue me," Chantel said. She stuck her tongue out at Agrona, and I chuckled.

My feet sloshed as I tried to take a step closer to Blayde. I glanced down and groaned. We were standing in a mud puddle.

I took a look around me. We were in a forest. Large pine trees mixed with aspen surrounded us. A small breeze blew leaves, and birds chirped in the trees. The crisp air smelled fresh like it had recently rained.

"Mud. Seriously, Chantel? Don't you have better aim than this?" I joked. My shoes would be toast if I didn't get out of here soon.

"I was under duress. You try transporting somewhere you've never been." Chantel gave me the stink eye.

While we trod out of the mud, Blayde's arm never left my waist. Once safely out, he pulled me close. I went to lean into him, but I stopped myself. His shirt was torn, exposing his blood-covered chest. My eyes and hands searched for any open wounds. I found nothing. Thank the Angels for Shifter healing.

My gaze met his, and I sucked in a breath. Only mere inches separated us. I swiped my tongue across my lips. The compulsion to close the gap was electrifying. Everything inside me was demanding it. It would be so easy to grab the back of his neck, to press my lips against his, and never let him go. But I didn't. I couldn't. Not yet.

Sensing my inner turmoil, he rested his forehead against mine. I closed my eyes, savoring the small, intimate gesture. I wanted him. Not just to kiss, but all of him. He made me happy. Made me feel safe. I needed to have a conversation with him, but first I had to learn more about fated mate bonds.

"Are you okay?" he whispered. Even coated in grime, he was still the sexiest man I'd ever seen.

I nodded, stepped onto the balls of my feet, and gave his

cheek a light kiss. Pulling back, I was captivated by the amber-flaked blue irises that burned with desire and longing. Without breaking eye contact, he brought my hand to his mouth. His touch lingered, sending a tingle through my entire body and deep within my bones.

Agrona cleared her throat louder than what was needed. "While I'd love to watch you two make out, we need to go."

Diverting my attention, I looked down at the dirt, trying to hide the crimson blooming on my cheeks. I risked a peek at Blayde. He flashed me a knowing smile and intertwined his fingers with mine.

"I'll lead the way," he said.

He inhaled a large whiff and started walking. I moved in sync beside him, enjoying the feeling of my hand in his.

I kept stealing glances at him. He was so attractive it pooled drool inside my mouth. His wild, wind-blown hair, his scruffy bread, and his broad muscles. A flawless male specimen. My stomach fluttered with each glance. He made me feel safe. He protected me against Jordan. And I had a sneaking suspicion he didn't kill Jordan because of me. I still hoped Jordan had good inside him, and Blayde respected that. Blayde cared for me not just physically but emotionally, too. Our bond couldn't make that up, could it?

"Are we there yet? I need a bath," Chantel complained. She lifted her arm and sniffed. "I smell."

"You have no one to blame but yourself. You wanted a road trip," Agrona said.

"I didn't think this would happen," she wailed.

With me in a mid-chuckle, a blur moved in my peripheral. I stared at the forest, and nothing seemed out of the ordinary. I shook my head. I must be going crazy.

Agrona touched my shoulder. "No, I saw it, too." She

stepped away and toward where we'd noticed the movement.

"Agrona. Stop," Blayde hollered, but it was too late.

Agrona flipped upside down and dangled by her feet. Her shirt clumped together, being dragged down by gravity. Her belly button was on full display along with her nicely toned abs—but whatever, I wasn't jealous—and dark locks masked her face. She brushed them aside, only to have it covered again. She threw her hands in the air in defeat.

Muffled snickers were uttered from behind me. I looked over my shoulder. Chantel covered her mouth, damping the sounds of amusement. My lips twitched, threatening to release a giggle.

"I'll..." *laugh* "go..." *laugh* "help her," Chantel said, unable to contain her laughter. "Sorceress to save the day!" She strolled to Agrona, still snickering.

"Chantel, wait," Blayde called after her.

This time, I couldn't suppress my joy. Chantel flew through the air, flipping upside down, screaming like a girl at a nineties boy band concert. Even Agrona was guffawing. I freed my hand to wipe the tears from my eyes.

"Oh, you think it is funny to laugh at a Sorceress?" Chantel asked Agrona. "Let me show you!"

Chantel flailed, swinging in every direction. She wasn't even close to hitting Agrona. Watching her made me laugh even harder. I could always count on Chantel to be entertaining. Some things never changed.

I glanced at Blayde, who wasn't grinning. Actually, he wasn't even there anymore. I spun in a circle, trying to find him, but he was nowhere to be found. What I did find were animals and Humans coming this way. And they didn't seem friendly.

"Uh, guys," I said in a panic. I didn't know what to do.

Blayde was gone, and the other two were hanging upside down.

Bears and wolves separated the beefy-looking Humans carrying guns. Shifters.

"Run," Agrona shouted.

But I couldn't.

I couldn't leave them. I *wouldn't* leave them.

A white wolf growled and bared its teeth at me. I hopped a few steps back in reflex.

"Well, well, well, what do we have here? A couple of trespassers?" the biggest guy said. He took a long sniff. "A Sorceress, Vampire," he took a whiff, "and a Hunter. Christmas came early this year." He smirked, his eyes never leaving me.

A circle of men formed on the ground under Agrona and Chantel. The biggest guy and the animals stalked toward me. They were predators, and I was their prey.

"Why don't you come with us, little girl?" the biggest guy said.

I peered over my shoulder, and no one was standing behind me. Then it hit me. Who was he calling a little girl? I huffed and crossed my arms over my chest. *Little girl? Little girl!* I was a grown woman, thank you very much. If he kept that up, he would learn how grown-up my vocabulary could be.

"We won't hurt you. We'll protect you from these women." He moved slowly, putting his gun in a holster. He raised his palms in the air in a gesture of peace.

"There was someone else with you. A Hunter. Where did he go?" he asked.

Huh. He didn't realize I was the said Hunter he was smelling. He mistakenly thought I was a Human. And he thought they'd kidnapped me.

I relaxed my stance and forced myself to seem small and frightened. I needed to get Chantel and Agrona and run, then we could find Blayde. Together.

When the biggest man was in front of me, I turned on the waterworks. I let moisture stream down my face. It wasn't hard. After today, I had enough tears to fill up a bathtub.

The animals stayed at the heels of the man as he stood a foot from me. "I promise we will make the Vampire pay for what she has done to you."

I glanced around him to see Chantel and Agrona staring at me. Waiting for me to give them a sign. Not yet. If I got closer to them, then Chantel could transport us. First, I need to teach this guy not to call a grown woman "little girl." So insulting.

I measured up the man standing before me. His size alone was intimidating. Like he must be part tree huge. No wonder why he was the leader. He had bronzed-kissed skin and black hair. If he hadn't wounded my pride, I might have admitted how attractive he was.

"Hey, you okay, little one?" he asked.

Like flipping a switch, I stopped crying. I took a step and closed the distance between us. I used my anger as momentum and thrust the heel of my hand into his nose. He grunted and his giant hands cupped his sniffer. But oh no, I wasn't going to stop there.

"I'm not a little girl!" I grabbed his shirt, pulled him to me, and slammed my knee into his manhood. Hopefully, he didn't want kids anytime soon.

Moaning, he dropped to his knees and hunched over. I couldn't tell which move hurt worse. My guess was the latter. I seized the opening and made my escape.

I sprinted past him and straight for my girls. Wolves and

bears charged at me with snaps and growls. Fear surged in my chest. Kneeing their leader wasn't my smartest idea. But it felt so good.

The Shifters in animal form closed in on me and blocked my route. I slid to a stop, and dirt and twigs covered my scuffed Adidas shoes. I glanced at my friends, and they were struggling with a man underneath them. The man twirled Chantel's wand in his hand, taunting them. It must have fallen when she'd flipped upside down. Unless Agrona could do something, no one was escaping.

"Crap. Crapcrapcrapcrapcrap," I muttered.

A white wolf growled and showed each pointy canine. He prowled toward me and locked his predatory gaze on me. I stepped back, only to have a black wolf at my rear snap its teeth. I was trapped.

What to do? What to do? I didn't have time to come up with a plan.

I heard it too late. The black wolf behind me lunged and tackled me. My head slammed into the dirt, giving me whiplash, and immediately I knew I would have a headache.

The black wolf restrained me, and I reached up to keep the wolf's muzzle away. It snarled, and its sticky breath soiled my cheek. The wolf was strong. So strong that if I didn't have fear and adrenaline coursing through me, I didn't know if I'd be able to hold the wolf's chomping jaws at arm's length.

I fought the instinct to turn my head to the side. I didn't want to expose my throat. My jugular. One little bite on my neck and it would be bye-bye Cedar.

"Gah. What are they feeding you? Steroids?" I pushed the words out, attempting to mask my dread with humor.

Should I use my Huntress power now, or wait till I was

with Agrona and Chantel? I had to make it count. I only had one shot at the element of surprise.

A growl echoed through the trees. I knew that growl. In a blink, the black wolf was off me. I scrambled to my feet to see what was happening.

Blayde.

Blayde in wolf form, to be exact.

He was snarling at the black wolf that was pinned beneath him. The animals closed in on me, and my heart thumped in panic. We were goners. All four of us.

A wave of magic burst from Blayde, and I stumbled. The animals retreated and bowed. The wolf under Blayde whimpered. Wolf Blayde scanned, looking each animal and Human in the eyes. He was asserting his alpha powers and claiming his dominance.

One of the men under Agrona and Chantel threw a knife at their ropes, cutting them. It sent them plummeting to the ground.

"Our apologies. We weren't informed that you were with Blayde, son of the Alpha King and future alpha," the man said to Agrona and Chantel.

Blayde sauntered over to me with his head held high. He stopped next to me and nuzzled my leg. I stroked his salt-'n'-pepper fur. It was soft. If he would ever allow me to shave him, his fur would make the softest, warmest blanket.

Son of the Alpha King and future alpha. This must be Blayde's pack then.

Blayde hunched down, growling, baring his teeth for all to see. Almost like he was staking his claim. He nestled against me once more, marking me with his scent before he trotted to the far side of a tree.

I walked to Agrona and Chantel. I was hyper-aware that practically everyone was staring at me. I was used to stares, but after that encounter, I still wasn't sure how I felt about them.

"You didn't have to drop me on my skull," Chantel yelled at the man who'd cut the rope. "You could have given me my wand and I could've gotten us down safely. But nooooo, Mister Fancy Knife had to be a showoff!"

"Your *Vampire* friend saved you before you hit the ground," he said. He spat out Vampire like it was the dirtiest word he had ever left his lips.

Chantel waved her arms in frustration. "I fell on top of her on accident, but that's not the point!" Her face was red, and she sounded like she was about to boil over.

I set my hand on her shoulder, and she jumped.

"Gah! Cedar, don't do that!" She placed her palm over her heart.

I embraced Agrona and Chantel, happy that they weren't harmed. Their arms encircled me, and I was immediately filled with relief. Someone, my someone, cleared their throat behind me. The girls relinquished, and I turned.

I beelined for Blayde. I wrapped my arms around his waist and lay my head on his chest. He pulled me in tighter.

"Where did you go?" I whispered. I looked up at him to watch his eyebrow inch up. "Not now, but when the attack guard came out."

Blayde brushed back my hair and thumbed my cheek. "I knew there were traps along the way, and they are easier for me to find in wolf form, so I went to shift behind a tree. I saw the enforcers come out, and I wanted to see what would happen. I almost lost it, seeing Josh tackle you."

Josh was the black wolf. I'd have to remember that in case I ran into him in Human form.

Blayde stepped back and faced the Shifters. "These three are with me. No harm comes to them, or you'll answer to me."

I glanced at the Shifters, and the look of shame graced each of their faces. I knew Blayde's dad was the Alpha King of North America, but hot dang, I didn't know Blayde had this type of power. I had a feeling that being on pack land would be a baptism by fire education.

Blayde nodded to the Shifter who had called me a little girl. "Lead the way."

Just like that, we hiked the rest of the way with a band of Shifters. Agrona was silent and emotionless. Chantel grumbled the entire time. Blayde kept his hand intertwined with mine, almost like he was afraid to let me go.

We walked for who knew how long. But once we arrived, all my preconceived notions about what I was going to find were shattered.

Chapter Nine

I, Cedar Hastings, admit that I formed preconceived notions about how Shifters lived. And I was wrong. Very wrong. Somehow, I had gotten in my mind that Shifters lived in trailers or cabins or even in an old Western village.

The town we were brought to was modern—like a small town nobody had ever heard of had a baby with a big city. The buildings appeared to have been erected a few years ago. How was that possible? Magic. Magic was the answer. Magic was almost always the answer. Of course, their town was contemporary. We were talking about magical beings, after all.

They directed us to a building that screamed, "I'm filled with cubicles." I glanced at the sign and read "Woodpine Town Hall."

I rolled my head back and took in the height of the structure. It was at least five stories high and towered over the establishments next to it. The black-tinted windows were more like mirrors and reflected their environment.

How Shifters were able to build this was beyond me. I whistled at its sheer magnitude.

Blayde chuckled beside me. "You grew up with rich people. I didn't think a town hall would impress you. If that is all it takes, I'll make sure to show you the library, too." He winked.

I smiled in response. "I'll be thoroughly impressed if the town has a chocolate factory."

"Alas, we don't have that, but we do have the best ice cream shop. Maybe I'll take you there on our date."

My spirits perked up at the thought of the frozen treat. It was almost enough to distract me from the anxious energy surrounding dating Blayde. He tugged on my hand and led me into the building.

My face fell. It wasn't as fancy and cool on the inside as it was on the outside. I felt misled. Tricked. Bamboozled.

It was plain. Plain u-g-l-y. It was as if a great-grandma with no taste had decorated it. The lobby's waiting room furniture belonged in the seventies. Tan floral couches and chairs that didn't have matching patterns. The only thing that made it seem like it had been done on purpose was all the tan. Tan walls. Tan flooring. Tan ceiling. Tan furniture.

I rubbed my temples. My headache from being tackled was getting worse. I was going to blame it on being tortured by TAN.

I must have let my disgust manifest because Blayde snickered. "It is pretty bad, isn't it?"

"Understatement of the year."

"Oh! Is that some blue over there? Just kidding, it's tan," Chantel said.

We all laughed, even Agrona, who had been the epitome of emotionlessness.

We were ushered into a room that appeared to be used

for community meetings. It wasn't tan like the lobby. There was a slight variation in color. Brown. Tree-bark brown. Was this entire building a different shade of brown?

There was a large desk on one side of the room, which was similar to the desk the Council had when I met them. It was a half-circle. The other side had a few rows of chairs.

Doors banged open, and Blayde stiffened next to me. His arm wrapped around my waist.

Three oversized men entered in a triangle formation. The biggest led the way. Beefy was how I'd describe them. They all appeared to be in their late fifties, but since they were Shifters, I knew they had to be older. Each sported patches of gray hair and were visually appealing. The leader was definitely president of the hot old men's club. Above all, each radiated power. It oozed from them.

"Blayde," the leader rumbled, sounding like we were a paper cut on his finger.

"Father," Blayde greeted. He didn't grumble. He didn't gripe. His tone held a sort of reverence and respect.

If this was Blayde's father, then this was the Alpha King. Well, crap. Was I supposed to curtsey?

I glanced at Agrona for a clue. Her face was a mask of indifference. The only sign of discomfort was the twitch of her nose. She never did like the smell of Shifters.

Chantel magically cleaned herself up and was staring at the trio. Her expression was flat, showing no emotion. Which was weird for the Sorceress—thoughts flowed off her tongue without a filter.

The leader took a seat behind the desk. The chair seemed to be higher than the rest. He wanted everyone to understand who was in charge.

The Alpha King leaned forward, elbows resting with his hands pressed together, tapping his mouth. He was sizing us up or maybe just me. Either way, I struggled to not squirm under his gaze. But Caroline had taught me grace and confidence under pressure, and that was exactly what I was going to exude. I lifted my chin ever so slightly to let him know I wasn't scared.

"Father—" Blayde stopped the second his father raised his hand in the air.

"So this is her. The *Huntress*." His lips puckered.

He'd already decided he didn't like me. Well, I'd show him. I'd charm the pants off him. Wait, no. I'd just charm him.

Blayde's hold on me tightened. "Not just a Huntress. Cedar is my fated mate."

I side-eyed him, and he shot me a pleading look to not fight him right now. I didn't like everyone calling us mates when I still haven't sorted through my feelings.

"*Hfmp*. We'll see. Everything can change. You will be Alpha King and will need a strong Shifter by your side. Besides, there have never been fated mates between a Shifter and a Hunter." He glared at me.

Did I say he disliked me? I meant hated.

"There is a first time for everything, Alpha King Hilt," I said. I didn't avert my gaze even though I desperately wished to.

Waves of power rolled off him. Dang, alpha powers. It annoyed me when Shifters sought to assert their dominance over me.

"Now that's out of the way. Let me welcome you back, Blayde, along with your gorgeous friends," said the man to the left of the Alpha King.

Blayde leaned over and whispered, "That is my father's beta, Herrick Nielsen, and to the right is Kerr Wulfric. He is the battle commander."

"Your timing here couldn't have been more perfect even if you had tried." His smile was friendly and without a trace of a hidden motive.

"I don't know if it is appropriate to explain what is occurring in front of our guests." Kerr's words teetered on the line of politeness and annoyance.

"Nonsense. It's obvious Blayde explicitly trusts them, or he wouldn't have brought a Vampire onto our land," Herrick argued.

Clearly, Kerr was on the Alpha King's side and Herrick was more of the peacekeeper, the loveable Shifter. I liked him already.

Hilt grumbled. He knew Herrick was right, but he wanted Kerr to be. He waved his hand in the air, allowing Herrick to proceed.

"Things have been...disappearing. And temper levels have been high."

That was cryptic. Shifters were losing their marbles and going all Hulk. It didn't seem like something that needed to be kept secret. It sounded like a start to a bad action movie or one of Ricardo's jokes.

"Disappearing like abracadabra?" Chantel piped in.

I snorted, earning me an icy glare from the Alpha King. I grinned sweetly in response. Nobody was going to piss in my Coco Puffs.

Herrick shrugged. "Maybe. Items are being stolen, and we aren't sure how or who is doing it."

"There is a thief in your midst," Chantel obviously stated.

"We gathered that much." Kerr relaxed in his chair and crossed his arms.

My eyebrows rose. They didn't pull their punches here.

I wondered how frequently they allowed pack members to mouth off to them.

"What about the tempers?" Blayde tried to return the focus to the matter at hand.

"Even though we, Shifters, tend to have temper issues, there have been an alarming number of fights," Herrick said. "Not just verbal but physical altercations, and when they come down from their anger trip, they can't remember what triggered them."

"Is magic influencing them?" Blayde asked, keeping his touch steady on me.

"We haven't sensed any, but with the help of your Sorceress friend, we are hoping we can find out what is happening." Herrick smiled.

I glanced at Chantel, who didn't seem excited by her new "assignment." If anything, she appeared to be a little bored. My sight moved to Agrona, who still remained emotionless, motionless like a wax figure. I itched to throw out that Shifters weren't T-Rexes and could still see her, but I thought better of it. The Alpha King already hated me. I didn't need to add more fuel to the dumpster fire.

"We'll speak more of this later. Right now, we will have you shown to your accommodations," the Alpha King said with a mischievous smirk.

The doors opened, and a modelesque woman stepped through. She tossed her white-blonde hair over her shoulder, and her curls bounced as she walked. Her sundress swayed around her hips, and the *click-clack* of her high heels was the only sound in the room. Her attention landed on Blayde, and a smile lit her face.

I immediately wanted to punch her and mark him as mine. Instead, I swallowed my urge and peeked at the Alpha King.

His gaze was glued on me, and he grinned as if he had just called checkmate. A bad feeling swam in my gut. The Alpha King wasn't going to make my stay easy. Luckily, Caroline had taught me how to handle social crushing situations.

"We'll let you all get acquainted and see you for dinner." Herrick shot me a sympathetic glance.

We watched the Hot Old Men Trio leave. Once the doors shut, the woman's glee grew, and she sauntered toward us. Blayde's touch hardened, and his fingers dug into my hip. Whomever she was had made Blayde anxious.

She threw her arms around Blayde's neck and kissed his cheek. "I'm so glad you're home!"

Blayde used his free hand to push the woman's body away from his. My jaw clenched so strongly, I might have cracked a tooth. I craved to spring into action, smack some sense into her, and inform her that Blayde was *mine*.

But I didn't.

I stood there shaking with rage. Every cell vibrated, screaming for retribution.

Blayde pulled me into his torso and pressed his lips to the top of my head. He was claiming me as his territory, and I didn't mind it one bit.

"Ashley, let me introduce you to my mate, Cedar." Blayde's smile didn't reach his eyes. It was strained but polite. Not one he would give a friend or even someone he liked.

It settled my nerves, but I was still wary.

"Mate?" She laughed. "We'll see."

Something snapped inside me. I wanted to rip her Barbie hair out of her head. I wanted to scream and gnash my teeth. I wanted to show her who was boss.

I lunged, but I didn't go anywhere. Blayde's hold on me was secure and unwavering.

"How about you go get someone to show us where we will be staying?" Agrona said flatly.

Even though her voice didn't hold any emotion, I knew she was attempting to get Ashley to leave for my sake. That's what best friends did.

Ashley narrowed her eyes. "Who said you could talk, viper?"

"Ashley, quit it." A wave of power rolled off Blayde, and Ashley stilled. "She is my guest, and you should treat her as such."

Oh snap!

She turned her attention to me and shot a quick glare before smiling at Blayde. "Of course. How about I find someone to escort them to where they will be lodging, and we can catch up like people who are engaged to be married should do."

Fiancée?

Blayde had a fiancée?

My stomach turned, and acid threatened to escape. Why hadn't he told me? Why hadn't he prepared me for this? Wasn't I supposed to be his fiancée? No, I hadn't decided if I wanted to be his mate yet.

A growl came from Blayde, and he shook with rage, but his grip on me never loosened. "We aren't engaged, Ashley. So, stop pretending as if I asked you in the first place."

I worked to school my emotions and keep everything in check. But it was so hard! I was getting emotional whiplash. Blayde had a fiancée. Blayde didn't have a fiancée. Whatever the answer, it didn't make me want to rip her scalp off any less. Taking a deep breath, I tried to settle the possessive surge that washed over me.

"He didn't tell you," Ashley said in mock innocence. "He didn't tell you that our marriage has been planned since we were little? My dad—Battle Commander Kerr Wulfric—and the Alpha King wanted to unite our bloodlines. Besides, we have been together longer than I can remember. And we look oh so good as a couple."

I stiffened as the impact of her words hit me. She'd done this on purpose. She'd meant to throw me for a loop. But why? Clearly, Blayde didn't want her, or he wouldn't have called off their engagement. Was she trying to drive a wedge between us? To get him back?

Regardless of her reason, I wouldn't let her get under my skin. I was a freakin' Huntress, for crying out loud.

I clamped down on my pain and permitted the rage to rise to the surface. I gave her a friendly smile.

"It's sweet of you to inform me, and to care about my feelings, but what you thought was between you and Blayde was in the past. Nothing more." I tossed my hair over my shoulders, acting like the bomb she'd dropped hadn't exploded in my face. Caroline had taught me how to control a room, and I had prematurely thought I had left this juvenile nonsense behind me. Shifters were more dramatic than an angsty teenager.

Pressing onto my tiptoes, I placed a soft kiss on Blayde's cheek. I lay my hand on his muscular chest and traced figure eights with my fingers. I forced my thoughts to stay on the conversation and not about Blayde's rockin' body.

"Besides, we don't keep secrets from each other. And this delusion you are carrying around isn't worth my time. Now please bring someone to show us our accommodations." I let my spoiled rich-privilege-girl voice drip into each word. She needed to learn real quick she couldn't mess with me. I wouldn't put up with her defecation.

Her jaw dropped, and she crossed her arms. "Are you going to let her talk to me like that?" she asked Blayde.

He shrugged, and amusement danced at the corners of his lips. "I don't muzzle my woman. Plus, I didn't hear anything wrong." He glanced at Agrona and Chantel. "Did you guys?"

They agreed with Blayde, but it was hard to detect anything over Ashley's shrieks.

"Just you wait till Daddy and *your* father hear about this." Bimbo Barbie stomped out of the room and slammed the doors on her way out.

I released a long breath and relaxed into Blayde, laying my head against him. I forgot how much energy it took to seem cool and collected. I might be out of practice, or they were really big jerks. Or both. *Nah.* It was totally them.

Chantel laughed. "You already made enemies, and you haven't been here long enough to sit on a toilet."

I groaned. She was right. It was clear Hilt, Kerr, Ashley, and the guy whose nose I broke in the forest weren't my biggest fans.

Let's get this party started.

Chapter Ten

"What was that all about?" I asked, staring at the doors.

I half expected Ashley to walk in and throw herself at Blayde again. Her exit wasn't her giving in. She was biding her time to come up with another plan.

Blayde placed his hands on my hips, turning me so I faced him. I quickly averted my eyes. He had kept her a secret. A secret fiancée. And I hated to show how it had cut me.

"Our fathers have desired our union since we were children. To strengthen our bloodlines. I have never been interested in Ashley. It was clear when we were teenagers that she was not someone I'd choose to spend the rest of my life with. Even my wolf doesn't like her. We are not a match in any way. When I first saw you at that club, something drew me to you. Then in the woods when my wolf met you, he knew you were the one. After that, I called my father and told him I would have nothing to do with Ashley or any woman they tried to set me up with. And that I had found my mate."

I stared at the brown hardwood floor, not making eye contact. I didn't want him to see how hurt I was that he hadn't told me about her. I was blindsided. Not to mention the jealous, possessive monster that raged inside me. It despised that Blayde had a previous girlfriend, let alone an ex-fiancée. It wanted him. It wanted all of him, and it wanted to stake its claim.

Blayde nudged my chin, and I closed my eyes, still refusing to meet his.

"Hey." His voice was gentle and full of love. "Hey, none of this. She means zilch to me and never will be anything more. You are my future. You've captured my attention and my heart ever since the moment you had a drink spilling down your shirt."

I snorted and met his fierce gaze. His amber-flaked blue eyes searched mine, and I let him see my pain. How much it hurt that he'd kept this from me. And above all else, how much I cared for him.

Blayde's stare didn't waver. "I am *so* sorry. This wasn't some deep, dark secret. I didn't bring it up because she's in my past, where she will remain. Also, because I would rather talk about us. About our bond."

Sincerity dripped off each of his words, so much so that I could feel it in my soul. Was that a product of the mate bond? Or was it because I relied on him?

Not trusting my voice to not crack, I gave a small smile and nodded that I understood.

He smiled back and leaned in. His lips brushed against my ear. The warmth from his breath sent shivers down my spine.

"I care about you more than anything in this world, and that will never change." His tone was low and husky.

His voice registered somewhere deep within me.

Surfacing warmth rose in me. I wanted to thread my fingers through his dark hair and pull him down to me with our lips meeting in the middle. I wanted to feel him against me. To press my body to his. The desire to have his luscious mouth on mine was overwhelming.

He pulled back, and our eyes connected. His pupils dilated, overtaking the pools of blue. The heat from his gaze warmed every inch of my skin, making me feel like I was his walking fantasy. My lips parted, and I tilted my chin up, inviting him.

His hand on my lower back tugged me closer, flattening me along the hard contours of his body. His free palm cupped my cheek, and I knew without a shadow of a doubt he desired me as much as I did him.

"Just kiss him already," Chantel blurted, popping our bubble. "Oof. Why did you elbow me? They were taking forever. My grandpop has more game."

"You ruined their moment. You deserved more than an elbow to the gut," Agrona hissed.

The doors opened, and we all turned to see who would walk through the door.

"Saved by the doors." Chantel clapped.

Once I could get Chantel alone, we are going to have a lengthy talk—lecture—about interrupting a kiss between Blayde and me. If she did, you'd best believe I'd be there to break up any kissing in her future. *Sisters before misters, my butt.*

A woman walked through the tree-bark-brown doors with a long-forgotten elegant grace. With her high cheek-bones, flawless skin, and voluminous blonde hair, I had a major girl crush. She had to be no more than fifty. With every step she took, I wanted to be like her when I grew up. She carried herself with such confidence, that it was evident she didn't need a man to stand beside her, but the smile assured me she had the joy of a loving relationship.

Blayde dropped his hands and stepped toward her. Smashed was my girl crush, and envy fueled. His pace quickened before they embraced in the center of the room. Red spots clouded my vision. Two females in a matter of minutes, hugging and throwing their arms around him. If this was going to be an hourly thing on pack land, I might go a little crazy. Okay, a lot crazy.

"Mom, I would like you to meet my mate." Blayde gestured to me.

Mom.

This woman standing before me was Blayde's mom? No wonder why Blayde was so hot. His parents were presidents of the hot people club.

A soft smile lit her face, and she effortlessly glided toward me. Her eyes appraised me, and I wondered if she had the same opinion as her husband. Instead, she flung her arms around me and pulled me into a hug. She squeezed softly before she finally released.

"Welcome to the family, sweetie. My name is Tammy Daniels," her Southern accent rang.

I think I died and went to mother-in-law Heaven. If only her husband could be as sweet.

"Thank you." I mirrored her kindness.

"I wanted to meet my son's mate before you were shown where you'd be staying. Blayde has told me so much about you. I already feel like you are my daughter."

I softened. She wasn't glaring or scheming. She was being sincere and genuine.

My heart ached for the only mother I knew—Caroline. I needed to call her and have a tête-à-tête.

"When you have time, maybe we could get together and learn about each other a little more," I said.

Anxiety ping-ponged in my chest. I hadn't wanted a mother's approval since I was sixteen—Caroline forced me to participate in a cotillion, and I wanted to make her proud.

"I'd love that, sweetie." She applied reassuring pressure to my hand.

The doors opened again, and I swear to the Angels that if another woman walked through and launched herself on Blayde, I was going to L-O-S-E IT.

But luckily, I wouldn't have to.

A boy, who looked to be twelve years old, shuffled in. He was slim and didn't have much muscle like all the other Shifters I had seen. Maybe he hasn't bonded with his animal yet.

During my stay at the academy, the first thing I learned about Shifters was at the age of sixteen, they traveled to an island. On this island, there were animals of all different species. While there, the Human and animal found each other and became one. How exactly this happened, I had no idea. In class, we didn't go into depth because the bonding experience between human and animal was sacred.

"Trevor, perfect timing," Tammy said. "Trevor here will show y'all to your accommodations. Blayde, dear, your father would like to speak to you regarding some responsibilities you'll need to attend to while you're here."

Blayde growled and shot his mother a glare.

"Hush, child, I changed your diapers. I taught you the growl and glare. It doesn't work on me." Tammy gave Blayde a cheeky smile and patted his shoulder. She was slowly becoming my personal heroine.

Chantel, Agrona, and I made our way to the door. Blayde snatched my wrist, bringing me to a halt.

"I'll come once I'm done with my father, okay?" Blayde asked.

I nodded.

He bent and pressed his lips lightly against my forehead. The gentle peck pooled heat within me. Peeking through my eyelashes, I watched his mouth tug up into a smirk. He knew what his small smooch did to me. My cheeks deepened the crimson color. That jerk. It wasn't fair I was the only person suffering.

I shuffled my feet closer to him, flashed my best "come hither" expression, fisted his shirt, and dragged him to me.

I leaned in and whispered, "Two can play this game."

I placed a lingering kiss just below his earlobe, and his hand gripped me tighter. I eased back, allowing space to form between us, and batted my eyelashes. A low growl escaped him, vibrating over my skin and landing in the fervor accruing in my belly.

"Come on, tell lover boy goodbye." Agrona yanked my arm, dragging me with her.

With a finger wave, I left Blayde standing with his intense gaze locked on me.

* * *

Trevor led us down the street where pack members openly gawked. Some curious. Some friendly. Some hostile.

I didn't know if they were all for me or directed at Agrona and Chantel. Only time would tell.

The street Trevor took us down seemed to be their main road; businesses lined it on both sides. Clothing, books, restaurants, and my personal favorite, ice cream. There was even a doctor's office. When the Shifters developed their town, they thought of everything. Each structure was modern and seemed to be recently erected. It had me wondering how old this town was.

"When was Woodpine built?" I asked.

"Way before Humans came out west and settled here, ma'am," Trevor answered.

Ma'am? Did I look like a ma'am?

I sighed. He was only being polite.

"Then how does the whole town look newly constructed?" I stepped to the side of him. It was starting to feel like our accommodations were on the outskirts.

Trevor nodded. "Renovations are done every ten years or so."

"That must get pricey."

"Sort of. We pay a Sorcerer to come here and renovate with magic. We like to stay modern, and paying a Sorcerer is much cheaper than doing it manually."

Huh. So, their decorating style was like a mullet—modern on the outside, tan on the inside.

"Here we are," Trever said at the edge of town.

It was either a large house or a cramped apartment building. I studied the building for a moment and noticed three different doors. It was multiple townhouses crafted to resemble one enormous house. Clever.

Trevor brushed his fingertips along the exterior, moving past it. Maybe our door was in the back?

Anxiety buzzed in me, lighting up each nerve as we walked past the house entirely. The small comfort was that Agrona and Chantel were by my side. And that if Trevor led us to a trap, Blayde would eventually come for me.

Aspen and pine trees greeted us as we traipsed into the forest. Fear and paranoia overpowered my instincts and screamed for us not to follow. Maybe this skinny boy was really a psycho Shifter.

I glanced at my girls. Chantel fisted her wand, ready for anything. Agrona's eyes were glued to Trevor, watching his every move, their expressions laced with suspicion.

We didn't have to journey too far before he announced that we had arrived. In front of me was a log cabin. Exactly how you would picture one. It wasn't teeny-tiny, but no bigger than two bedrooms.

Trevor strolled up to the front door and pulled out a key. Once unlocked, he pushed it open and gestured for us to go inside. My eyebrows rose. I couldn't tell if this was an ambush or if he was being chivalrous.

"You go first, Human," Agrona snapped.

Human. It confirmed my thought that he hadn't bonded with an animal yet.

The boy stepped through the threshold with a scowl. He clearly knew we didn't trust him. He tossed us the key, and Agrona caught it in her palm.

"There you go. I'm sure Blayde, son of the Alpha King, will make sure you are comfortable. I'd say if you need anything, holler, but since one of you is a Vampire, I don't see that going well. So yeah." Trevor exited and headed the way we'd come.

I had an intense urge to yell "holler" to see what he would do, but I dropped it. He was just a boy.

"Stay here while I check it out." Agrona placed her hand to stop Chantel and me. She disappeared into the unknown edges of the cabin.

"Do you sense any magic?" I asked Chantel.

"Nope," she said, placing emphasis on the p. "But she is a Vampire and she doesn't trust Shifters. It is easier to let her scope it out rather than fight with her."

Agrona reappeared with a grim expression.

"Traps?" I asked. My heart pounded faster by the second.

"No. I'll let you see for yourselves." She moved aside, and Chantel and I entered.

It opened up to what would be considered a TV room, but it lacked, well, everything. There was only one plain wood bench that fit two people. Unfortunately, it looked like if you sat on it, it would crumble. There were no couches or tables. No TV or end tables. No artwork on the walls. Nothing that would make the cabin feel welcoming. Above all that, the air was stale, humid, and miserable.

"This isn't even the best part," Agrona's voice dripped with sarcasm.

Off the main room, there were two doors. Each opened to what would be considered bedrooms. They were a carbon copy—a single yellow-stained mattress on the floor. Don't even get me started on the smell.

"That's it? All of it?" I asked in disbelief.

"No, come see." Agrona directed us to the main space and gestured to the only window.

Ugh.

A lone shack stood a short distance from the cabin with a crescent moon carved into the wood. An outhouse.

This was a nightmare.

I didn't expect to be received like royalty. Just to be treated like a human being. Oh, wait. Was that what they were trying to inform us? That we were beneath them. That even Humans were beneath them?

Chantel pulled out a phone and snapped pictures of everything. I quirked my brow.

"First, Ricardo will think this is hilarious. Second, before and after photos."

Before and after what? Sometimes, I didn't understand what transpired in her mind.

"If you both will please step out of this condemned cabin while I work my magic?" Chantel pushed us outside. She cackled, slamming the door in our faces.

Agrona rolled her eyes at her shenanigans. After a minute of us kicking rocks, Chantel emerged and beckoned us in.

I stepped through the threshold, and I hadn't anticipated this. Maybe a few pieces of furniture, but not this.

The inside of the cabin resembled a luxury hotel room but farmhouse style. There was shiplap on the walls, painted gray and light blue. The floor was a sand-toned laminate. Couches were white, and I was afraid to sit on them. A little chandelier hung in the middle of the ceiling. Where one of the bedrooms used to be was now a kitchen like you would find in an extended-stay hotel. Narrow counter with a mini fridge and a microwave. A small sink was in the corner.

I wandered and peeked into the bedroom. There was a matching white dresser and end table with a three-person bunk bed. Each had a white comforter and pillow. I flopped on the bed, and it was like landing on a cloud. Soft. Comfortable. Fluffy.

"The only thing I couldn't completely fix was the bathroom. Sorry. I wasn't sure how to configure the layout to attach the bathroom to the cabin. Although, I did add a shower to it, so now we won't be stinky. But unfortunately, you will have to walk out there." Chantel stated. "Now let's take some after pictures to settle Ricardo. He was NOT happy about the situation."

"You don't say?" Agrona's mouth twitched.

"No hay buena trampa mortal," Chantel mimicked

107

Ricardo's accent. "Then something about biohazard horse crap or whatever. When he began to tell me about the Shifters who walked into the bar, I hung up."

I laughed. I couldn't help but laugh. And man, did it feel good.

Chapter Eleven

Chantel helped me stash the journal. I was adamant it wouldn't fit, but she proved me wrong. We magically placed it in the pole of the bunk bed and sealed it up with an incantation. I was just going to hide the journal under my mattress again, but Agrona and Chantel scoffed at my lack of hiding abilities.

After taking—what could only be described as ridiculous—pictures, Chantel sent them to Ricardo to appease him. To reassure him that things were under control. We even modeled in the photos to send the point across that everything was fine. After successfully making sure Ricardo didn't explode with worry, we napped. Napped on our glorious beds. I was actually considering writing poetry about my bed. Even with all of my parents' money, I hadn't slept on a mattress this comfortable.

Being woken up by a series of loud bangs was not ideal. With adrenaline spiking through my veins, I bolted up and dashed out of my covers. Agrona darted ahead of me, and Chantel brought up the rear.

"Cedar! Open the door now," Blayde roared.

My epinephrine dipped, and a sense of yearning rushed in me.

"Is there a back way out of here?" I joked, not wanting to deal with the big bad wolf.

Chantel chuckled and shoved me toward the entrance. I opened it mid-knock and sidestepped to prevent Blayde's fist from connecting with my nose.

Without a moment's hesitation, he drew me into his arms, squeezing me against his torso. He took a large inhale, and I rested against his chest, listening to the rhythmic pounding of his pulse. With his head on top of mine, he nuzzled me, marking me with his scent. Something that Shifters did to mark what was theirs. You would think that by being hesitant about our relationship, I would hate that he was staking his claim. Instead, I loved it. I loved knowing he wanted everyone to know.

He held me until his heart rate slowed. I pulled back. Traces of anger lingered on his face.

"What's going on?" I asked, trying not to show my enjoyment of being in his embrace.

"When I got back to my place, your scent was nowhere. I panicked. You were supposed to be staying near me. Usually, mates stay in the same room, but I knew you wouldn't be pleased with that. Once I was told that Ashley had been in charge of your accommodations, I lost it. The worst scenarios ran through my mind. I followed your scent to the old cabin," he bit out. His upper lip curled, and a small growl escaped.

Ashley had done this. I suspected this was a part of her plan from the beginning. She was sending me a message. A message that I shouldn't get complacent. That I wasn't accepted. That she wielded the power. If she thought she could steamroll me, she was in for a rude awakening.

Reaching up on my tiptoes, I planted a peck on the edge of his mouth. I wanted to give him a proper kiss, but I didn't want to do it with an audience. Or at least until I figured out my feelings.

"Of course, your crazy ex did this. She got booted out of power and she wants it back," Agrona said.

"Pleeeease let me hex her. I have this idea for a really fun hex, and I've been dying to try it out." Chantel was all but bouncing up and down.

Her excitement made me laugh.

My girls had my back to the end, even if it meant taking a Shifter on pack land. They were my ride-or-die.

Blayde growled. "Cedar is mine to protect."

Something possessive grabbed a hold of me. I *wanted* him to protect me. Always. But I wouldn't allow him to do anything doltish because of me. I couldn't pit him against Shifters. It would only turn their hate into loathing.

I placed my hands on the sides of his face, cupping his cheeks. "You make me feel safe."

His pupils dilated, and his intense gaze bore into me, sending heat to flood my body. I closed my eyes, breathing slowly, still feeling his stare on me, pricking my skin. I needed to calm down, to focus on the topic at hand, to take a cold shower.

Reluctantly, I opened my eyes. None of the passion from his attention had distinguished. If he kept this up, I would be in trouble. Big trouble.

"I can handle this. We—" I gestured to Agrona and Chantel, "can handle this. When there is a bigger threat, you can join in. But right now, you need to let this go."

The fire simmered in his eyes before dying out, but longing remained. Something else lingered, and I knew I wasn't ready to explore that...yet.

111

"I will let you handle matters for now. If things get out of control or your happiness is dampened, I *will* step in. Your happiness isn't negotiable. Got it?" Blayde's lips pressed together to produce a thin line.

My heart soared, and, on the inside, I melted into a puddle. He was going against his protective instincts to make me happy. To prove to me that he cared.

I nodded, knowing my voice would give my emotions away. He released a long breath.

"Now that you are settled and have DIY'd the cabin." Blayde smirked. "Let me show you where you will be training."

Ugh. Couldn't I go one week without training? I was hoping for a mini vacation before my babysitters threw me back into practice, but alas, no such luck.

* * *

I clipped my chakrams to my belt, and Blayde led the way into town. He intertwined our fingers, showing everyone I was his. He walked down the street with his chin held high and with an air about him that warned you not to mess with him. The only ones who approached him were little old ladies. He was sweet to them. He treated each as if they were his own grandma. I laughed when one of them grabbed his cheeks and pinched.

We arrived at a building that looked similar to a Human gym. It had open windows that showed cardio machines, and in the back were the weights. We walked in, and a receptionist nodded to us. Blayde stopped and glanced down at me.

I raised my eyebrow, struggling to discern why he was staring. I ran my hand over my face, making sure nothing was on it. Without feeling anything, I took in my clothes. Nada.

Blayde chuckled and shook his head. "What are you doing?"

"I was trying to figure out why you were gawking at me. I thought something was on my face or somethin'.'"

"I was wondering what you thought of the gym?" He smiled.

"It stinks like feet and wet dogs," Agrona cut in. "Can we move along now?"

I rolled my eyes. I could tell this Vampire vs Shifter prejudice was going to be a problem. I hoped no Shifter with anger issues overheard. That was the last thing I needed.

Blayde ushered us to an elevator, and we went to the top level. There were only two floors, so it didn't take long.

The elevator pinged, and the doors revealed a gym similar to the training rooms at the academy. There was a small bleacher that had two rows off to the left side. Mats took up most of the space for sparring. One wall contained different weapons and a bullseye for target practice. Off to the side of the mat, punching bags and practice dummies.

"I need to introduce you to someone." Blayde steered us over to three beefy guys sitting on the bleachers.

Once we got closer, one, in particular, looked familiar. *Uh-oh.* My palm had gotten intimate with his nose. At least it had healed fast and wasn't crooked.

"Cedar, this is Kanyon. He will be your new trainer." Blayde gestured to the guy whose expression promised revenge.

"Wait—why does she need a new trainer?" Agrona asked. She eyed the three guys with disdain.

"There are some...things...commitments I must oversee

while I am here." Blayde's hand wiped down his face. "When I am on pack land, there are obligations I am required to attend to. I hoped my father would've allowed me a respite from those duties, but he did not. Instead, he added to my existing responsibilities. He seems quite determined to keep me away from Cedar."

"That is exactly why you should still train her and not let these *animals* do your job." Agrona gestured to the three Shifters.

"Stick it to the man!" Chantel pumped her fist in the air.

Kanyon growled, and the others took steps toward Agrona. Blayde brought up his palm, stopping them. He inclined his head to the elevator. The two Shifters glowered at Agrona and stalked out of the gym.

"For now, this is how it has to be," Blayde said through clenched teeth. He pulled me to the side and held both of my hands. "My father is being stubborn. I'll do everything in my power to be present as much as I possibly can. Even now, I don't want to leave you. Learn from Kanyon. I trust him not only with my life but with yours, and that is more important to me than anything." Blayde pressed his lips to my forehead, and before I was ready for his touch to dissipate, he was gone.

I turned to watch the elevators close and gave Blayde a small smile. My heart twisted, and all I wanted to do was run to him and throw my arms around his neck. But I couldn't. He had a job to do, and so did I. It seemed the more time I spent with him, the faster my feelings developed. More than that, I felt drawn to him.

I focused my attention on Kanyon and sized him up. He was big. Like, bigger than Blayde. His muscles had muscles. He had to be Dwayne Johnson's size, if not larger. With bronzed-kissed skin and black hair, he was as sinful as the Devil. If only he hadn't called me a little girl, I might have been able to like him.

"Is this the part where you are in awe of me because I'm a Huntress, and you go 'girl, you the bomb,' and I go, 'tru dat'?" I asked.

"No. That will never happen. I am your trainer, and you'll do what I tell you to," he spat.

Putting my fists on my hips, I shot him a glare. My annoyance went from zero to a hundred in three seconds flat. He wasn't going to boss me around like I was beneath him...or like a little girl.

"So, you think you can teach me, eh? What are your qualifications? Or are your muscles for show?" I taunted and allowed my irritation to seep into my voice.

His eyes grew into tiny slants, and his mouth became a hard line. Somebody didn't like me questioning his manhood.

"By the looks of you, you need all the help you can get," he said.

Agrona barked out a laugh. "We don't need your help, cub."

He took a few steps, stopping only inches away from Agrona. "You want to go a few rounds, viper?"

Viper? That was the second time Agrona had been called that. I was starting to think it was an insult to the max.

"Why did he call her that?" I leaned over and asked Chantel.

"Sometimes I forget that you didn't grow up in the magical community and then you ask a question like that, and BAM, it reminds me how new you are to all of this," she said.

I stared blankly at her, wishing she would get to the point. Agrona and Kanyon were still locked in their Mexican standoff, and who knew how long we had until it exploded?

"Viper refers to the way they execute their magic. They have to bite someone with their fangs like a snake. It isn't a nice term, as you can imagine. Usually, people don't take it well being called a snake." Chantel flashed a cheeky grin and turned her scrutiny to Kanyon.

I swiveled my attention to my new instructor. I needed to break the tension before the three of us did something to disappoint Blayde.

"Why did Blayde assume that you would be an appropriate trainer for me?" I worked to school the ire in my voice.

He was silent for a moment, and when he did speak, his gaze never left Agrona. "I'm the top enforcer in the pack."

"So, you're the toughest, baddest guy in the Woodpine pack." I tried to joke, but it fell flatter than a bottle of open soda.

With an eyebrow quirk, he adjusted his attention to me. "I'm the toughest in North America. The North America Alpha King's head enforcer, to be exact." He gave me a wide, cocky smile, showing all his teeth.

I wanted to roll my eyes but resisted. "Well, Mister Big Shot, we got some training to do."

I spotted an iPod connected to the wall near the punching bag and walked toward it. Choosing the song for my warm-up was my therapy. Angry, rock music. Happy, pop music. Sad, slow country music. Sassy, rap music. There was a genre for every mood. Picking wasn't just therapy, it was something I had control of. A little taste of freedom.

I scrolled through, not finding anything that sounded appealing. So instead, I pressed shuffle. A song popped on that I wasn't familiar with, but it had a good beat, so I went with it. I stepped up to the punching bag and started with the sequence Ricardo had taught me.

Punch. Cross. Hook. Knee. Repeat. I turned my hip into each hit and waited for the endorphins to rush through me.

After a few rounds of it, the tune abruptly shut off. I spun. Kanyon stood next to the iPod. Anger snapped in me. He was ruining my favorite part of training. I didn't get much independence in my life anymore, but the single thing I could always pick was the music.

"Excuse me, what is your problem?" I yelled and stomped in his direction.

His arms crossed his chest, and he stood in front of the iPod, guarding it.

"You will train how I say you train. The music is throwing off your concentration." His voice was commanding, and I was sure it would've worked on other Shifters. Good thing I wasn't one.

"It makes me better." I lifted my chin, challenging his statement. Surely, he must have realized I wasn't going to shrink.

He snorted. "If this is at your best, then you're in more trouble than I thought." His condescending tone dripped with arrogance. It was clear that someone needed to pop his ballooning ego.

"Turn it. Back. On," I said through clenched teeth.

"No. I'm your trainer, and you'll practice how I say." He stepped toward me, closing the distance. The vein on his neck bulged, and his muscles puffed up. He towered over me, trying to assert his dominance.

117

That cocky, pompous jerk!

My mind reeled. I didn't think the three of us could get away with his death looking like an accident.

He mistook my silence for acceptance. With his back facing me, he walked to the weapons. I used this moment to go to the iPod and searched for the first song that popped into my brain.

"Fergalicious" by Fergie.

"I challenge you to a dance-off!" I marched to the center of the mats. If he assumed he could strip my last bit of freedom away, his underestimation of me would be the death of him.

His head jerked, and he bristled. I swear his muscles got bigger. I clamped down on my fear. I wouldn't let him know he intimidated me. Because he did.

Stopping a few feet away from me, he stated, "We don't have time for your shenanigans, little girl."

Now he's done it!

I started walking around him, and I let my body shake and shimmy. I was going to educate him in the art of dance fighting.

I stopped in front of him and broke out my finest nineties moves. Running man. Voguing. Cabbage Patch. The Sprinkler.

He cannot touch this.

No matter what move I threw out at him, his stoic facial expression never changed. I would settle for the corner of his mouth twitching in amusement. This guy needed to lighten up.

I transitioned into my best boy band, diva dance moves of the 2000s. My hand moved in a Bye-Bye-Bye fashion, and I felt like I was showing him the evolution of dance.

I refused to submit. To cower. I wouldn't permit him to

eliminate the last remaining bit of my freedom. I wouldn't live with him treating me like a little girl.

Instead, I was going to get him to lower his inhibitions and make him meet his inner child. No one—and I meant no one—could resist Fergie's insatiable beats.

I flowed into hip-hop steps, and he still supported his surly demure. I was starting to think he used to be a Buckingham Palace guard.

I didn't understand how he was so heartless. So emotionless. I was a volcano of rage, and if he didn't crack soon, I was going to explode.

"Get it! Get it!" Agrona shouted over Chantel's catcalling.

At least my girls had my back.

Then the most amazing thing happened. The song hit my favorite part. You know the portion where Fergie raps, and the beat drops.

Mister Grumpy Goose broke out in a crump. A smile split across my face. I had gotten to him. No matter what type of dancing he did, I won. I won this round.

He shook his booty, and I couldn't stop the laughter from spilling out. Chantel and Agrona joined us, and it ended up a group cavort. By the end of the song, Kanyon was beaming.

Maybe he wasn't so bad after all.

It was all fun and games until the spawn of the devil walked in.

Chapter Twelve

I always thought that the spawn of Satan would inspire more fear. More intimidation. But no. All I felt was anger and annoyance.

"How embarrassing. I sincerely hope that isn't what you call dancing." Ashley snickered.

Two ditzy girls flanked her sides. One a blonde, the other a brunette. Both were slim, even by Shifter standards. They gave off the vibe that they went shopping on a regular basis—not that there was anything wrong with that. I missed the trips Agrona and I had frequently taken. The three of them wore designer clothes as a symbol of status.

A judgmental lump lodged in my throat. I used to look like that. I hoped my attitude didn't mirror theirs. In the past few months, it amazed me how much I'd changed and grown.

"That's the best you got? Really? How unoriginal," I shot back.

The laughter died. The lines around her eyes tightened, and her upper lip curled. Her face reflected a cold desire to knock me down a peg.

"I see they have Kanyon teaching you. They have the nothings paired together. How sweet. They couldn't spare anyone of value to help you. That should show you how worthless you actually are."

I fought my eyebrows that threatened to shoot up. Kanyon said he was the top enforcer, but Ashley was saying he was nothing. Something wasn't adding up. Two plus two didn't equal five.

"Is there a reason why you are here?" Agrona asked, sounding bored.

Ashley glowered, an expression of pure hatred and disdain. "Don't speak to me. You're less desirable than she is."

My blood boiled. I desperately itched to slap some manners into this woman. "Get on with it. I'm sure there is a plastic surgeon somewhere waiting to fix your nose."

Her sidekicks scoffed. Ashley didn't need a nose job. She had perfect bone structure. But that didn't stop me from attacking her precious vanity.

Ashley pursed her lips and focused all of her evil attention on me. She stalked toward me, letting her eyes flash, alerting me that her animal was close to the surface. Coercion tactics might have worked on someone else. Unfortunately for her, I'd seen scarier creatures.

"I'm only going to warn you once. Stay. Away. From Blayde. He's mine." Her voice was low, as if she were trying to make it frightening.

I snorted. Possessive instincts swirled in me. Blayde was mine, and only mine. I wanted to drill that point home, but I couldn't use my fists.

"He'll never be yours. You can try, beg, plead, but he will never love you."

Rage flickered over her features. I had struck a nerve.

"You think you are so special, but I'll clue you in. Blayde is using you. That's right. He is using you because you are a Huntress. Being with you puts his foot in the door for future politics. But he'll eventually break your heart. You can't rule by his side. You don't know what he needs." Ashley's hands opened and closed.

"I know it's not you." I might not be cognizant of everything Blayde needed, but without a shadow of a doubt, I knew she wasn't it.

She laughed. It was forced, and she was trying to make me feel like a speck of dust. "You will never be enough."

Fury ignited in me. Every inch of me craved to lash out. To show her I couldn't be pushed around. I would've liked nothing more than to let my fists do the talking. But I realized if I did, I would only earn Blayde's and Caroline's disappointment.

"And you'll waste away waiting for something that will never happen, cow."

"I'm a wolf, actually." Ashley flipped her—clearly dyed —white-blonde locks over her shoulder.

"I stand by what I said." I smirked. "Now run along. We have work to do."

"Well, my father will be hearing about this," she yelled, stomping away.

We all watched the doors on the elevator close. Instantly, the burning ball of fire in my belly extinguished.

"Girl, you the bomb," Kanyon said.

His words brought a smile to my face. He was referencing what I'd mentioned not only twenty minutes ago.

"Tru dat." I could feel that this was the start of a beautiful friendship.

"Dang, girl! You got some claws," Chantel said proudly.

"She's going to be a problem." Agrona crossed her arms

over her chest.

I almost cracked a Sherlock joke for stating the obvious, but my irritation was still palatable. Ever since we arrived on pack land, my emotions had been crazy. I wanted everyone to understand that Blayde was mine, but that meant claiming him, and I wasn't ready. I needed to find out more about fated mate bonds.

"Ashley has always been trouble. She's after power and status. Even though Blayde is my brother, she deemed me beneath her. She is still a shank in my side," he said. He walked over and grabbed a staff off the weapons rack.

Hold up. Kanyon and Blayde were brothers? Besides both having ripping muscles and dark hair, they didn't look similar.

Tossing the staff at me, he said, "I'm adopted."

He'd said it as if it was the key to understanding everything. But it wasn't.

"Being adopted, he doesn't have the Alpha King's blood through his veins. Many Shifters place bloodlines on pedestals," Agrona added.

Chantel rolled her eyes. "You make it sound like Shifters are the only ones who do that." She focused her gaze on me. "Every species place bloodlines on a pedestal. It's stupid. And very annoying. Thinking about it is giving me a headache."

"Most Shifters respect me, like I'm the Alpha King's natural born. Blayde has never treated me as Ashely does. Our brotherly love is thicker than blood. We have been best friends since we were little."

Huh. This was the missing piece. This was the reason Blayde trusted Kanyon with my training.

"You'll have to tell me what Blayde was like as a child. I'm dying to collect any dirt on him. Hopefully something juicy enough for blackmail." I gave Kanyon a mischievous smile. The idea of teasing Blayde made me stupidly happy. I really needed to get these emotions in check.

"You can do that later, but first Chantel needs to do a binding spell," Agrona said.

"Binding spell?" I asked.

"On you and Kanyon."

Kanyon's eyebrows furrowed, and the corner of his mouth turned down. He didn't seem overjoyed to be bound to me. Whatever that meant.

"For what?" What would it do? Would I be stuck with Kanyon forever? What would Blayde say?

"You should see your face right now. You look like a deer in headlights." Chantel giggled. "Nothing too crazy. It will bind Kanyon to you so he can't reveal anything about you without your permission."

Oh. That would actually be nice. I trusted Blayde, and he trusted Kanyon. But the more people knew about my abilities, the more likely Jordan—or worse, the Dark Master —would find out.

All eyes were on Kanyon. What was going on in his mind? If he said no, I knew without giving it a second thought, Agrona wouldn't allow Kanyon to train me. She didn't have faith in many people, and clearly, she was skeptical about Shifters.

Kanyon was silent for a long time. His expression lacked emotion, not showing what he was thinking.

"Blayde is head over heels for you. Ever since he found you, he hasn't stopped talking about you. I never thought I'd see my brother care about someone as much as he cares about you. It is quite annoying, actually." Kanyon let out an exaggerated sigh. "He has always had my back, and now it's my turn. I'll help protect who he deems more precious than anything in this world." He moved closer to the Sorceress. "I'll do it."

"You need to grasp each other's forearms." Chantel pulled out a blue silk ribbon and her wand.

Kanyon stepped toward me and extended his arm to me. I clasped my hand to his forearm, and he did the same. Chantel wrapped the glossy ribbon around our joined arms.

"*Vinculum sigillum copulare,*" Chantel repeated three times, pointing her wand at our fastened arms.

Small glitter specks swirled on the ribbon, mesmerizing me. After a moment, it ceased. Chantel removed the ribbon and stuffed it into her pocket along with her wand.

"There. All done. Now he can't share anything about you unless the person already knows Blayde, Agrona, Ricardo, or myself," Chantel said.

I released his arm and exhaled the breath I had intentionally been holding. Relief washed over me like waves against the shore. I didn't have to worry about accidentally slipping in front of Kanyon.

"Now, does someone want to tell me why I needed to do that? What's the secret?" Kanyon asked.

"I'm so glad you asked." I smiled.

It was a pleasure to finally teach Kanyon I wasn't a "little girl." That I was a grown woman with prowess.

* * *

I couldn't claim I could win a fight against him again. Kanyon was skilled, and the element of surprise only worked once. Oh, how I wished I could've taken a picture of the look on his face when I was able to not only use Shifter ability but also magic and Vampire speed. It was glorious knocking him on his derriere and placing my foot on his chest. I'd hold this over his head until it stopped being amusing.

Oddly, we bonded. There was an unspoken level of trust between us now, and not because of the binding spell. Blayde was the common factor. I trusted Blayde's faith in Kanyon and vice versa. It helped that I told Ashley where to stick it, and that went in my favor. Also, I kicked his butt, and that I wasn't totally defenseless. I wouldn't say we were besties. No, we had a long way to go. But we formed a weird, gruff friendship. He didn't take my crap, and I wouldn't take his smelly pile of dung.

After the match, Kanyon had some enforcer duties he had to attend to. Before he left, he showed us to the pack's library. I needed to learn more about fated mate bonds and more about the ornaments the Angel had given the first Council.

We found a table easily. Not many Shifters were hanging around stacks of the written word. I didn't know why, seeing how this library was every nerd's dream. Columns of books from floor to ceiling. Completed with a second floor. The building itself wasn't like a public library, it was magnificent and looked like it held some of the greatest treasures. Or like a fancy mansion.

We walked in, and there was an information desk before a grand staircase and chandelier. The railing appeared to be made of gold, and I couldn't say for sure that it wasn't. Marble flooring everywhere. It was the nicest library I have ever seen. A part of me wished I could move in and never leave.

"What are we looking for?" Agrona asked.

"About the first Council. Who were they? What were the ornaments gifted to them? I'm hoping to find a starting location. Also, maybe, if I knew their names, I might discover something about them in the journal," I said. Personally, I wanted to find information on fated mates.

With a collective nod, we began our search. Agrona retreated to a computer, and Chantel and I headed to the stacks to seek any book or title that seemed beneficial. She went one way and I another. The faster we could find information, the faster we could destroy the Dark Master. Or locate someone who could.

Ways to Kill a Vampire. I already knew how.

Everything to Know About Serenading a Female. Nope.

Hierarchy of Shifters. Still nope, but that might be something I should learn a little more about.

Bonding with Your Animal. That would be an interesting read. But not right now.

101 Ways to Cook Wild Game.

Acting Normal Around Humans.

Living the Simple Shifter Life.

Nope. Nope. Nope. Nope.

I'd gone down rows and rows and hadn't found a single thing. I wished I had help finding what I needed. The longer this took, the easier the opportunity Jordan and the Dark Master had to track me down. More time to plan to murder me.

I walked by, sweeping my fingertips along the bindings. I think I chose the wrong section of the library. I hoped Chantel and Agrona were having better luck than me.

I turned down another row and felt a tug. With every slow step, the tug grew stronger. Pulling me closer and closer. It didn't feel wrong or malicious. It was as if my deepest desire was leading me forward, directing me.

It stopped in the middle of the row. I skimmed the titles, and my gaze landed on one.

Truth About Fated Mates.

I reached out, touching the deep-red tattered cover with reverence. This was what I wished to find. What I was seeking. Fate must have played a part in this. There was no other explanation.

I gripped the book in both hands and held it close to my chest, near my heart. I gave up my pursuit and ambled to the table.

Agrona was seated with a volume lying in front of her. I slid into the chair next to her.

"It was the only book about the first Council in the computer." Agrona's hand brushed against the material.

Chantel placed a leather-bound book on the table. It had a string that tied it together.

"My magic led me to this. A journal belonging to a Crispin Mannering. I have no idea who he is, but hopefully, his diary is helpful," Chantel said.

I put my book down, and Agrona leaned over to read the title. Her eyebrows shot up, and she gave me a questioning look.

Heat stained my cheeks. "I just want to be sure," I whispered, my voice wavering.

"If you need to talk about anything, we are here for you. Always," Agrona said, and Chantel nodded in agreement.

Screw mates or boyfriends. What girls really needed were best friends who were there for them through thick and thin. Friends who knew you and didn't shy from the worst parts of yourself. Friends who knew when you were struggling and supported you. They helped. Guided. Protected. Chantel and Agrona would be my girls forever. Not even death could end our friendship.

I put my book aside and snatched Agrona's. I cracked it and riffled.

*Councils are made up of a Hunter, Vampire, Shifter,
Sorcerer, and Fae. Together, they form a group that has the
best intentions for the magical community. Without a single
ruling party, one species cannot overthrow or exterminate
another.*

I read the same paragraph over and over. I couldn't
concentrate, not when my curiosity over fated mates ate at
me. It was right there. A book containing all the answers I
was seeking.

I caved and grabbed the book I was genuinely interested
in. Opening it, I flicked through the first couple of pages.

*Fated mates are rare; they are two halves of a whole. The
mating of the pair was ordained by the Angels.*

Whoa. Heavy. Blayde and I were destined to find each
other...to be each other's mate.

I flipped through a few chapters, trying to identify
anything about feelings produced by the bond.

*Fated mates are drawn to each other. If they fight it, the bond
will only grow stronger, attracting each other like magnets.
The speed at which mates fall in love is rather fast. Being two
halves of a whole, their soul recognizes the other and there
isn't a need to hold back, making it easier to fall in love and
complete the mating bond.*
*The fated mate bond doesn't force the pair to fall in love or to
complete it. It shows them their soulmate, the person who
will complete them. Rarely, people don't choose that.
Completing the mate bond to their fated mate makes them
feel whole and right, and brings forth abilities only they can
have.*

I sighed. The bond couldn't compel me to love him or manipulate my emotions. It only drew me to him. But to claim him—and to complete the bond—was my decision. I wasn't being forced. And that eased the weight off my shoulders. I still had the freedom to accept.

"Some light reading?" Blayde whispered in my ear.

Gah!

I slammed the book shut and tossed it away from me. My heart jackhammered. I felt like a kid getting caught stealing a cookie.

He chuckled, turning my chair so I faced him. His grin hit me with a strength I didn't expect. It crinkled the lines encasing his eyes. A flirty glint shone through. This smile was all for me.

Still with him only inches from me, I swallowed the desire to reach up and kiss him. Knowing the bond wasn't producing affection, I now had to decide if I wanted Blayde forever.

"It's okay. It can be our little secret." Blayde's warm breath sent shivers down my spine.

It took me a second too long to realize he had gleaned what subject I had been studying. He knew I was learning more about our mate bond.

"It was...uh...I mean...I just..." I sucked on my bottom lip and nibbled it. I didn't have an excuse to give him. And after reading the book, I was embarrassed to admit that I thought the bond had been controlling my feelings.

"It's okay. We will talk about it when you are ready." His soft lips brushed my cheek, leaving it burning.

Heat rose to the surface, and I touched where his peck had been.

If I wasn't careful, I would lose all of myself to him. And the worst part? I wanted to.

130

Chapter Thirteen

"**D**id you guys learn anything?" Blayde asked, stepping away from me.

I fought the urge to reach out and pull him to me. I was starting to act like a lovestruck teenager. I was a grown woman. Dang it!

"Crispin Mannering was the original Shifter on the Council." Chantel's voice was full of boredom.

Agrona gripped her book. Anger and hatred shot from her gaze toward something on the page she was reading. At that moment, I wouldn't have been surprised if fire came out of her eyes and burst the paper into flames.

"The originals were Crispin Mannering, Shifter. Desmond, a knight, Hunter. Ada, Fae. Gerald Webb, Sorcerer." Agrona paused, clenching her teeth. "And Vladimir Ward, Vampire."

"Vladimir? Any relation to Vlad the Impaler?" Chantel asked with a smidge of excitement.

She didn't know Agrona and Vlad, aka Dracula, had a past. Agrona had told me that she loved Vlad, but in the end, she'd left him. I didn't think she had truly gotten over him.

Thanks to Dracula, the media portrayed Vampires as bloodsucking, ruthless creatures who couldn't be in the sun. Now, I hadn't met a lot of Vampires, but most of them weren't bad. Agrona certainly wasn't. Vampires did bite people, but it was so that they could use their magic. Hypnotism, paralyzing, poison, turning the victim's blood into ashes, and healing—the healing venom had been rumored to be long gone. Only some—made or turned—Vampires drank blood, they could walk in sunlight, and they lived forever unless killed by decapitation or by fire.

"Yes," she bit out. "Vlad is a family name."

"Great!" Chantel clapped her hands together. "Then he should be able to give us the ornament the Angel gave the Vampire, or at least tell us more about it."

"No! We are *not* speaking to him. We don't need his help." Agrona's resolve was firm.

There was no talking her out of it. If she didn't want to speak to him, then I wouldn't push her. And I for sure wouldn't talk to him in secret.

"Well, in that case, I recommend we visit someone who might be able to help us, but be warned, we have to go on a small hike to get to him," Blayde said.

With a shrug, we got up and followed Blayde. He led us to the desk where we could check out our books. We could've left them in the library, but it felt weird leaving the information we needed behind.

We dropped off our research materials at our DIY cabin before setting off on our hike. We took a trail just beyond the outhouse. The forest was breathtaking. It was calm and peaceful. Breathing in the fresh air and the hint of pine helped dispel any worry or panic.

"You feel it, too?" Blayde asked, joined our fingers. A light tingle ran up my arm. I didn't think I'd ever get used to that.

"Feel what?" I asked, unsure what he was referring to.

"The connection to the forest. The feeling of being grounded. Happy. At ease."

I took another deep breath, letting my senses expand. A lightness settled in my chest. I did feel more relaxed. Back home, we had acres of woods where I grew up playing hide-'n'-seek with my dad. We even built a treehouse. Being there always made me feel peaceful. Balanced.

Was this one more aspect of my unique abilities? Or did Fate design me this way, knowing my fated mate would be a Shifter? More questions with little answers.

I nodded, and an easy smile rested on his lips. We walked in silence, enjoying the beauty of our surroundings.

But it didn't last long.

"Are we there yet? My feet hurt," Chantel complained.

"Toughen up, buttercup. Blayde said it was a hike," Agrona teased.

"This is cruel and unusual punishment! I'm not made for this," Chantel whimpered.

"Aren't Sorcerers supposed to be attuned with nature? To feed off its energy?" Agrona asked.

"What's your point?"

"My point is, shouldn't you enjoy the outdoors and being on hikes?"

Chantel scoffed. "I am not an Earth Mage. Yes, I can be in tune, but I do not worship Mother Earth like a Mage. I do not spend hours outside. I do not enjoy hiking, and the only walking I do is from shop to shop." Chantel pouted and jutted out her bottom lip.

I choked back my laugh. I really didn't want to snicker

at her pain, but I couldn't help it. This trail wasn't difficult. It had been at a steady incline, but my calves weren't burning.

"Sorcerers need to work out more," I said.

A chuckle finally escaped me, and Blayde and Agrona joined in.

"I am very fit, thank you very much," Chantel replied.

I raised my brow. She was fit? I'd never seen her exercise.

"I would like to see you run a mile," Agrona taunted.

"Me too," I piped up. "I would pay money to see that."

Chantel narrowed her eyes. "How much?"

I looked at Blayde, not knowing what to say. I hadn't expected Chantel to ask. He shrugged, not helping me at all.

"Uhh... I don't know..." I stopped talking as we came to a rope suspension bridge linking two cliffs together. The rope was frayed and tattered. The wood planks were deteriorating and well-worn. Some of the pieces had broken off.

Was that thing even sturdy?

Blayde placed his hand on my lower back and leaned in. "Nothing will happen to you. I'll be right here beside you. I've crossed the bridge a dozen times. I wouldn't knowingly put you in danger, I promise."

My heart pounded at how near he was. I wanted him to wrap me in his arms and never relinquish me. Our eyes locked and, like a magnet, I moved toward him.

"Oh, heck no! No. No. No. No. You cannot make me! I won't do it," Chantel wailed, breaking the intensity between Blayde and me.

I withdrew from him to see Agrona nudging Chantel to the bridge with a teasing smile on her face.

"Don't be such a baby. Just cross it. I'll be right next to

you. If you plummet to your death, so will I." Agrona chortled with clear amusement.

"Nope. Not happening." Chantel dug in her heels and struggled to stop.

It didn't work. Agrona had twice the amount of physical strength in her pinky than Chantel had in her entire person.

I shook my head at their antics. "I'll go."

With an inhale, I stepped onto the bridge. And another. And another. Until I was in the middle.

This wasn't too bad.

I glanced over my shoulder, and Blayde was only a few steps away. I had been so focused on not falling that I hadn't noticed him right behind me. Knowing that he was so close soothed my jackhammering pulse.

A blast of wind swayed the bridge. I gripped the frail rope tighter than before. A knot formed in my stomach. I closed my eyes and willed my fear to dissipate. With a gulp of bravery, I continued forward.

Another gust rocked the rickety structure, and I lost my balance. I stumbled, tripping over my own feet. A wood plank broke, and I plummeted through the bridge. With my increased reflexes, I grabbed the next wooden board and clung on. A scream pierced the air, and I realized it was mine.

A third burst of wind tossed me back and forth like a boat on choppy waters. The sheer force of it loosened my grip. I struggled to readjust but failed. My heart thumped a million miles per minute. My fingers ingrained into the wood and clutched to it for dear life. Because literally, my life depended on it.

Tan hands wrapped around my wrists and yanked me up from dangling from my doom. My body trembled.

Breathing erratically, I tried taking long, deep breaths, but I couldn't focus. I was too shaken.

As if sensing what I needed, Blayde pulled me into an embrace, and I eased into him, letting his scent and closeness calm me.

Safe. Home. Right.

He was slowly becoming my everything. He had been anticipating my needs even before I knew what I lacked.

I could've fallen to my death. I almost had. Everything could've been gone in an instant. But instead, I was here because he'd saved me. He had kept me safe as he'd promised.

I didn't want to fight the bond anymore. I didn't want to fight *us*. I still wasn't a hundred percent sure I wanted to complete the mating bond, but I wanted—no, needed—to give us an opportunity to thrive. I didn't want to look back and wonder "what if?"

Glancing up, his fiery gaze hit me. His pupils dilated and the amber flakes burned bright. I swallowed my nerves. I needed to tell him. Now.

"Blayde—" I let out a long breath. My palms were clammy, and my throat tightened. "We need to talk ab—" I started to say, but the fire in his stare died, and his brows furrowed.

Pain and sadness swirled in his blue eyes. I reached up, hoping to smooth out the wrinkles when he retreated.

He unwrapped his arms from around me and stood. My rib cage pinched like he'd removed a part of me with him. *What just happened?*

Blayde led the rest of the way across and only briefly made contact with me when our fingers touched as I got off the bridge. He quickly put space between us, crossing his arms, more closed off than I'd seen him since our bond had formed.

My eyebrows puckered. Something had distanced him, but what? Had seeing me almost fall forced him to realize he didn't want me? My heart twisted, and my stomach tightened. My soul couldn't take his rejection, not now that I wanted a chance to see where this would lead.

I took a step toward him, wanting to clear the air. But I was blocked. Sorceress blocked. Chantel materialized in front of me. Annoyance bubbled in my chest.

"You could've transported all of us over the bridge," I spat. If I wouldn't have fallen, then maybe Blayde wouldn't be so aloof.

"I didn't think about it till now," she spat in defense.

"Liar," Agrona said beside me.

"Fine!" Chantel threw her hands up. "I was curious to see if y'all were stupid enough to cross that death trap. How was I supposed to know that Cedar was going to fall?"

I shook my head, and the corners of my mouth twitched. Even in a tense situation, Chantel's antics made me smile.

Feeling a smidge lighter, I looked at Blayde. A flicker of pain crossed his face before a cold indifference settled in. A pit forged in my stomach. Whatever had happened wasn't about to subside.

Chapter Fourteen

With a slight nod, Blayde spun and led the way. We walked with Chantel's nonsense chatter about cruel and unusual punishment—and something about revenge on us all—until we happened upon a house. Cottage? Small fortress?

It was as if a cinder block and a modern-style house had a baby. All sides were concrete, with one giant corner of the dwelling crafted out of glass. That was the only window I could see.

A soft buzzing sound caught my attention in the trees. Camera. Whoever lived here was watching.

Blayde stopped and waved at the camera. It zoomed in.

"Let us in. It's important." Blayde glanced at the three of us. "I brought guests. Lower your weapons."

Blayde stayed where he was, not moving an inch. A click sounded, and he started forward. It made me uneasy that a weapon had been aimed at me and I hadn't even seen it. I fought the urge to ask. I didn't want to seem weak or defenseless.

The door flung open by the time we reached it.

Standing there was a balding, white man. Only a thin crown of hair remained on his head, while sunlight bounced off the top of it. He was about my height—five foot six inches—which could be considered short for a man. Black-rimmed square glasses framed his face. He had little muscle tone, and his hands rubbed each other subconsciously.

"Come in, come in. Hurry," he said, shooing us through the threshold.

I was learning that Shifters had expensive taste. The room was huge and expertly decorated like a page out of a magazine. And no tan in sight.

It was the perfect bachelor pad. Black, gray, brown. All neutral colors, except for the works of art on his wall.

I turned my focus to the man in the green-and-blue paisley shirt and gray slacks. With his chin tilted up, he took a large sniff, scenting the air.

He looked at Chantel. "Sorceress."

She smiled politely in response. He pointed at me. "Huntress. The mate."

My gaze darted to Blayde, but his expression was clouded. What went wrong?

With a second whiff, the man's eyes went wide. "Snake! You brought a snake into my house. My sanctuary." His voice was high and shrill.

"Trash panda," Agrona bit out.

Ohhh, a raccoon. The man before me was a raccoon,Shifter.

"Trash panda? Trash panda! Now you listen here, lady, this is my house. You came to me. I didn't seek you out, then insult you. So, if you are wanting to bite someone, you'll have to hunt for another neck," he wailed and wrapped his hands around his jugular in an effort to protect himself.

Agrona ground her teeth. She hated to be called a snake

or viper. I could only imagine the strength it took to hold her tongue.

"These paintings are amazing. Where did you get them?" I stepped toward the artwork. I hoped to be able to lighten the mood and to move into the spotlight.

"Funny story. I—" the man started to say.

"He conned a thief," Blayde finished for him.

The man's head jerked, and his mouth gaped as if he couldn't believe Blayde had stolen his thunder and cut the story short. If the artwork angle wasn't going to work, then I needed to approach this differently.

I faced him and stuck my hand out. "I'm Cedar Hastings."

He stared at me, then my hand, then back at me. He was searching for something. I just didn't know what.

Blayde let out an annoyed sigh. "This is—"

This time, the man cut him off. "Don Plate...wall...shire. My name is Don Platewallshire."

Clearly, that was a fake name. But I wasn't going to ruin his fun.

"Nice to meet you, Don Platewallshire." I kept my hand extended until he took it.

Blayde stiffened and didn't relax until "Don's" hand left mine. "For Pete's sake. This is Griff."

"Dang it, Blayde! Out goes my anonymity. Now the government and Council have something they could use to find me." Griff rubbed his cracked hands and paced.

"Why would you be worried about the government and Council finding you?" I asked.

First, he'd conned a thief, now he was worried about people locating him. He was one coo away from coo-coo-ka-choo. I was suddenly very anxious to get out of here. I tried to remind myself Blayde promised he wouldn't knowingly place me in danger, even if he was now acting cold. Frozen tundra, cold.

"Why wouldn't they? I'm onto them. Onto them and their dirty secrets. I have perfect recall, so if they found out that I know what they are covering up, they would kill me," Griff said as if it were completely logical. Which it wasn't.

"We are here to talk about—" Blayde began.

"The thefts and the anger flare-up." Griff nodded, assuming that was why we were here.

Not going to pass up the opportunity, I asked, "What do you know?"

"Come, come. Let's discuss this over tea...or hard liquor? I'm having a hard time reading the room," he admitted, his eyes shifting between the four of us.

I glanced at Agrona and Chantel. They mirrored my uneasy expression. This guy seemed off his rocker. One marble too loose. Riding the cuckoo train. However you put it, this guy was crazy.

"How about you show us what you know?" Blayde suggested, his voice diplomatic.

Griff bobbed his balding head a few times before heading out of the room. He escorted us down a long plain hallway, stopping at the door at the end of it. Twisting the brass knob open, he gestured with his hand for us to enter. My eyebrows shot up. When he led us here, I hadn't expected this.

It was every gamer's, or hacker's, dream room. On the back wall, rows of TVs hung, covering half of it. A giant map of the United States was pinned on one of the side walls, and the other had newspaper clippings and strings from article to article.

In the center of the room was a huge desk with not one

but four computer monitors. The two screens on the outside were vertical rather than horizontal.

Griff sat in the black wheely chair and covered the keyboard with one hand while he typed in his password with the other. He was paranoid, that much was obvious.

He clicked on a file on his computer and pulled up various images of some of the Shifters who had been getting into fights.

"I've been trying to find a connection between the first five Shifters who first started showing signs of irrational aggression. If they ate the same foods, wear the same brand of clothes. But I realized that was stupid," he said.

Stupid? I wasn't sure what he meant.

"Why is that stupid?" I felt foolish that I didn't understand.

"I forget that you are a Hunter." His tone didn't indicate if it was an insult or not. "On pack land, there is only a single place to buy food and only a handful of shops, so the whole pack generally eats the same food and shop at the same stores unless they venture from pack land."

Blayde opened his mouth, but Griff stopped him. "Before you ask, none of the first five have left recently. I already checked. So, I searched for different factors. Where they lived. Their names. Jobs. Hobbies. I even went as far as to find out their favorite colors. Also, none of the items taken were particularly rare. I haven't found anything linking them together. Yet."

Blayde swiped his hand over his face, pulling the skin from his cheeks down. I hadn't noticed till now that the thefts and anger flare-ups had been causing him stress. My first instinct was to comfort him, but I hesitated. The cold distance Blayde had been giving me made me think twice.

"What did they steal?" Chantel asked.

"Jewelry mainly. Some watches, books, art, and even a TV," Griff answered.

"Any pattern to the robberies?" Blayde asked.

"I haven't been able to find rhyme or reason," Griff admitted.

"So what? We wait around until more happens to establish a pattern?" I hoped that wasn't the answer.

"Yeah, that sums it up," Griff said. "But I know you couldn't have come down just for that. Why else are you here seeking my expertise? My unique skill set?"

"What is your skill set? Are you some type of Shifter detective?" Agrona asked with a hint of joking in her tone.

"No, no, no. I wouldn't stoop so low by joining those no-nothings," Griff scoffed.

"Griff is a hacker," Blayde supplied.

"Not just a hacker. I'm a great technician, one of the best. Among other things, I have connections that support my true specialty: knowledge. Knowledge that no one else can get, or at least I get first."

Hmm...no wonder Blayde thought this guy could help. I glanced at Agrona to see if she was comfortable with me asking Griff. She shrugged.

"You're right. We are seeking information on something else. On the first Council. Specifically, anything an Angel might have given them." I left out the connection to the dagger. I wasn't sure how much to tell him.

Griff rubbed his silky-smooth chin. His worn loafers tapped the beat to "Old McDonald Had a Farm." He swiveled in his chair and faced his computers. The tapping of the keyboard was furious and rhythmic until his final tap, and he sat back with his arms folded.

"*Hfmp*. Not much comes up about them. We have their names, their accomplishments, and a painting. Looking at the dates, this would have to be around the time that the first Hunter was created. If I can find anything that cross-references, I'll send them your way along with everything I currently have." Griff paused and tilted his head to the side. "Why are you wanting particulars on them? Was there a cover-up? Did they secretly take out a king? Did they discover the magical room in the pyramids? Are they connected to the mole people who live in the tunnels under the pack town?"

A crazed twinkle in his eyes caught my attention. The possibility of stumbling onto a conspiracy made him worse than a sugared-up kid at a birthday party... I guessed, technically, he wasn't wrong. The Dark Master was conspiring to kill me, and I was bent on stopping him.

The prophecy had haunted my every hour. *For she is born to protect the magic, faithful warrior, strong and true. Complete the crystals to wield the dagger. Rule with truth and might or chaos and death, she must decide, to find what the Angel of Crystals has scattered.*

"Do you have any details or material on the Dark Master?" I was taking a shot in the dark. No one has been able to tell me much about him, only that he was bad to the bone and wanted to murder me.

For a moment, Griff's blue eyes went round before he touched each shoulder, then his forehead. He clasped his hands and muttered words that sounded like a prayer. "You say his name in my house. Bad juju follows him. I'm going to have to cleanse my whole house."

"I'm sorry. I didn't think it mattered since he wants to put me six feet underground." I tried to make my voice sound lighthearted.

"Why would he be after you?" he asked.

"The Huntress prophecy..."

"What Huntress prophecy?" He turned back to his computer.

A growl came from Blayde, and the amber in his irises brightened. His fists were clenched by his sides, his muscles swelling. I glanced at Agrona to gauge her reaction. Her head tipped back, and her eyes rolled.

"The Huntress prophecy isn't widely known. Hunters keep that under lock and key. It's also so old that anyone who would've known is most likely dead." Agrona shifted her weight to her left leg.

"There is a conspiracy," Griff exclaimed, typing faster on the keyboard.

I thought the prophecy was common knowledge. I was surprised that for all the boasting Griff did that he hadn't heard about it.

"Ha! Hunters think they are so smart. Spoiler alert, they aren't!" Griff laughed. "Here it is." His lips moved in silence as he read what was on the screen. "Huh."

Huh? That was all he had to say?

"I'd have to do more research, but it's vague. In any matter, if I find anything, I'll email you," Griff added.

I flashed him a grateful smile.

My stomach decided it'd had enough and loudly grumbled so that I had every set of eyes on me. It rumbled again, and I rubbed the back of my neck. I was just realizing how hungry I was.

"We should head back and get some food," Agrona said.

Thank heavens! That girl always had my back.

Griff stood and handed me a piece of paper and a pen. I wrote down my email and returned it to him.

He ushered us out the front door, closing it softly, and the lock reverberated a loud clunk. When we got far enough from his concrete fortress, a click sounded, letting us know his weapons were functional. I never wanted to get on Griff's bad side. Even though he was odd, he sure had everything ready at the touch of a button.

We followed Blayde back through the forest, and every time I tried to step next to him, he sped up. He kept his distance. Hurt pinged in my heart. A thousand daggers would've done less damage. Maybe he just needed to calm down. Or maybe he was hangry. Yeah, that was it. It had to be. Because if it wasn't, I wasn't sure I would survive.

Chapter Fifteen

Whoever said absence made the heart grow fonder was full of crap! Absence didn't make my heart grow fonder. It pissed me off. Ragey. Wanting to punch a hole in the wall.

I hadn't seen Blayde in two days. Two whole days! Kanyon informed me at the beginning of our training session that he was alive and well—just busy.

Just busy, my booty!

That wolf was avoiding me. After he hadn't shown for dinner, I'd thought he needed more time to calm down. Then the next day I hadn't seen him at all, but I sure heard that Ashley had. That brat.

I wanted to destroy something. Set the room on fire and watch it burn. A scream burned on my tongue, and I sent the punching bag sailing through the air, slamming into the wall. My soul-crushed chest rose and fell quickly, and the air cracked and sizzled around me.

"Deep breaths, Cedar. In through your nose, out through your mouth," Kanyon said in a soothing tone. A tone that would be used on a caged animal.

Normally, I would let his deep-honey voice wash over me, but not now.

"Come on, Cedar. Breathe with me." Kanyon stepped beside me.

"I don't want to," I said through gritted teeth.

Kanyon's gaze darted past my shoulder for a brief moment before he placed his calloused hands on my shoulders. "Control your emotions. Don't let it control you."

Sure thing, Yoda.

I closed my eyes and allowed my senses to expand. Quiet footsteps sounded behind me. I focused on them until they stopped near me. I peeked through my eyelashes to see Chantel and Agrona.

"Maybe you should practice with your chakrams. The more you train with them, the more you'll be comfortable fighting with them," Agrona suggested in a light, easy tone.

"Oooooo, you haven't named them yet. Let's do that. Then you can practice against Kanyon. It will be loads of fun," Chantel squealed.

"Why would I name them? Like, is it similar to naming your car?" I asked.

"No. Naming your weapons lets you bond with them. It gives the weapons more power," Kanyon said.

"My chakrams are alive? Is this some weird *Toy Story* thing?" I arched my brow.

Kanyon shook his head, and a smile tugged at his lips.

"Go sit on the mats," he instructed

I parked my butt in the middle of the mat and placed my chakrams in front of me. The three of them sat opposite me.

"You need to feel the connection between you and your chakrams. Feel the magic. Let it flow from you to the chakram and back," Chantel instructed.

With an inhale, I let my senses amplify, closing my eyes. Lingering anger stirred in me. Blayde should be here. But he wasn't. The muscles in my jaw ached, and my shoulders were tight. After I was finished here, I was going to give Blayde a piece of my mind. I wouldn't stand to be treated this way. I was not a doormat.

"Relax," Kanyon said in my ear.

I had been so focused on my indignation that I had blocked out my surroundings. Kanyon's words had recentered me.

When I calmed down enough to not dwell on my negative emotions, I gestured for him to continue.

"Now imagine an empty place. A space with just you and your chakrams. In this space, talk to them. Get to know them, ask them their names."

I opened one eye, making sure I wasn't being punked. The three of them stared at me. Agrona tsked, compelling me to close my eyes again.

With a cleansing breath, I relaxed my arms on my legs. I guessed it was time to try this crazy nonsense. If it didn't work, then I'd totally rub it in their faces. If it did, I might consider getting my brain scanned.

Exhaling, I imagined a barren room. White everywhere. It stretched on for miles with no walls in sight. On the ground lay my two chakrams.

All right, buddies. I'm a Huntress. My name is Cedar Hastings. Recently, my life got turned upside down, and I have no idea what I am doing ninety-nine percent of the time. I'd love to bond and know your names, I thought in my head.

A warm, kind feeling rose in my chest. Was that from my chakrams? Was I somehow communicating with them?

Let's try this again.

My favorite thing to eat is chocolate. I like to go dancing with my best friends. My favorite color depends on my mood. In the past few months, I haven't had a lot of reasons to dress up, so I mainly wear a lot of exercise clothes and jeans. Oh yeah, the Dark Master, along with some other evil people, are trying to kill me, I thought again. At least, I hoped I wasn't saying this out loud.

Feelings of humor, then fury flashed over me. My chakrams found my intro to Cedar 101 funny and hated the Dark Master as much as I did–or more.

"You know my name, but what's yours?"

Flashes of names popped into my mind. But they didn't linger long enough for me to catch them, and there were a lot of them. And it felt like they were both telling me at once.

Whoa, whoa, whoa. Too many, I thought.

I studied the chakrams. I picked one up, and it hummed. I rotated it and noticed the flame had a tint of black to it. Wild and carefree.

I set it down and picked up the other chakram. It also hummed in response. This one had a pink-tinted flame. Grounded. Happy.

I sat it back down next to the other. I knew what I was going to name them.

I opened my eyes to see Chantel, Kanyon, and Agrona watching me intently. Unmoved from their positions.

"So? Did you figure it out?" Kanyon asked.

I nodded. His eyebrows rose in question, and he waited for me to tell them.

I picked up the chakram that felt wild. "This one is Blacky." I gripped the other. "This one is Pinky." The chakrams hummed rhythmically as if they were letting me know they approved.

At that moment, Blacky's flame took on more black, and Pinky's more pink. Their colors intertwined with their blue fires. They were taking on their names with pride.

"Pinky? Blacky?" Agrona questioned. "You didn't want to go more traditional?"

I chuckled. Yeah, their names were childish. I was sure a five-year-old could've chosen better names. But it fit. It *felt* right.

"Names kept flashing in my head that were a mile long. I wasn't going to remember them all. Think of them as nicknames. Everyone has a nickname." I shrugged, trying to seem cool and collected.

Kanyon's brows pinched. "I've never been called anything other than my name. Well, if you disregard being called 'Blayde's brother.'"

A ping spread through my chest. Everyone deserved a nickname.

"How about we call you Sourpuss?" I suggested.

"Muscle Man," Chantel provided with a saucy smirk full of innuendo.

"Smokey," Agrona said.

I snorted. Smokey as in Smokey the Bear...because Kanyon was a bear... I thought it was hilarious. Kanyon's expression said otherwise.

"We'll work on it. We have time to come up with something good," I said.

A slow smile lit his face. He acted all big and mean but was a gooey teddy bear. A gummy bear. Just like Blayde.

Blayde.

An eruption of anger burst inside me. That was it. I'd had enough. If he didn't want me, then he could at least say it to me directly. I refused to mope while he pushed me to the side. Oh, heck no. I refuse to be led on.

I pressed off the ground and stood. I attached my newly named chakrams to my belt and headed for the training room elevator.

"Where are you going? You need to practice with your chakrams," Kanyon yelled.

"I'm going to go knock some sense into your brother," I answered without turning back. I might have to literally knock some sense into him. It didn't understand how he could be patient for weeks on end—be kind and thoughtful —then BAM. A complete personality change.

The three of them muttered to each other, but I couldn't discern their words over the pounding in my ears. I tried to take a few calming breaths, but it didn't ease. My rage was chaotic. Wild. Destructive. It felt...powerful.

I waited for the elevator doors to open, and Kanyon appeared at my side. "I'm going to come with you."

Glancing over my shoulder, I noticed Agrona and Chantel stayed where I'd left them. "Why aren't they coming along?"

"Because Blayde is out running, and it is better if Agrona's scent isn't there. It could cause bouts of anger flares. Chantel is staying with her because, you know, the buddy system," he explained.

Sure, whatever helped him sleep at night.

"Lead the way, Baloo." I gestured for him to enter first.

A twitch of his cheek let me know he got my reference. I couldn't wait to see his reaction when I eventually called him Winnie-the-Pooh.

* * *

I followed him to the forest, fuming with every step. I didn't want to let Blayde go without a fight. I was going to call him on his crap and give him the chance to explain before I went all vengeful shrew on him. He at least deserved that for how wonderfully he had treated me in the past.

I just hoped he didn't realize we wouldn't be good together. My heart couldn't take that. Not when I was ready to immerse myself wholeheartedly.

Kanyon stopped and sniffed. His eyes narrowed, and he cocked his head. We stood in silence. Me in confusion, and Kanyon looking like he needed to take a dump.

I opened my mouth to ask what in the world we were doing standing here when Blayde popped out from behind a bush.

His abs were on display in all their glory. My gaze traced each sculpted muscle. I swallowed the burst of heat that settled in my stomach.

No. I needed to rein in my hormones. I was mad at him. I wouldn't let his well-defined-muscles distract me. At least for not long.

"What is she doing here? Cedar would be better protected in town," Blayde snarled. The fury in his eyes bore into Kanyon.

Kanyon lifted his hands in the air in surrender. A tiny smirk played at the corners of his lips. "Cedar here couldn't wait to talk to you." Kanyon moved backward before turning and retreating completely.

Blayde's attention shot to me. He searched for any sign of injury, but he still contained the fiery intensity burning in his irises.

We faced each other, neither one of us uttering a word. Remaining motionless. I was giving him a moment to say something—to say anything. But my temper was ready to blow. I could no longer be silent.

"What the heck, Blayde? What is wrong with you?" I yelled, taking a few steps toward him.

His head tilted to the side in confusion. "You'll have to be more specific."

Did I have to spell everything out? "Oh, like you don't know."

"Please," he growled, "tell me what is so important for you to risk your safety?"

"You. You big dumb idiot!" I screamed.

"I really don't know what you are talking about." The fire in his eyes died, replaced with disbelief.

Did he not think I would catch on to him ghosting me? That I wouldn't realize he was avoiding me?

I closed the gap, stepping shoe to toe with him. My fingers twitched, wanting to trace the outline of his abs. Instead, I poked him in the chest. Hard.

"If you didn't want me, the gentlemanly thing to do would've been to tell me! But no. You avoid me. Shut me out. Put distance between us. How dare you! I trusted you." I jabbed my index finger repeatedly into stone-solid pecs.

His hand wrapped around mine, thwarting my poking. "What are you talking about?" he asked, feathered in frustration.

My hands trembled. I had been holding too much pent-up emotion, and now that I had let some steam out of the pot, I was going from spitting mad to crying. Moisture welled up in my eyes, and like a balloon, I popped. Droplets streamed down my face, and it felt like the world was caving in.

"Hey. Shhhh. Hey, tell me what's going on." Blayde tugged my wrist, discharging a tingle down my arm, and brought me against his torso.

He enveloped me in an embrace, and I rested against

154

him. Tears touched his skin and ran down his sculpted body. I forced myself not to follow the trail.

Sobs escaped my mouth. This was the beginning of ugly crying. How did I get here? Why did I want to confront Blayde just to hear he didn't want me anymore?

His hands leisurely rubbed my back, sending calming waves down my spine. Only a few short days without his touch, and now it was as if I had tasted chocolate for the first time. Being in his arms felt right. Down deep, my soul was singing hallelujah.

Blayde lay his head on top of mine and sighed. Maybe he missed my touch as much as I'd missed his.

"Are you ready to tell me what has made you so upset?" Blayde picked up a strand of my hair and twirled it around his fingertips.

I swallowed the lump in my throat. It was now or never.

"Are you done with me?" I asked into his sternum.

If this was the last time he would hold me, I didn't want to pull away.

"Done with you?" Shock colored his voice. "I will never be done with you."

I will never be done with you.

My mind swirled. Could it be that he had just been busy? No...he's been distant for a reason. I needed to know why.

I withdrew reluctantly to look at him. I was prepared to watch for any signs of a lie.

"Aren't you breaking up with me? You've been so distant...so cold." My voice was small, hesitant, and unsure.

Pain and longing peeked out of his eyes. My heart pounded. I was afraid of what he would say.

He tucked a piece of my hair behind my ear. "I'm sorry."

That was it? That was all I was got?

"Why? Why would you do that to me? Aren't we... mates?" I had never admitted that out loud for fear that it would further bond us. Sure, I wanted to explore a relationship with Blayde, but I wasn't emotionally equipped to take the next step in the bonding ceremony.

The edges of his mouth tugged up, but a hint of sadness lingered. "You've never said that before."

"You've never been this stupid before," I snapped.

His head tipped back, and he laughed. His joy made me want to wrap my fingers around his throat. Here I was, concerned he was leaving me, and he was laughing.

Once he stopped, he placed his hands on either side of my hips and held me in place.

"You said you wanted to talk, and I assumed the worst. Never before had you acknowledged that we were mates, and I thought you'd finally decided you were done. I panicked. I hoped that giving you space would change your mind." He rubbed the base of his neck.

"We should work on our communication skills. I was going to say that if you still desire to, we should give us a fair shot. I'm not ready to move forward with our bond, but I would like to see what we could be. What our future could hold." I gave him a bashful smile, fully aware of the brush forming on my skin.

Blayde hauled me up against him and swung me in a circle. We both laughed and enjoyed the happiness in that moment.

Blayde set me down. His fingers ran up my arm. Brushed over my shoulder and grazed up my neck to cup my cheek. His gaze was deep, searching as if he was trying to see into my soul.

"I vow to never give up on us, on you. I can't promise I'll

be perfect. We both know we'll make mistakes, but I'll never stop trying. Never stop trying to give you what you need. To be enough for you. You're my everything." Blayde tilted his head toward mine, and my breath hitched.

A small pinch of panic bubbled in my throat, and my lips parted. He was going to kiss me. Was I ready for that? My hormones screamed yes!

I held my breath. I wasn't sure if it smelled bad. Blayde let out a soft sigh that I would've missed if I hadn't been focusing on him. Instead of him pressing our mouths together, his forehead tilted and rested against mine.

He'd promised to take it slow weeks ago. It was sweet that he was still trying to keep it. I needed to make the first move, to show him I was ready.

But before I had a chance, Blayde spoke, "Tag. You're it."

Chapter Sixteen

Tag. A game that involved two or more people chasing the other players in an attempt to "tag" them—by touching with a hand. This was usually played by juveniles. Coincidentally, it was also a favorite game of Shifters.

I gawked dumbly at Blayde's back as he dashed away. I was going to kiss him...and he started a game of tag.

He started a game of tag.

Was there a malfunction between his brain and lips?

He'd said I was his everything. That he wouldn't stop trying. I'd seen it—the spark of heat in his eyes. What I didn't understand was why he wanted to play a child's recess activity instead of swapping affection.

I had a few options. I could stand here and pout like a spoiled rich girl who got her daddy's credit card revoked. Or I could go after him and show him who was boss.

Option two.

I pushed off the dirt, heading for Blayde. He was now far enough ahead of me that I couldn't see him. I paused, allowing my senses to open, and I listened for any sign that he was near.

Birds chirped, and the leaves blew in the light breeze. Nothing. There wasn't a single noise that could be him. That was, until a snap cracked behind me.

I turned a moment too slow. A large salt-'n'-pepper wolf pounced and knocked me to the ground before I had the chance to dodge. The wolf's paws lightly pressed into my shoulders. It cocked its head from side to side. Its tail wagged rhythmically like a metronome. I lay frozen beneath the giant animal. Adrenaline coursed through me and pricked every nerve. A wet tongue licked my cheek, leaving a trail of slobber. *Yuck*.

Blue eyes with flecks of amber stared at me. Blayde. My big fluffy dog. I squirmed just a little that he eased off his stance. I seized the opportunity and snaked my arms around his belly and squeezed.

I pulled back and watched. The hacking sound gave me pause. Either he was laughing or choking. By the wag of his tail and the almost grin on his face, it was probably the former.

I wiggled from underneath him and touched his spine quickly before I scurried in the opposite direction. "Tag!"

A howl erupted. The crushing on twigs and leaves followed. I didn't need to look to know he was following.

Knowing that we were playing, I didn't try to tap into my Vampire Speed. I knew that without it, he wouldn't have a hard time catching up with me. I was a willing prey.

With a small growl and a bark at my heels, I sped up. Not to be left behind, Blayde caught up and ran beside me. He matched my speed like it was nothing—what clued me in was the tongue hanging out of his mouth.

From my battle strategy class, I knew I couldn't outmaneuver him. He had hundreds of years of various tactics in his head. I couldn't compete with that no matter how hard I tried.

I increased my pace and gained some distance. I skidded to a halt. I spun to face him and noticed that wolf Blayde had stopped running. He crouched, ready to pounce at a moment's notice. He bared his teeth and growled. The only sign he was still playing was the steady wag of his tail.

"What are you waiting for?" I taunted and gestured for him to come.

He sprang and charged. If this was any other wolf, I would've been scared of the giant creature plummeting for me. But this was Blayde. He would never hurt me.

I moved toward him, intending to leap and pin him when he got close enough. A crack thwarted my plans, and I whirled around to the sound.

A menacing growl came from behind a tree. Blayde placed himself between me and the prowler. A black wolf, smaller than Blayde but bigger than a normal wolf, stepped out and stalked toward us.

"Is he pack?" I whispered.

Blayde nodded. The black wolf and Blayde stared at each other. I imagined they were communicating via mind link.

Blayde hunched down and bared his canines, emitting a loud, fierce snarl. The black wolf copied and crept forward. My eyes went wide. He didn't seem friendly. *What gives?*

Wolf Blayde snapped at my feet and barked. I retreated in panic. Blayde was trying to get me to leave. My mouth dried, and my breathing increased. He would only tell me to go if it wasn't safe.

Blayde snapped again, and I jumped back, fear pumping new life into my veins. Blayde leaped at the black wolf, tackling him to the ground, breaking twigs and sticks on the way down. Blayde snarled, and I knew it was time to vamoose.

With a heavy heart, I sprinted away. I hated how cowardly this was. I was Defensive Huntress of the Year. It was possible that if I helped, it would do more damage than good.

"Must go faster. Come on, come on. Hurry," I muttered and swerved in and out of the pine and aspen trees.

I sprinted through the forest, and I wasn't quiet. I aimed for speed over stealth. A resounding yelp made me pause.

"What have I done?" I cursed.

Overwhelming guilt shredded my chest. I would never forgive myself if Blayde got injured when I could've stayed. When I could've fought next to him. I sucked in a long inhale and exhaled with my decision.

I raced back toward Blayde. I had to correct my mistake. If I couldn't fight the black wolf, I could lead him in a game of chase. My advantage—Vampire speed. It wasn't the most brilliant plan, but it was all I had.

By the time I got back to Blayde, he had the situation under control. He didn't need my help. The thought swelled me with pride and sadness. He was fearsome and could handle anything. I, on the other hand, had to run away with my tail between my legs.

"Thank the Angels." My voice was quiet, and my palm lay over my breastbone.

The black wolf was pinned on its side, whimpering. Red cascaded down its neck and back. Blayde snarled, declaring who was dominant. Blayde looked relatively unharmed. I couldn't tell if the red on his fur was his or the black wolf's.

With my approach, I slowed down, erring with caution.

Blayde stiffened as I came to the side of him. His attention swung to me, and he gnashed his jaw. I bowed my head and tried to appear submissive, nonthreatening.

"I won't be made to feel guilty about my decision to come back. There's nothing you can say that would change my mind." I lifted my chin. I wouldn't concede.

Blayde growled at the black wolf one last time, then walked over to me. I took a tentative step and brushed against his fluffy coat.

"Are you hurt?" My voice wavered, showing more emotion than I intended. I entangled my fingers in his salt-'n'-pepper hair and stroked the small patch of clean fur.

He shook his head, and a giant anvil lifted off my chest. He nuzzled me and touched his nose to mine.

My heart sped up. What I would give to spend the day with him. To lie in the grass and have the sun warm us.

But alas, we needed to find my girl squad and talk about what had happened. I nudged Blayde.

"Do you think it was an anger flare?" I asked.

Blayde nodded.

"Do you think it is safe to leave him here?" I glanced at the black wolf. He hadn't moved since Blayde had restrained him. His slow and steady breathing led me to believe that the black wolf was sleeping.

Blayde nodded again.

"Tag...come get me if you can!" I scrambled up, taking off in the direction of the DIY cabin.

Hopefully, continuing our game would put Blayde in a better mood.

Glancing back, I noticed that Blayde wasn't as fast as normal. He must have been more injured than he'd let on. I decelerated my pace, letting him catch up. He nipped at me playfully before we settled into a comfortable side-by-side stride.

The cabin fell into sight, and I zeroed in on it. Soon, we'd be able to figure everything out and I could catch my breath. Only a few feet more. Blayde leaped in the air, tackling me to the ground. I tried to get out from under him thinking we were still playing.

He snapped and growled at me. I glanced at his tail—it wasn't wagging. It was pointed down, indicating a serious situation.

"What is it? What's wrong?" I asked, even though I knew he couldn't speak.

Wolf Blayde lifted his nose to the sky and sniffed. He looked at me, and his eyes were full of rage. I remained motionless to not exacerbate the moment and waited for his direction.

He eased off me and trod carefully toward the cabin. I followed with light and quiet steps—not wanting to bring attention to us.

It was moments like this when I was reminded of how inadequately prepared for danger I was. Yes, I'd trained nonstop for months, but when it came to a real threat, I didn't have the experience.

Blayde led us to the entrance. His ears twitched and listened for any intruders. Not a peep, tweet, not a sound.

I sucked in a breath. "Crap."

The door was ajar. Fear blossomed in me. I knew we had closed it when we'd left. Chantel had also put a protection spell around the cabin. Whoever broke in wanted us to know they could.

Blayde pawed the door and nudged it open. He shot me a scowl over his shoulder, and I knew he preferred me to stay here.

"If you aren't back soon, I'm coming in after you." I leveled a glare at him.

I would placate him for minutes. After that, I was going to barrel in. I wouldn't leave him by himself again. Especially when he wasn't at full strength.

Blayde disappeared into the fixer upper. My nerves buzzed and pooled the energy inside of me, just waiting to be let out. I paced back and forth to try to soothe my jitters.

After an unascertained time, Blayde reappeared. He nodded for me to enter. I stepped in cautiously and when I made it past the threshold, my stomach dropped.

"No," my mouth squeaked out.

Things were smashed and scattered across the area. The new couches Chantel had conjured up were sliced with the stuffing oozing out. The small kitchen appliances were smashed into pieces on the floor.

"Not again." The words faded into the carnage of the room.

Images of my apartment in Virginia flashed through my mind. Before I'd arrived at the academy, Agrona's and my apartment had been broken into and everything destroyed. We never had learned who was behind it. I'd always assumed it was Jordan or one of his lackeys.

I headed toward the bedroom door and prayed I wouldn't find it like I had found my bedroom—ravaged and pee-filled. Poking my head in, I choked back a sob.

Everything was in pieces. Every article of clothing, blanket, pillow, even some of the floorboard. Our three-person bunk bed lay in shambles on the floor.

Whoever did this, had done it on purpose. They had the magic and strength to break through Chantel's protection spell and destroy every item. They weren't just looking for something; they were trying to scare us. If they thought they could frighten us, intimidate us, then they were as delusional as a bear on skates. No more Miss Defensive Huntress of the Year. They were going to meet the Offense Huntress of the Year.

Glancing around the room, I scanned for the only object I cared about in this cabin.

"No. Oh, please, no," I pleaded.

I rushed over to the pile of wreckage and searched frantically.

It was gone. The Angel's journal was gone.

Chapter Seventeen

We didn't have to wait long for Agrona and Chantel to arrive at the cabin. Within minutes of Blayde shifting to his human form—and finding some sweatpants—they were back and up to date. They went full-blown mama bear on me and fussed until they were satisfied that I wasn't hurt.

"Have we heard from Ricardo at all?" Blayde leaned against the wall.

I glanced at Chantel and raised my eyebrows in question. She was the closest to him, and I had a hunch there was a little somethin' somethin' between them.

Chantel fidgeted with her fingers. "I haven't, uh..." She swallowed. "I haven't heard from him today. When we spoke yesterday, he was getting on a plane."

"Did he say where he was traveling to?" I asked.

Chantel moved her gaze down to her hands in her lap, but not before I saw the tears well up in her eyes.

"I don't know. He should've called by now. He told me he might not have reception, and that is the only thing I am clinging to." Her voice was tight and pinched, barely above a whisper.

"I normally would have someone inquire about it, but I don't want to draw attention to him. I'm worried that if we checked on him, it would alert others to his location, and he might not be able to get the item to help Cedar." Blayde cracked his neck from side to side.

No one spoke. Concern showed on each of their faces. Ricardo was one of the best fighters I had ever seen. I had faith in him. I refused to lose hope.

"What are we going to do about the journal? As well as the angry black wolf." I chewed on a fingernail.

"The black wolf, Josh, was having an anger flare. By the end of the fight, his temper had disappeared. I will need to talk to my father about this and check if there are any leads yet," Blayde said.

"And the journal?" I focused on the floor. Guilt didn't even cover the twisted pinch in my chest. Bennett had entrusted it to me, and I couldn't keep it safe. Not to mention, I hadn't read it as much as I should've.

"Could it have been Jordan?" Agrona asked. An implacable expression crossed her face.

My brows knitted together. Jordan knew I had it, and he'd informed me that he wanted it. He was convinced it would aid him in locating the dagger.

"Maybe." I looked at Blayde. "Does this intruder smell like Jordan?"

Blayde shook his head and scratched his bicep. "No, but it smells faintly like the same perpetrator who destroyed your apartment. Whoever keeps destroying your living quarters wants you to know that they know where you are."

"I could make a potion that would let us see what happened," Chantel suggested.

"Do it and let me know what you find out." Blayde pushed off the wall and headed toward the door but stopped when he got to me.

"Where are you going?" I asked, lifting my gaze to him.

He bent down, making us eye to eye. "I need to speak to my father before I pick you up in a few hours."

I stared at him dumbly. What in Angel's name was he talking about?

His smile grew, and the laugh lines around his eyes crinkled. "I believe I promised you a date." He picked up a strand of my hair, twirling it, and then placed a lingering kiss on my forehead. Sighing like it was physical torture, he left.

"Ooooo, girl, whatcha going to wear?" Chantel beamed.

My face fell. All my clothes were destroyed. I had nothing to wear besides what was on me. I peeked down at the dirt and soot on my blue t-shirt and jeans. I hoped Blayde wasn't taking me somewhere nice. Agrona elbowed Chantel in her side.

"I forgot about our clothes. No problem, I'll pretend to be a fairy godmother, and you can be Cinderella." Chantel clapped her hands together in excitement.

I was a little afraid of what Chantel would put me in. I prayed it wasn't a fancy ball gown. For one, they were terribly itchy and uncomfortable. Two, they weren't my style.

"We should make her put on a fashion show," Agrona said with a teasing glint in her eye. She was enjoying this too much. Well, two could play this game.

"Only if you guys join me. It can't be a one-woman performance." I smirked.

"Yes!" Chantel fist pumped.

Agrona stood and extended her hand to help me up. I grabbed a hold of it and let her pull me up.

"So, what should I wear?"

* * *

After parading around in ridiculous outfits, we finally decided on the perfect ensemble. Dark skinny jeans, a flowy floral blouse, a black leather jacket, and charcoal stiletto heels.

Chantel wanted to use magic to do my hair, but Agrona refused. Agrona and I used to do each other's hair before we would go out, and it was apparently a tradition she wanted to hold on to. She ended up transforming my locks into soft loose curls and gathered the top half back with an elastic.

As Agrona pulled and tugged on my tresses, my thoughts wandered. The journal was gone. I needed to retrieve it somehow. I had to. It was my only lead. My only chance to get a step ahead of the Dark Master. My only way to acquire true freedom was to defeat him. And that starting place was now missing. At least I had friends to help keep my mind off of it, not to mention a hot date.

I was all ready by the time Blayde picked me up. I had to stop the drool from escaping at the mere sight of him. His fitted white t-shirt hugged his muscles and complemented his bronze-tinted skin. Jeans hug his butt and—ooh wee—I couldn't peel my gaze away as he led me out of the cabin. The gel in his hair finished assembling the perfect image, as if he were late for a *GQ* photo shoot.

Blayde chuckled, and he laced his fingers in mine. *Oops, did I say that out loud?*

"I was thinking the same thing. You never fail to leave

me breathless." Blayde brought my hand up and gave it a light kiss.

My cheeks collected heat, and I didn't need a mirror to know they were pink.

We ended up at a restaurant where I was sorely under-dressed. We were seated at our table, and I glanced around at the other couples. They were dressed up in suits and dresses, and here I was in jeans. If I had known, I would've asked Chantel to put me in a dress.

As if psychic, Blayde said, "You're perfect. Every woman in here wishes she was you."

A smile played at the edges of my mouth. "Only because I'm with you."

"Nah. They wish they could make your outfit look as sexy as you do. And I know for a fact that every man would kill for a shot to be sitting across from you. Don't underesti-mate the effect you have on everyone...especially me."

My heart melted like a popsicle. Not wanting to ruin the mood, I swiped my tongue along my lips. Blayde's eyes darted to the movement, and I resisted the urge to lick them again.

Was it getting warm in here or was it just me? If he kept saying things like that to me, I wasn't going to last through dinner.

The waiter appeared. Dumbstruck and flustered, I couldn't get my vocal cords to work. With a chuckle, Blayde ordered for me. It didn't take long for the food to be deliv-ered. A big juicy steak and two fist-sized scoops of mashed potatoes. A second plate was set next to it. A Caesar salad, which was bigger than my head. All the portions were oversized.

"This is a Shifter restaurant. We tend to eat a lot due to our fast metabolisms. Shifting burns thousands of calories."

Blayde sliced into his steak and put it in his mouth. He slowly dragged out the utensil. Who knew a fork could be so sexy? I sure didn't.

I sipped my water in hopes it would cool off the fire in my belly. Blayde reached out and clasped my free hand, sending a tingle through my arm. It was five times more intense than normal. The bond we shared was growing stronger.

"So, what kind of first-date topics should we talk about?" His expression was blissfully happy. He looked as if the drama from today hadn't occurred. As if our date was the best thing to happen to him—because, at least for me, it was.

Reluctantly, I untangled my hand from his. I couldn't cut my steak with one hand. I diced my chunk of meat into little pieces just in case Blayde held my hand again.

"Umm...How about what is your favorite color?" I asked. His favorite color seemed like something I should know.

"Blue. And yours?"

"Yellow."

"That fits you. You are definitely the sunshine in my life." He scooped up some mashed potatoes and turned the spoon over in his mouth, slowly pulling it out. First a fork, now a spoon. I was a goner.

I swallowed my dollop of potatoes before asking another question. "Any siblings besides Kanyon?" It stung a bit that in the time I'd known him, I hadn't known he had a brother.

"Nope. I wanted to bring him up a hundred times, but we never really had a get-to-know-you setting, and blurting it out as you throw a punch at me seemed weird." He chuckled.

"I guess that will suffice for not telling me. What is your

vivid childhood memory? You already know about my treehouse."

He was thoughtful as he chewed. "One day, my father was away visiting another pack. It was just my mom, Kanyon, and me. Kanyon and I were being typically boys, driving our mother crazy. Frogs in the shower, snails in the fridge, mud on the couches. You know, boy stuff. Needless to say, we drove our mom past her limit. She was fuming when she found out that we had put worms in the casserole she had made. She sent us to our rooms and threatened to send us to bed without dinner."

Blayde drank some water, then continued. "She yelled for us to come down from our rooms and into the kitchen. Lined up on the counter were ingredients for her casserole. She demanded that we make a new one. She helped us step by step until we were done. After it was cooked, my stomach was growling so much, in typical youth fashion, I thought I was starving to death. Instead of digging in to eat it, she covered the casserole with tinfoil and required us to deliver it to an older couple down the street. This was the first occasion I had met them. The husband had been crippled in an accident, which was rare considering how fast we heal. The wife worked full time to provide for them. What I didn't know was that my mother often made food for different families in the pack. It was her way of taking care of everyone and making the pack family. It was then I realized how much my pack relied on my mother, how she was just as in charge as my father. That day changed the way I viewed being a leader. Being Alpha wasn't only about being the strongest or the bravest. It's about not only protecting your pack but caring for them. Being compassionate. Making sure everyone is taken care of."

His eyes were soft and full of pride for his mom, for

showing him how to serve and be sympathetic. I glanced around, and the restaurant had fallen silent. The other customers had heard what he said and looks of respect were on their faces. Blayde was going to be an amazing Alpha, and they all knew it. He would be hard and strong when needed, but also kind and benevolent. Their pack was lucky to have him.

I was lucky to have him.

This was my moment. I was ready to tell him how I felt about him. To open my heart completely, to shatter every wall that I had built.

Wiping my palms against my jeans, I ignored the deep-seated fear of rejection in my belly. I reached across the table and took his hand in mind. His thumb drew small circles that sent me a burst of tingles. I smiled, and his face mirrored mine. My pulse was the biggest traitor—it beat so furiously I was sure the entire establishment could hear. I blew out the tension like I was blowing on a pinwheel.

"Blayde, I—"

"Blayde! There you are," a shrill voice cut me off.

I closed my eyes and counted to ten. When I reopened them, Ashley was beside our table. Moment ruined.

"The Alpha King is calling a meeting, and he wanted me to come get you." Ashley's red polished fingers caressed Blayde's bicep.

"You can inform my father that I won't be attending. I'll have Herrick catch me up on what I miss," Blayde growled.

"You wouldn't want me to go against orders, would you? Alpha King told me that I personally needed to escort you. Besides, we have so much to talk about...like our upcoming wedding." She beamed and batted her eyelashes. She knew she was interrupting our date and was purposely ruining it.

I turned my attention to Blayde, and his irises flashed

amber. His grip tightened around mine and squeezed to the point that it was almost painful. His lips pressed into a firm white line. Tension bracketed the edges of his mouth. If I Googled "angry expressions," his face would be the number one search result, followed by mine.

"If by wedding, you mean Cedar's and mine, then I'll let you know I haven't asked yet, but I fully intend to. If you're implying anything else, then allow me to tell you once again. There will *never* be a you and me. I will *never* mate or marry you. Cedar has my heart and always will. The next time you try to insinuate that there is something between us, I'll oversee your punishment. Am I clear?"

I didn't know how he managed to put Ashley in her place and simultaneously be swoon-worthy, but man, he did it well.

Ashley huffed and crossed her arms. "We'll see," she mumbled. "I'm still supposed to escort you, so shall we?"

"No. I'm busy. Go away." Blayde waved for her to disappear, consciously not looking at her.

I'd prefer to not attract the wrath of the Alpha King. He already disliked me, and if he knew Blayde skipped because he was with me, it would only make things worse.

Going off the high his words had taken me on, I pushed the remainder of my anger into a box that I would release later. It was time to wear my mature big girl panties.

"You know, I've never been to a Shifter meeting before. And since you and me," I gestured between us, "are an item, it would be nice to see what you do."

A mischievous smile spread across his face, but anger lingered in the shadows of his eyes. He understood I didn't really want to go, but he loved hearing me admit that we were a couple.

"Well then, we don't want to be late." Blayde stood and

extended his hand to me. I took it and intertwined our fingers. Holding his hand was becoming second nature.

Ashley's cheeks were puffy and red. She threw her arms in the air before stomping out of the restaurant on her four-inch heels. If her attitude was indicating how the rest of the night was going to proceed, I was in for a whole lot of fun.

Chapter Eighteen

False hope evaporated that they would change the decor since I was last here. The brown meeting room would star in my nightmares for the rest of my existence. Maybe I should have Blayde introduce Chantel to their interior decorator. Food for thought.

The Alpha King's upper lip curl was so minuscule that if I hadn't been anticipating his reaction, I would've missed it. His disgust at Blayde holding my hand was schooled quickly before we finished walking in. The Alpha King knew what he was doing when he'd sent Ashley to escort Blayde to the meeting. He never suspected that I would come along to foil his plan. Oh, it was the simple things in life that brought me joy.

Blayde led us over to the front row of chairs. I was more of a back row sort of girl myself, but I speculated this was some type of formal seating arrangement, so I kept my mouth shut. Or at least I assumed I had until Blayde chuckled at my groan.

"The front is reserved for Alphas or next Alpha, so they

might make their presence known," Blayde leaned over and whispered.

Turning my head, I hovered my lips over his ear. "Wouldn't it be better to sit in the back and watch the reactions of everyone else? It would be much more insightful."

A flash of awe crossed his face. "You know, I've never considered that. Usually, my presence demands order and respect. To keep attendees from getting rowdy. But you're right. It would be valuable to observe unconscious body language and to unknowingly take in the temperature of the group. I'll have to talk to my father about it."

It was my turn to be shocked. It had rolled off my tongue more as an offhanded comment, but he took it seriously and saw value in it. My heart swelled, warming me all over. He was treating me as his equal. Someone to have at his side. Someone who had merit.

"Now, let's start the meeting." Herrick hit his fist once against the desk like a javelin.

Kanyon sat next to me and bumped his shoulder into mine, grinning. The remaining stragglers claimed their seats, and a reverent hush fell over the room.

"We have asked you all here to discuss a new development. Five kids have gone missing. Peter, Sarah, Julie, Brian, and Markus," Alpha King said.

No one spoke, not a mutter, not a whisper. Infuriation and sadness descended into the crowd like a dark fog. I didn't even know the kids, and I ached for them and their families.

"First the anger flares, then the thefts, and now this! What's next!" a man two rows behind me stood and shouted.

There was a collective mumbling in agreement around

him. The Alpha King arched his eyebrow, and the man slumped in his chair.

"We don't know if they're connected. We have been searching for any type of connection but have found nothing so far. The only thing they have in common is that they are all Shifters, and you can see why that hasn't provided a solid lead," Herrick said.

"We are open to any suggestions you may have." Kerr gestured to the floor.

The three of us sat in silence as a few people stood and spoke, each ranging from a different degree of implementing a new protective measure. They weren't bad ideas, but none of them were going to help find the missing kids.

"It's the Vampire's fault!" the same man two rows behind me shouted. "Vampires are cold-hearted snakes! We should've never allowed the viper to be on our land!"

Shouts of agreements followed, and the atmosphere went from respectful to mob mentality.

My blood sizzled. No one—and I meant no one—talked about my best friend like that. I thrusted onto my feet to give them a tongue-lashing, but Blayde's firm grip yanked me back to my chair.

"Now isn't the time." Blayde's voice was cool and collected. Anger clouded his eyes, and his clasp tightened around mine. His voice and eyes told me two separate things.

I opened my mouth to speak, to demand the right to defend Agrona, but I was beaten to the punch.

"That *Vampire* you are implying had something to do with any of this is innocent. She wasn't here when the anger flares or the thefts started. She has been too busy to even consider harming any of us, let alone children. She is a guest and will be treated as such." Kanyon's booming words echoed in the room. Waves of power rolled off him, and his bear peeked through his eyes. Kanyon was the Head Enforcer. He was doing his job and solidified the Alpha King's ruling.

A hush descended over everyone for the second time. Kanyon's show of dominance had the intended effect. After glaring around the room, he sat back in his spot. I shouldn't have doubted Blayde's intention. Clearly, there was a protocol that I wasn't familiar with. A mere second after Kanyon relaxed, the outraged cries erupted.

"He is in on it!"

"Vampires are going to overrun us!"

"Traitor!"

"Viper-loving hippie!"

Kanyon's speech hadn't pacified the Shifters. No. Instead, it made their prejudice burn brighter than a neon sign. Honestly, I was surprised that food wasn't thrown at him.

Blayde's hand vibrated in mine. A glance at his face only confirmed that he was barely controlling his rage. He was right—adding to the contention wouldn't solve their problem. Nothing could pierce their stupidity.

"Enough!" the Alpha King boomed. "We are not here to discuss the Vampire." His voice didn't hide his disgust.

"We need to be vigilant," Herrick said. "We need to take extra precautions, locking our doors and valuables. We need to keep track of the little ones. No one goes on a run without a buddy. In fact, no one should go anywhere without accompaniment. Until we can pinpoint who is behind this, and *if* all three are connected, we need to have coherent minds. We need to solve this before a council member gets involved. They are a pain in my—"

The more he talked, the more I liked him. He seemed wise and level-headed.

"Now that everyone is up to date and clear about moving forward, you are all dismissed," Kerr interrupted and terminated the meeting at the same time.

Blayde and Kanyon remained seated, so I followed their lead and watched the rest of the rows exit. Ashley and a few others glared in my direction. I wasn't a hundred percent sure that all the glares were for me.

Once the last attendee had left, the Alpha King narrowed his eyes at the three of us. The longer he stared, the more I felt like I was in the principal's office.

"That could've gone better," Herrick said.

Kerr snorted.

Alpha King reclined in his chair and shook his head. "Kanyon, next time, a tad bit more force. You didn't use as much dominance as you should've. Normally, for this small of audience, it would've been fine, but with their tempers, you needed more. And Blayde—your anger was visible. Nobody saw it only because their focus was on Kanyon. You cannot show them that their words and opinions have affected you. You did well by not saying anything and letting our Head Enforcer manage it."

My jaw dropped open. The Alpha King seemed like a—dare I say—a good father? He was instructing his sons how to handle pack members and be leaders. There wasn't any malice in his voice. He was just teaching them.

"Now, I want the three of you to visit Griff. See if he has come up with any leads. None of the investigators or enforcers have discovered anything," he said.

Kanyon bowed his head slightly at the mention that his division hadn't brought forth results.

Wait...did he include me?

"The three of us, uh, Majesty, sir?" I asked.

Herrick's lips twitched, and he coughed to cover a chuckle. Yeah, he was definitely my favorite.

Alpha King's brow quirked. "Griff has requested you personally. He hasn't been able to shut up about you since he met you."

I hoped that was a good thing. I liked Griff. He was unique. Plus, I was slightly afraid of what he could do if I got on his bad side. That man had everything at his fingertips.

"Oh, Blayde. I hope you had the chance to speak with Ashley about your future. There are some details about upcoming events that need finalizing," Kerr said.

For a brief moment, I'd forgotten that he was Ashley's father. I disliked him even more.

"I'll repeat this a final time. There is no Ashley and me. There never was and never will be. Cedar is my mate. If I hear anyone talking about Ashley and me as a couple, I will forcedly beat those thoughts out of their skulls. That includes you three. I will not stand for my fated mate to be treated this way." Blayde held the gaze of his father. Neither moving. An intense stare to claim dominance.

Alpha King broke first by blinking then averting his focus. Blayde released the tension in his shoulders. Herrick's and Kerr's eyes widened, but they didn't utter a word. Blayde had won, which I had a feeling wasn't a normal thing against his father. I, once again, was in awe of Blayde.

"We will let you know if we find anything out." Blayde nodded before dragging me alongside him.

If this was how all Shifter meetings went, I'd pass on the next one.

* * *

We stopped briefly at the cabin, which Chantel had magically cleaned up. Upon us walking over the threshold, she told us her potion for seeing who was behind the theft wasn't successful. The thief wore a dark hooded cloak that obscured his or her features.

It was decided that only Blayde, Kanyon, and I would go see Griff. Agrona needed to lie low, and Chantel would stay with her. Shifters naturally liked Sorcerers, so her presence with Agrona might not cause more agitation.

We hiked to Griff's house without any incidents. It was a miracle. I didn't fall off the bridge, and no one got gruffy.

Kanyon spearheaded the way while Blayde was at my side, our fingers intertwined. Ever since our talk, it seemed as if he had to have one hand on me at all times or I might change my mind. I enjoyed his touch, so I didn't protest.

Kanyon waved and announced our arrival to the camera. With a click, Kanyon walked forward. We got to the concrete fortress front door, and before Blayde was able to knock, it opened. The overexcited balding man greeted us. I'd only met Griff once, but this greeting felt abnormal.

"Cedar! I was hoping that you would come. Please, I have a new piece of art I would like to show you." He tugged on my wrist.

I tried to release Blayde's hand, but instead, Blayde's lip curled, giving me a warning growl. So, I allowed Griff to lead me along with Blayde in tow.

He took me to the kitchen, where a framed picture covered the length of the wall. I tilted my head from side to side. It was hideous.

"Is that a chicken?" I squinted.

Griff clapped. "Close. It is a rooster!" He beamed.

He was so proud of his ugly farm animal.

"Why is the rooster on a rowboat about to be swallowed by a shark?" Blayde asked.

"No, the real question is why the pool of water is depicted as spit in a whale's mouth," Kanyon added.

"I painted this. I felt so inspired after meeting you." Hope and excitement shone in Griff's eyes.

I wasn't sure if the artwork was a good or a bad thing. It looked a little deranged.

"It's...different. Unique even. Just like you." I touched his shoulder, trying to not show my true feelings.

"Thank you. Finally, someone understands and appreciates my genius. When's your birthday? I'll paint you something." He clasped his hands together in glee.

"Oh, no need to. I already had my birthday this year. Thank you, though, it is a sweet gesture." *Please, oh please, don't paint me something.*

I purposely didn't tell him my birthday, but if he really wanted to know, it would only take him a second to find it online.

Blayde cleared his throat and pulled me closer to him. "Any updates on the cases?"

Griff's smile fell. "Fine. Follow me."

He led us into his tech cave, where he positioned himself in his black chair. He typed a few things before the word "NOTHING" appeared on every screen.

"That is what I've uncovered, and it is frustrating. There is no video surveillance of any of the thefts or kidnappings. We do have recordings of the anger flare-ups, but zilch on the cause." Griff folded his arm across his chest with a defeated *humph*.

I give him points on style. I was starting to get a feel for Griff's sense of humor. It was drier than I expected.

"Are the homes that got robbed the same homes that had the kidnappings?" I was grasping for any correlation.

"No, and before you ask, the anger flare-ups haven't had thefts or kidnappings. I haven't been able to find any overlap."

"For all appearances, they seem to be three very separate cases, but my gut is telling me that they are connected somehow." Kanyon frowned.

"The kidnappings—did the thefts occur to friends of the kids who were taken?" Blayde asked.

Griff turned to the computer and typed for a moment before he reclined in his chair.

"I have it running a program to check for that connection. It may take a few hours, seeing how I don't know the name of all the friends, so I'll be basing it on camera footage of seeing the kids together a couple of times. I will let you know," Griff said.

"What about, um, anything about the first Council?" I asked.

"Nothing significant. I did find that the other species do have books on the first member, like we do with Crispin Mannering. If you have any connections, you could get them. Oh! I found a painting of them, and I had it digitally enhanced. Let me email it to you." Griff typed on his computer and looked satisfied when he hit send. "I do have a contact inquiring about it, and if he finds anything, you'll be the first to know."

Disappointed didn't even cover how I was feeling. I thought Griff would've had more. No leads. No clues. Nada.

"I'll have my enforcers check out the kidnapped kids' friends. It might give us a starting point," Kanyon said.

And just like that, our visit was over.

Chapter Nineteen

"**D**on't be such a baby." I adjusted Blacky in my hand. Bending and straightening my arm, I practiced the motion of throwing my chakram. My technique needed to be flawless.

"You'd whine, too, if some crazy chick was going to throw a sharp object at your skull," Kanyon complained and transferred his weight from one foot to the other.

I bet his eye was twitching.

A week had passed since the journal had been stolen, and I had used every moment I could to train. To become a better fighter. When I'd told them I wanted to become Offense Huntress of the Year, they all but threw me a party with how elated they were. Blayde's demeanor changed— more relaxed, happier, calmer. Relieved.

My only regret was that Ricardo wasn't here. He would've said one of his lame jokes, but we would've celebrated all together that I was finally doing what he hoped for me to do all along. We still hadn't heard from him, and it was taking a toll on Chantel's mental and physical health. She kept up the facade of happy and cheerful, but we all

185

could see through it. Her eyes looked sunken and were lined with dark bags.

In the past week, my skills had improved significantly. I could almost best Agrona without tapping into my Vampire speed. Blayde had stepped back in to help me with my Shifter competency, giving us another excuse to be around each other. Chantel started to teach me advanced spells that left me exhausted. Kanyon changed his lessons on weapon training. More importantly, my chakrams.

And that was how we'd got here today.

Kanyon touched the apple on top of his head, making certain it was centered. "I'm not sure I'm confident in your ability to not kill me."

Booming laughter broke from Agrona and Chantel on the metal bleachers. I drummed up the brilliant idea for Kanyon to be an active participant in today's lesson. Kanyon would stand against the wall while balancing an apple. I would aim a chakram from twenty feet away and nail the fruit. Without much effort, I'd hit the bullseye every time. I was ready to take it up a notch. Chantel and Agrona loved my plan. Chantel because, well, she was crazy. Agrona because she didn't like Shifters, even though I suspected she considered Blayde and Kanyon friends.

"Waaaaaaa. That's all I'm hearing right now. Don't you trust me?" I joked.

"This is a bad idea," Kanyon grumbled.

"What was that?" I smiled. Thanks to my increased senses, I was able to hear him, but I pretended not to.

"If you kill me, I'm coming back to haunt you." He straightened out, his posture going rigid.

"I'm looking forward to it!"

Wanting to mess with him, I threw Pinky at him. My

chakram sailed through the air and landed near Kanyon's feet—exactly where I intended it.

"Oops. Let me try again." I stifled a laugh.

Life wouldn't be fun if I didn't get to mess with my friends now and then.

The color drained from Kanyon's face, going baking-flour white. His Adam's apple bobbed up and down, gulping. I didn't know if it was reassuring or not that he so easily believed my lie. Now was not the time to dwell on that. I had a chakram to throw.

I tightened my grip around Blacky, and it hummed with delight. I was getting better at sensing emotions from my chakrams. We were bonding beyond mere buddies.

Blue-and-black fire erupted on my chakram. It didn't burn me. It was warm against my skin. Pinky's and Blacky's fire couldn't harm me. Chantel thought their magic and personalities were an extension of my own. I wasn't sure about her theory, but it didn't feel wrong either.

I shifted my stance and brought my left foot in front with my right behind. I placed all my weight on my back leg, I brought my right arm up. I gripped Blacky tighter and moved it close to my ear. Exhaling, I altered my weight to the front and extended my forearm, sending Blacky sailing.

Crunch.

Blacky punctured the apple and sliced it in two. My chakram had embedded itself into the wall, and the red halves fell to the speckled gym floor.

"That could've gone wrong in so many ways," Blayde announced from the elevator door, startling me.

My palm went over my thumping heart. "Don't scare a girl like that," I chastised.

"I waited until after you were done to voice my

concerns. If I hadn't, I might not have a brother right now. Actually, I don't know why I didn't say anything."

Amusement lit his face, and I knew he was joking. He'd tease his brother, but he loved Kanyon and would do anything for him.

"I see how it is, brother. My life flashes before my eyes by your mate's hand, and now I have to find out how you feel about me. Shame on you." Kanyon strode toward me with a jesting smile.

Blayde and Kanyon arrived by me at the same moment. They stood side by side, making me wish that I had a sibling. Caroline and my father took great care of my every whim, but I had missed out on sibling affection.

The thought of home reminded me that I needed to speak with Caroline. Over the last few months, what I considered a betrayal had been defrosted. No matter what our DNA said, she was my mom through and through. She'd changed my diapers and stayed with me when I was sick. We had our differences, but she would forever be my mother. I'd been wanting to call her, to tell her I forgave her, but it felt impersonal doing it that way. But I was coming to realize my life might not slow down anytime soon to go visit her—the phone would have to do. I made a mental note to call her later.

Blayde planted a kiss on my forehead. "Not that I don't love seeing you or watching my brother be used as a training exercise, but I'm actually here to speak to Chantel."

My interest was piqued. Why did he need the Sorceress?

We walked over to the bleachers, and for the first time, I noticed Kanyon had one of the apple halves in his hand. Taking a bite, he glanced in my direction and shrugged. He wasn't going to let a perfectly good apple be wasted.

"My ears are burning. One of you was talking about me." Chantel touched the sides of her head.

"You heard Blayde, you dork. Stop acting like you didn't." Agrona elbowed Chantel in the waist.

I chuckled at Chantel's antics. I swear "silly" was her middle name.

Chantel stuck her tongue out. "Fun sucker."

Blayde waited patiently for Chantel's and Agrona's quips to cease. I was starting to think he had patience like feathers on a bird.

"Why did you require Chantel?" Kanyon asked before taking another bite.

"Chantel, would you be willing to do some calming exercises with the Shifters who experience anger flares? Maybe there are some new techniques you can teach them?" Blayde asked.

Why Chantel? She wasn't an overly calm person. Shoot, she would rather see me almost fall off a bridge for her own amusement.

"I'm not a Mage. I'm not well-versed in helping Shifters connect with Earth and magic. This is not my area," she scoffed and looked a little offended. "But I could do it. I am a Sorceress after all. It could be entertaining to make Shifters do some yoga." A mischievous smile appeared on her face. That was never a safe sign.

She got off the bleachers and headed for the elevator.

"Wait, nothing crazy, Chantel. Soothing techniques." Blayde grabbed her arm. "Promise me."

"I promise," Chantel grumbled the rest of the words, rendering them inaudible.

"You promise what?" Kanyon asked next to Blayde.

"I promise to lead them in calming exercises," she said innocently and batted her eyes.

Kanyon snorted. "Yeah, calming exercises for a psychopath. Try again."

Chantel huffed. "Fine. I promise no one will die or be seriously traumatized. You take the fun out of everything."

"Wait. No. Chantel, relaxing methods, please!" Blayde panicked.

Chantel's mouth moved, muttering a spell. "See you in the common area." She plastered on a smile before touching her wand to her head. In a blink, she disappeared.

Those poor Shifters had no idea what they were getting themselves into.

* * *

Somehow. Some way. I got roped into attending Chantel's "calming exercises." Actually, Blayde dragged all of us into it, claiming we were keeping an eye on her. Whispering that secretly, he just wanted to spend time with me.

Ever since I'd told him I was all in, he'd tried his best to woo me and to be affectionate. My heart kept murmuring that pesky L word. No matter how much I struggled to squash it, it bubbled to the surface.

In the past week, he'd gifted me a new black leather jacket and a Barbie night t-shirt—exactly like the one he'd purchased from the mall weeks ago. Since my belongings were all destroyed, he even took me shopping. Never complained once. Flowers also showed up at the cabin, with a note signed "Blay Blay." He was weaving himself into my soul, and I didn't know if I'd ever be able to extract him.

"Now, maggots, drop and give me two hundred. Go! Go! Go!" Chantel barked at the Shifters.

Two hundred push-ups were nothing to me now, and I assumed it was similar for all the Shifters here, but I was wrong. Most were panting, with beads of sweat rolling down their faces. Blayde, Kanyon, and Agrona didn't appear to be tired from the physical strain. Chantel put us through a boot camp-style workout, and it was all too clear that she was enjoying herself. Hopefully, this was a part of the plan and not something she wanted to do for fun.

"Come on! I have teddy bears tougher than you," she yelled. She circled the Shifters with her hands clasped behind her. She'd missed her calling as a drill sergeant.

After about thirty more minutes of exercising, she had us partner up and sit across from them. Agrona went to take a seat on the grass in front of me, only to have Blayde grumble and growl. He was staking his claim, and I couldn't say I was mad about it. I wanted to spend as much time as I could with him. With a dramatic eye roll, Agrona and Kanyon became partners.

"Sit cross-legged with your forearms resting on your thighs," Chantel instructed.

Blayde and I did, with our legs almost close enough to touch. Our gazes locked. A magnetic force drew me to him, creating the desire to press myself against him. But I held back. My first kiss with Blayde shouldn't have an audience.

My gaze slowly progressed to his lips. Plump. Luscious. Kissable. A fiery inferno burned within my belly. Did he want me as much as I wanted him? He must feel the connection between us, this irresistible urge.

His fingertips brushed my knee, delivering an electric jolt through me. Tingles lingered on my skin where his touch had been. His pupils dilated, and his hands stretched and clenched as if he was stopping himself from reaching out.

"Now close your eyes. Take four long breaths. Feeling

the magic between you and your partner." Chantel's tone dripped with honey.

Forcing my eyes closed, I inhaled. On my last exhale, I zeroed in on the magic between Blayde and me. If I thought it was hard before, it had nothing on this instance.

The invisible force of our bond ensnared me. In my mind's eye, it looked like a million strands connecting me to him. Without thinking, I reached forward, trying to grab a hold of one. I made contact, but not with what I was seeking. With Blayde. Our fingers intertwined, and the strings appeared to be growing bigger, thicker.

"Expand your senses. Feel the energy all around. In the grass. In the air. In the blood coursing through your veins." The crunch of greenery followed Chantel's footsteps.

I freed my consciousness, and instead of observing the magic surrounding me, I only felt Blayde. The magic in him. His soul. It was a bright light, beckoning me. I wanted to shy away from it, but it drew me in like a bee to a honeycomb. My spirit responded, stretching, searching for his. Shivers ran the length of my body, and magic swirled between us.

Each moment I spent assessing our bond, the more it intensified. Every fiber of my being wanted to inch closer to him, and it was a battle I was slowly losing.

Blayde released his grip, and immediately our bond dimmed in response. His arms pulled me to him, placing me on his lap. The bond flared, getting sharper and more brilliant, sending the message that we were stronger together than apart.

"Now feel the magic through your fatigued muscles. Allow it to course through you, giving you renewed life. New strength. Let it refresh you. We are magic. Each and every one of us. Every species has that power within.

Connect and let it restore you." Chantel's voice was just above a whisper.

The magic washed over me. I was ready and able to take on the world. My mind was clear and free of confusion. My heart screamed to complete the bond. I itched to comply.

With our bond flaring, I recognized that this was only the beginning. That once we took the next step, it would grow and blossom even more. It would be so easy to succumb and claim Blayde right here, right now.

A high-pitched blaring sound had me jumping out of Blayde's arms. Adrenaline rushed through me, cutting off my mind's view of our bond. Turning around in a circle, I found the source. Chantel stood with a grin on her face and a red blowhorn in her hand.

"Class is over," she bellowed. She honked the blowhorn again.

Before she could blast it a third time, Agrona took it from her and passed it to Kanyon. He smiled at her as he crushed the can in his hand.

"Sure, just take all the fun away from me," Chantel pouted. "See all of you tomorrow. Wear something to exercise in!"

The Shifters dispersed, leaving the five of us. My eyes met Blayde's, and I perceived he'd experienced what I had. There was one thing I knew for sure: I wanted to make him mine. And the sooner I did that, the better.

Chapter Twenty

B rave. Courageous. Bold. Daring. Everything I wasn't currently. If you were to say I chickened out, you'd be right.

Blayde and Kanyon were summoned for another meeting, and with every step toward the DIY cabin, the more I cowered in my decision to move forward in the bonding ceremony.

I didn't have an excuse for being a giant domestic fowl. Only the big ball of fear sitting on my chest.

By the time we were back in the cabin, I had split my lip from biting it. My nerves were getting to me. I was jittery and bouncy, like I had just consumed three energy drinks.

"What is going on with me?" I complained.

"Oh, sweetie," Agrona said, and she enveloped me in her arms.

We sank onto the couch, and tears welled up. This wasn't me. I wasn't someone who cried over a guy, especially when I lacked a reason to weep.

Chantel slid in on the other side of me and put her arms

around us. A girl group hug. It was comforting and reassuring that they were always looking out for me.

"I think having you explore the magic between you and Blayde strengthened your bond. Being edgy and pensive without your mate is a way your bond is trying to force you guys back together," Chantel said.

"Fated mates usually complete their bond quickly. The longest I've seen a couple last is a week... and you guys are past that." Agrona released me from her embrace.

Chantel let go and lay her head on my shoulder.

"All of this because I've been indecisive. Been keeping him at arm's length." A tear rolled down my cheek. I wouldn't be in any of this if I would've trusted the bond more.

Agrona mimicked Chantel's position on my opposite side, and I took both of their hands. I sighed and enjoyed the familiarity. It would be so easy to shut my eyes and take a little nap.

But no.

There was a burglar running free who had the journal, and I needed to retrieve it.

"Do either one of you have a computer I can use?" I asked.

I unclasped their hands, and they sat up, taking their warmth and closeness with them.

Chantel dashed to our bedroom and returned before I could ask what she was doing.

She deposited her magic bag on the couch, pushing her arm down into it. The fabric was up to her armpit. She stuck out her tongue as she moved inside the bag, searching.

"Ah! Here it is." Chantel lifted a laptop out and set it on my lap.

I opened it and coughed as dust came off it.

"Jeez, when is the last time you've used this thing?" I sneezed and swatted the air with my hand.

Chantel pursed her lips and tapped them. "Never? Once? Twice? Only in my dreams? I have no idea."

Luckily, it powered up. Logging in to my email, I found the image Griff sent me. I pulled it up and enlarged it to full screen. It was a painting, and even though Griff had enhanced the portrait, it still wasn't the best.

I tilted my head from side to side. *No. It couldn't be. Could it?*

Placing the computer on Agrona's lap, I asked, "Do any of them seem familiar to you?"

Her eyes squinted, and she brought the screen closer to her face. Her finger hovered over one of the first Council members. She sat back against the cushion and set the device on her legs.

"It can't be," she muttered.

"You see it, too, then?" I asked.

This was nuts. It couldn't be him.

"See what?" Chantel asked, sitting next to Agrona to study the picture.

"That guy right there," I pointed at the man in question, "looks like a bartender we know named Desmond."

"The hot one from the club?" Chantel asked.

"Yep," I confirmed.

"That can't be. He'd have to be really, really, *really,* old, and he didn't seem that much older than us," Chantel justified.

"You said that Desmond and Quin were two of a kind. Quin mentioned the Angel who helped create the Hunters was beautiful. What if they were there?"

"No...There has to be a different reason." She appeared perplexed.

"Well, there is only one way to find out." I jumped to my feet and headed out of the cabin to go locate Blayde. He would know how to contact Desmond and then, maybe, finally get some answers.

* * *

I left Chantel and Agrona at the cabin, wallowing in complaints. Not only did I want to talk to Blayde about Desmond, but I wanted to stake my claim on him, or at least see if that was something he was ready for. And I didn't want an audience for that.

Some nice Shifters told me he was at the meeting hall. Of course, where else would he be for a meeting?

I went into the modern building and passed the tan lobby toward the brown room. Voices bled through the door, and I stopped to listen. Blayde. Ashley.

My jaw snapped hard, and anger burst inside of me. I didn't want her anywhere near him. He was *mine*. All mine.

With my ear flat against the door, I tried to figure out who else was there with him. I kept my hand on the door-knob and opened my senses, not hearing anyone besides them. Slowly, I turned the knob, cracking the door just enough to peek.

My instincts screamed that I should barge in, but my heart gave Blayde the benefit of the doubt. What if the Alpha King was in there, and I barreled in and made myself into a bigger idiot? Then I would never be in his good graces.

"I'm better suited for you than some random girl, she

will never be woman enough for you. Come on, Blayde. We belong together. Our parents have planned this since our infancy," Ashley cooed and crept toward him.

Blayde stood there with his fists by his sides, rigid as a stone wall. At the angle he was at, I couldn't see his expression.

"Blayde. Stop fighting." Ashley slithered her palms up his torso.

With a quick movement, she launched herself at him. Blayde turned his face into his shoulder, and she pressed her lips against the intimate curve of his neck.

My vision flashed red, and I shook with indignation. I clutched the handle, crushing it. The anguish inside my chest called for justice. To make them pay.

In a blink, Blayde brought his hands onto Ashley's shoulders and shoved her. My inner rage monster demanded blood. It couldn't be reasoned with. My thoughts were clouded with nothing but vengeance.

But this wasn't me.

A sob escaped my throat, and I didn't wait for Blayde to realize I was here. I spun and sprinted out of the building.

I put all my energy into running. I moved faster than I ever had. If this had been in training, then I would've enjoyed the wind in my hair. But it wasn't.

Another woman's mouth had touched my mate. My heart cracked, slowly splitting. The scene kept replaying in my mind. I couldn't get it to stop. The thirst for revenge burned at my center. I wanted to smash something. To inflict pain.

I let the pain guide my feet, requiring a task to dull my agony.

I arrived at the training room, went up the elevator,

beelined for the music, and hit shuffle. "Monsters" by All Time Low blared through the speakers. Fitting.

I stood in front of the punching bag, and it was all too easy to imagine Ashley's face. I worked through my warm-up sequence, and tears welled up, blurring my vision. I didn't want to sob. Not over this.

So, I kept punching. Every ounce of fury and hatred was thrown into it. I smashed my fist into the bag, and it fell back, crashing into the wall.

Panting, I sank to my knees. Moisture broke free, and I couldn't contain my sorrow any longer.

Ashley had kissed him.

Ashley had kissed my mate.

Why would Fate do this to me?

Maybe Ashley was right. I wasn't enough for Blayde. She was a Shifter; she would be a good Alpha's wife. She was everything I wasn't. She had freedom. She wasn't the conductor of the hot mess express.

Tears dampened my shirt. With the back of my hand, I wiped my nose. I wasn't a pretty crier. I was the queen of ugly cry.

The two halves of my heart were hanging on by a tiny thread of hope. Blayde had pushed her away. She had kissed him, not vice versa. Maybe I should've barged in and demanded an explanation.

My head argued. That dumb brat had snogged my mate. *Mine.* It shouldn't have ever happened.

A blanket of anguish wrapped around me. Sobs became frenzied and frequent. I gasped between snivels, unable to assuage.

A hand touched my shoulder, and I didn't bother to look. *What's the point?* My heart was broken, and I was unsure I'd be whole again. Not without Blayde.

"Cedar, what's going on?" Kanyon knelt next to me.

"Blayde," I started, but the words wouldn't leave my tongue. If I told someone, it would make it real. My personal nightmare would become a reality.

"Blayde what?" he said softly.

My blubbering didn't ease. If anything, it was more harsh and unforgiving.

Kanyon pulled me into his arms and emitted shushing noises, like how you would calm a baby. His hands drew giant circles on my back, trying to relax and comfort me. But there was only one person I wanted right now. The mixed feelings inside me twisted in my rib cage.

After a very long few minutes, my wails dissipated into a trickle of tears, and I was able to find my voice. I told Kanyon what was tormenting me.

"Ashley kissed him?" Kanyon asked after a moment of silence.

I nodded.

"What did Blayde do after? Or did you not stick around for that part?"

"He pushed her away. I bolted after that. I couldn't stand to see them together. I wanted to cry and punch them at the same time," I confessed.

"Blayde pushed Ashley away. Let that sink in."

Blayde pushed Ashley away.

Blayde. Pushed. Ashley away.

"I know my brother, and I know he hasn't even looked at a woman since you walked into his life, so there is no way he would cheat on you. Ashley is conniving and would trade her left arm to be an alpha's bride. So, why are we here talking about this, instead of you speaking to Blayde?" he asked.

"What if he changed his mind? That he actually wants

Ashley? What if I'm not good enough? If we move forward in our relationship and this happens again?" My voice was small.

It was hard admitting my doubts. My insecurities.

"A part of being a fated mate is that there is no one more perfect for you. He is the other half of your soul and you're his. If you continue with the bonding, it will cause him pain to hurt you."

"But...What if I'm not enough for him? What if I'm not worthy of being an Alpha's wife?" I hated how vulnerable I was. How weak I was.

Kanyon laughed. "The real question is not if you are good enough for him, it is whether he is worthy of you. If he has the qualities to be a great Huntress' husband. You continually surprise me. Your abilities are like none I've ever seen. But I don't think all of these doubts are the real problem here."

I stared at him in disbelief. My doubts weren't the issue here? Was he nuts? Of course, he was.

"I think the real problem is that you haven't claimed him as your mate. You're kicking yourself for not realizing sooner how in love you are with him," he said.

Me? In love?

Could it be? Did I love Blayde?

I let the thought marinate for a moment, but I already knew the answer. I wouldn't be in my own personal hell right now if I didn't.

"Ah, you finally realize it. My job here is done." Kanyon stood and helped me up to my feet. "Go get him, tiger." He swatted my butt like we were football buddies.

It was time to go get my man. To claim what was mine.

Chapter Twenty-One

Love. An intense feeling. One that made you the happiest but also made you feel the craziest. To love someone and to be loved, in my opinion, was one of the greatest gifts you could give. You gave the most vulnerable parts of yourself and gave them the power to crush you or build you up. Love was one of the scariest things I had ever experienced.

It didn't take me long to find him. Seeing how he was standing against the elevator, blocking anyone from exiting. His gaze bore into me, drinking up every ounce.

"This is my cue to leave." Kanyon patted my shoulder before walking to the elevator. He stopped briefly next to Blayde and whispered something.

Blayde nodded, but his eyes never strayed.

I stood there like an idiot, frozen, as Kanyon left. The doors *chinged* as they closed. All the words I wanted to express lingered on my tongue.

Blayde pushed off the door and stalked toward me. This was my chance. I didn't want to let him go, not now, not ever.

His pace was unhurried, deliberate, as if trying to move without scaring me off. If he thought I was preparing to flee, he was in for a surprising discovery.

Blayde was too slow for the ball of nerves bouncing around in my chest. I didn't want to wait a second longer.

I sprang from my spot and rushed toward him, like I was in a desert, and he was an oasis. His stride picked up, and he ran. We met in the middle, stopping two feet from each other.

"Princess..." Blayde cleared his throat. "Cedar. I know what you saw. I can only imagine what is transpiring through your mind."

I stared at him with a blank face. I knew what I felt, but first I needed to hear what he had to say.

He didn't start talking again, so I raised my eyebrow to encourage him to keep going.

"She kissed me. Not that it is any excuse, but it is the truth. I pushed her away and gave her a verbal lashing. She is being sent to a different pack where she won't be even able to look at you sideways. I should've pressed harder the first time she was rude to you, and that's my fault. For that, I'm sorry."

He gulped and ran his hand through his brown hair. "I'm sorry you had to see that. I'm sorry that even took place. But I want you to know you are it for me. There will never be another. Just like a run during a full moon, I need you. Every second of every day, I want to be with you, but I also don't want to smother you, so I resist. I give you as much freedom as I can without feeling that my skin is the only thing holding me together. I'm all in, forever. I'll do anything to prove it to you. I'll give up my pack, my alpha status, everything for you. Just say the word."

Vulnerability shone through his eyes. His fingers tapped

his thigh. He was nervous. I suspect that he thought after seeing the incident, I would break the bond. But how could I give up someone who was willing to give up everything for me? He was kind, gentle, fierce, protective, sometimes a jerk, strong, possessive, funny, and I couldn't forget smokin' hot. Even with the bad, his good outweighed them.

Keeping my face neutral, I inched forward. "I just want you."

I wasn't sure who reached for who first. Maybe we both did. One of his hands slid behind my neck, inching me closer, while the other cupped my jaw. I gripped his shirt and tugged him down to me. In the middle, our lips touched. No hesitation. No fear. No worries. No regret. No Huntress. No Alpha. Just us.

Sparks exploded. Passion. Desire. Yearning. Months of pent-up longing and fervor. His hand drifted from my cheek and got tangled in my blonde locks. I moved my palms up his chest and around his collar, pulling him closer. I didn't want anything between us——not doubts, pain, or space. Nothing.

Our kiss softened, and only affection lingered. The kisses were light and full of promise.

We eased back, and my clasp was locked around him. His forehead rested against mine. Our bond felt stronger, more magnetic. One kiss wasn't enough to satisfy me. But there was more that needed to be said.

"I, Cedar Hastings, claim Blayde Daniels to be my mate," I whispered.

Euphoria exploded in his eyes and his smile was the biggest that I had ever witnessed. I thought I had seen what happiness on him looked like, but I was wrong.

His lips touched mine in a light, gentle kiss. "I, Blayde Daniels, claim Cedar Hasting for my mate."

Swirling lights of gold and silver surrounded us, cocooning us. Our souls reached for one another, dancing, similar to the first time only a few weeks ago. But in this instance, it was more intense, intimate.

For a moment, we became one, and everything felt right. When our souls finally separated, they took a mirror image back with them. A piece of Blayde would always be with me. Always there protecting me.

I didn't think I could explain this feeling, this experience to anyone even if I wanted to. It was special. Sacred.

Blayde wrapped me in his arms, and we sank to our knees. He pulled me into him until he was sitting on the floor, and I was on his lap. I rested against his chest.

We didn't need to speak. It was beautiful, and we were basking in the moment. I only wished I hadn't done it in the middle of the training room. There was only one more thing I needed to say.

I tilted my head back and looked into Blayde's eyes. "I love you."

His hands cupped my cheeks, and our lips met. He nibbled on my bottom lip before pulling away.

"I love you, too. You don't know how long I have waited for this. From the beginning, I have loved you. Every sassy comment, every time you pushed me away, I loved you. For the longest time, I believed I would never find my mate, nonetheless fated at that. But there you were. In a million years, I never thought I would feel this way. To love someone with not just my heart but my entire being. I am yours, Cedar. Forever and for all eternity."

Despite my flaws and his—this was perfect. I was in love, and I wasn't going to let anybody take this away from me.

* * *

After a small but passionate make-out session, I ran my fingers through my hair, putting it into a top knot with bobby pins and elastics securing it. He surprised me and took me out for ice cream. The first way to my heart was chocolate. The second was ice cream. Combine the two, and I was in heaven.

I took a big spoonful of my double fudge brownie chocolate ice cream, and my gaze roamed over Blayde. He relaxed into his chair across the table from me. His shoulders held no tension and a slight smile lingered at the corners of his mouth. He took a bite of his Graham cracker raspberry ice cream and slowly dragged it out. I'd never felt so hot eating a frozen dessert before.

Would it be weird to reach across this table and make out? Probably. Would it be fun? Heck yeah!

Before I had the chance to decide whether I was going to assault Blayde with my mouth or not, we were joined by three people. Agrona. Chantel. And Griff, who wore a trench coat and fedora.

Blayde released a miffed sigh, and I wanted to copy his sentiments. But I refrained. It seemed like our dates were always getting interrupted. Maybe, one day, we would have time for ourselves.

"What are you wearing, Griff?" Blayde asked.

Griff popped the collar. "*Shhh*...Someone might hear you. There are listening devices everywhere," he scolded.

Agrona's lips twitched in amusement.

"We're sorry. What's up with your outfit?" I asked.

"There are cameras all over. My clothing obscures my identity," Griff said, but after a moment added, "I also don't want to be recognized by Mrs. Johnson. She has never forgiven me for running over her rose bushes."

"Why did you run over her rose bushes?" Chantel asked.

Griff waved his hand. "That's beside the point. I found something. In one of Crispin's journals, he talks about the first Hunter. I have reason to believe that the man in the Council portrait wasn't the actual original Hunter. Someone else was." Griff paused and glanced around the table.

We all sat there in silence, waiting for him to continue. Why did he suspect that? Who did he think it was? He'd stopped on a cliffhanger.

"Is anyone going to ask me why? I left a dramatic pause, and nobody filled it," Griff whined.

"Why do you surmise it was a different person?" Agrona asked.

Griff gestured to Agrona. "The snake is the one who asks. I say, what is the world coming to?"

Agrona didn't appear to be annoyed. Instead, she rolled her eyes, slightly shaking her head. I peeked at Blayde. He still appeared to be irritated, but some of it had eased.

"Get on with it, Griff...please." Blayde pushed his ice cream away. If he wanted to let his ice cream go to waste, then whatever, but I wasn't. I scooped up a bite, and I immediately got a brain freeze.

"In the journal, it mentions another but doesn't mention his name. I was able to dig up a picture. The quality isn't the greatest. I tried to render it the best I could." Griff patted his pockets, searching for something.

Another picture. It reminded me of the first one. It looked like Desmond, and we could start there. If that didn't take us anywhere, at least we had this avenue.

I straightened my posture, anxious to see what Griff showed up. I couldn't help but smile. First, Blayde and I claimed each other, then ice cream, and now a second lead. Today was turning out to be a great day. I could almost kiss Griff for his brilliance—I wouldn't, but I could.

I took another bite and glanced at Blayde. Almost all the irritation had vanished. He didn't act as relaxed as before, but it seemed his mood had altered with a new lead.

"Ah, here it is." Griff drew out a phone, swiped it a few times, then placed it in the center of the table.

Without hesitation, I snagged the device before anyone else had the chance to. I studied the image. Placing my thumb and index finger on the screen, I zoomed in. Unfortunately, it did little to help. I zoomed back out and squinted.

It was of two men. One with dark hair that had been in the first picture. He had his arm around the shoulders of the second guy. The second guy had shoulder-length blond hair. It was possible he was familiar. It was hard to judge with how grainy it was.

I passed the phone on to Blayde, who examined it before giving it to Agrona. Impatiently, Chantel peeked over Agrona's shoulder.

"Could the blond man be Quin?" I asked.

"The cranky chef?" Chantel tilted her head and forced her eyes into tiny slits.

I filled Blayde in on my suspicion that the dark-haired Hunter was Desmond. I also mentioned that Desmond knew Quin, and Quin had confirmed it when I'd brought it up. With no one being able to tell me what species they were and only saying they were two of a kind, it was logical.

"But we would know by their smells that they were Hunters. They don't have the same scent," Blayde said.

"Maybe it is because they are the first. Maybe genetics have changed the essence over the last few centuries," I argued.

"Perhaps," Agrona said. Her tone let me know she wasn't convinced.

"Is there a way you can get me into contact with one of them?" I asked, looking at Blayde.

"Anything for you, Cedar Rosita Hastings," Blayde said.

Heat rose to my cheeks. I thought that after claiming him, he wouldn't affect me so much. Boy, was I wrong! The pull to be near him, to touch him, was even stronger.

"That's not my middle name."

"One day, I'll know all your secrets." He winked.

Chantel made a gagging noise. "Just kidding," she teased.

I chuckled and shook my head.

"I'll inquire about Desmond and Quin. I'll email you my findings." Griff stood and nodded to each of us. Just when I thought he would leave, he swiped Blayde's ice cream off the table.

"Good day." Griff smirked and exited with the frozen treat.

Once he was out of sight, I couldn't contain my laughter. First with the getup, then with dessert snatching. He was slowly becoming one of my favorite people.

Blayde pulled out his phone and glanced at me. "I'll be right back. I have to take this."

I watched him depart. He had a perfectly shaped butt. Dang, he could rock a pair of jeans like it was his day job.

"I'm glad matters are sorted out between you guys," Agrona said with a smile.

"Me too. Things aren't as fun when you and Blayde avoid each other," Chantel admitted.

Chantel shot her hand out, reaching for my ice cream. I quickly grabbed it off the table and pressed the bowl against my chest. "Get your own!"

She went to reach again but stopped when we got interrupted.

"Well, well, well. What do we have here? What is a viper doing in here, eating all of our ice cream?"

I groaned. We couldn't have a moment of peace.

Chapter Twenty-Two

F ate hated me. That must be it.

I was beyond tired of all the fights and interruptions. Didn't people have better things to do than ruin my life? Apparently not.

I peered up at the two goons standing behind Agrona. More like looming over her. They timed their confrontation well. Blayde had stepped outside, and *ping* they'd arrived. The Alpha King had announced Agrona was to be treated as a guest, and I sure hoped they didn't treat all their guests this way. Because this was crappy.

"What can I help you boys with?" I asked in an attempt to take the attention off Agrona.

"This *snake* is eating our ice cream," the first goon said. He was beefy. Clearly spent too much time working out. His shirt was too small, and my guess was that he did that on purpose. He was like a peacock trying to show off his feathers. *Yuck.*

Then it hit me. I knew him. I'd seen him before. He was the one at the meeting yelling, throwing a tantrum, that all the Shifters' problems were Agrona's fault.

"As you can see, she isn't eating anything. I am." I smiled as sweetly as I could, despite the fact that I'd love to throw a punch.

Goon Two placed his giant meat mitts on the table, getting in Agrona's face. "We don't like your kind here. So beat it."

Goon Two obviously was not the brains of this duo's operation. I mean, come on, who invaded a Vampire's personal space? That was just plain idiotic.

"How about you two scram, and we'll pretend this didn't happen?" This was their last chance before I switched from defense to offense.

Agrona remained stone-faced. Only the flaring of nostrils gave her emotions away, but I was positive the goon squad hadn't noticed.

"Snake needs to leave before she poisons the place. Get lost or we'll make you get lost," Goon Number One responded.

Chantel bolted from her seat, standing toe to toe with stupid. She was like a doll next to him. He was all brawn, and she was all wand. She was dainty and looked like she could curl up in his hand if she wanted to.

"You need some calming exercises. I'm hosting a class tomorrow morning. You and your friend would benefit from it." Chantel's voice was full of bravado. She put her hands on her hips, showing she wouldn't be submissive.

Goon Two lingered in Agrona's space. What was the deal? Did Shifters and Vampires have such extreme prejudice against each other that they couldn't even be in the same room? Whatever the reason, he was earning the title of Stupid Shifter.

Goon One pushed Chantel's shoulder with two fingers.

"I don't think so. I don't want to hurt a Sorceress, but I will if you don't get forgotten."

Something inside me snapped. No one messed with my friends. No one. I tried to be patient. To be understanding. We'd given them many opportunities to take off, and still, they acted like cavemen.

"Neanderthals, this is your last opportunity. Leave. Now." I slowly scooted out of my chair, mimicking Chantel's power pose.

Goon One pushed Chantel out of the way, tossing her aside. She caught herself before her head hit the floor. She glared up at the goons. Her hand slid into her pocket and pulled out her wand. It rested in her palm, waiting for the chance to be used.

The goon squad bristled. Goon Two approached me from behind, finally getting out of Agrona's face. Goon One took a few steps toward me. I edged to the side, creating space from the table, and dragged the chair with me. I was the turkey in a goon sandwich. Right where I wanted to be.

I gripped the chair with my left hand and lifted my bowl of ice cream to my mouth with the other. I darted my tongue out and licked my ice cream as if it were in a cone, and I hid my smile from their sight. This was almost too easy.

Goon One stepped up against me. The magic in me was repulsed by him. His chest brushed mine, making me feel violated. My chakrams hung heavy at my side, attached to my belt. I would've reached for them at the start if it wouldn't have caused so much damage. I really didn't want to destroy an ice cream shop.

Goon One's eyes were red. Deep red. Fur on his arms kept appearing and disappearing. I imagined this was an anger flare, and it would be frowned upon if they were "permanently" taken care of.

Goon One snarled in my face. His breath was hot and pungent.

"Someone needs to introduce you to a Tic Tac. Pee-ew!" I quibbled.

I didn't get a snarky retort. Instead, his arm came up, ready to smite.

Agrona was there in a blink and grabbed his wrist. I smashed my dessert in his face—something I would mourn later—and sent the chair backward into goon two.

Goon One swiped at his eyes, clearing his vision. Goon Two toppled to the floor and scrambled to stand.

"That one is mine," Agrona growled and pointed to Goon Two.

I shrugged. *Whatevs.*

Agrona pounced on Goon Two, and I focused on my own opponent. I brought my arm back, gaining momentum. I released and met the intended target: Goon One's ugly mug.

He cupped his nose and roared. Letting go, he huffed and puffed. If he was a cartoon, steam would be blowing.

"Olé!" Chantel jumped in front of me with a red washcloth.

Goon One bolted for us. We jumped out of the way, and he turned, spinning around.

"This reminds me of a joke. Cedar, a Shifter walks into an ice cream shop—" Chantel started.

"This isn't the best time for that," I reprimanded. For a brief moment, a flicker of yearning to hear Ricardo tell a joke hit me. I shook my head and threw myself back into the fight.

I got into a fighting stance. My left leg forward and my right leg behind, and beckoned Goon One to attack.

"Enough!" a deep, powerful voice bellowed.

I stumbled as a wave of magic swept over me. The goon squad froze but still struggled in their anger.

"I said *enough*," the voice boomed.

A ripple of magic washed over me, and I swayed. The sounds of footsteps had me turning.

Blayde.

Blayde followed by Kanyon. Blayde was terrifying. He was in his Lycan form—half animal, half man. He had grown a couple of feet. His face had elongated and formed a snout. Salt-'n'-pepper fur covered his body. His clothes were held on by a thread. Literally.

It would've scared me if I hadn't instinctively known it was Blayde. Shoot, the sight of him probably would've had me peeing my pants, though I was never going to admit that. Kanyon was still in his Human form but had a wicked glare. A shiver ran down my spine. I was so glad I wasn't the object of their ire.

Blayde moved toward the goon squad. They whimpered and made themselves seem small. Kanyon waved his hand, and four beefy Shifters came in and dragged the goon squad away.

Walking slowly, Blayde kept his focus on me. His claw-shaped hand took a strand of my hair and rubbed it together between his fingers, his brow quizzical as he cocked his head from side to side.

I inched nearer to him, reached up, and brushed his fuzzy torso. No more tingling sensations had occurred since we had claimed each other. But now a deeper longing had developed. I wanted to touch him, to calm his worries.

I gave him a lazy smile, I said, "You don't scare me."

Taking my thumb and index finger, I flicked his chest. A weird chuckle-growl rumbled out of him. With another step closer, I lay my head against him and wrapped him in a hug. His furry arms enveloped me and gave me a gentle squeeze.

"Blayde, if you will escort the enforcers, I'll make sure Cedar makes it home," Kanyon said behind me.

Without letting me go, Blayde snarled. His possessive trait was still going strong, I saw.

"Come on, man. You need to shift, and you don't have any clothes with you. You can meet us at the cabin afterward and give your girl a proper goodnight kiss." Kanyon winked.

After a long moment, Blayde nuzzled the top of my head before withdrawing. I watched him exit, and it was as if a part of me went with him.

There stood Kanyon, Chantel, Agrona, and me in the middle of a busted-up ice cream parlor. Our little rumble caused property damage. I wasn't winning any points with the Shifters.

"How about you two," Kanyon pointed to Agrona and Chantel, "use the buddy system and head to the cabin? Take some showers and relax. Cedar and I will remain here and make sure the mess gets taken care of."

Agrona narrowed her eyes. I knew she didn't like leaving me behind, but Shifters didn't necessarily enjoy her company, and I needed to get on the Alpha King's good side. If cleaning up would achieve that, then so be it.

"I can stay and help," Agrona bit out. "Or Chantel can fix it with magic."

"Don't be silly. It will go a long way for my reputation if I put in the effort. Winnie and I have it covered." I smiled and Chantel giggled.

Agrona's lips twitched, and I waited for Kanyon to get my Winnie-the-Pooh joke.

"Winnie? What does that mean?" Kanyon's brows furrowed.

"Don't worry about it, hot stuff." Chantel patted his shoulder with a grin on her face. "Agrona and I will go back to the cabin."

"It would be nice to shower all of this off me," Agrona finally conceded. I knew she meant wash the Shifter smell off of her.

Not bothering to watch them leave, Kanyon found some brooms, and we started sweeping.

* * *

When all the broken furniture and glass had been swept up, Kanyon promised the ice cream parlor owner that the damages would be paid for. He thanked us by giving us ice cream to go. Guilty, I took a bite of the ice cream and smiled. We stepped outside and sat on the curb on the sidewalk to eat.

"Things seem to be going well with you and my brother," Kanyon teased, elbowing me gently in the ribs.

"If claiming each other is going well, then heck yes, we are!" I beamed. I didn't remember a time when I was this happy. "Any ladies in your life, Winnie?" Secretly, I loved that nickname for him.

Kanyon raised his eyebrow. He still had yet to make the connection. "What do I get to call you?"

"Umm...Blayde calls me Princess. Even though I have no idea why. Hey! Don't change the subject!" I took another bite.

He sighed. "No ladies in my life. After seeing all the

hassle Blayde has gone through, I don't want to be in a relationship." He chuckled. "I'll think of my own name for you...How about Pain in My Butt? Though that is a mouthful."

I stuck my tongue out at him to stop the laugh that threatened to escape. He grinned, taking a spoonful of his ice cream. When I had finally thought of a comeback, movement caught my eye.

Past Kanyon and down the street, there was a skinny man beside a young boy. The boy appeared to be around ten years old. The skinny man had a slimy air about him. His hands kept scratching his arm, and his head twitched every thirty seconds or so.

"Winnie, do you know him?" I gestured to the skinny man.

Kanyon turned around to look at them. He sat his ice cream on the sidewalk and stood. "No. I've never seen him before in my life. And as the Head Enforcer, there isn't anyone visiting that I haven't seen."

"What does that mean?" I copied him, setting my ice cream down, and stood next to him.

"It means he shouldn't be here. If he or someone is hiding that he is here, then there is bound to be trouble. Let's observe for a moment to see what he is doing here."

We remained side by side, watching them. The boy handed an item to the skinny man. A necklace? A watch? I wasn't sure, but the illumination from the streetlight bounced off it.

Another boy came over and gave the skinny man an object. Both boys beamed up at him. He nodded, stuffing the objects in his pockets. His head twitched, and he said something to the adolescents.

I had a bad feeling about this.

Taking a step forward, Kanyon popped his arm out, almost clotheslining me.

"I need to call for backup enforcers. Plus, Blayde will kill me if you get mixed up in this. Angels help us if something ever happens to you."

The skinny man turned and walked away. The boys followed him like baby ducks.

"The boys are leaving with him. We can't just stand here! What if that man hurts them, or worse? Could you live with that? Because I can't." I started after them. I couldn't let the boys leave with him.

After a beat, Kanyon was by my side. We power walked to catch up to them—well, I power walked, Kanyon strolled. When the skinny man and the boys were in sight, we slowed. We had moved out of the town and into the forest. Thankfully, Shifters and Hunters had an increased sense of sight, so it wasn't hard for us to see in the darkness. It also helped that the moon was out and shining in all its glory.

Staying as close to trees as we could for coverage, we pursued them. The boys sprang behind the skinny man in exuberance. Either they didn't know where they were going, or they did. Both possibilities sent a shudder through me.

I didn't know how long we trekked. My guess would be about fifteen minutes. Not too far from the pack town. The forest began to clear, and Kanyon pulled me to the far side of a pine tree.

We watched the skinny man lead the boys to a cabin. The three of them disappeared into it, and the door shut. I inched forward, and Kanyon yanked the back of my shirt.

"It could be a trap," he whispered.

"It probably is," I agreed. I took another step and once again was stopped.

"I need to call for backup, and you need to go home. I can't allow you to be here."

"*Tsk.* By the time your enforcers get here, the boys could be hurt or dead. Nothing good can happen by letting those boys be alone with that man." I crossed my arms over my chest.

"We don't know what or who is in there. There could be ten guns with silver bullets inside. We would be walking to our deaths." Kanyon frowned.

Taking my thumb and index finger, I flicked him between the eyes. His upper lip curled into a snarl.

Okaaaaay...apparently, that only works on Blayde. *My bad.*

"I don't care if we could be digging our own graves. I'm making the deliberate choice to continue, even with the small chance of success. Those boys need us. Call it luck, call it destiny even, that we were in the right place at the right time. Those boys are a part of your pack. I wouldn't be able to live with myself if something happened to them. Could you?" I stared at him, waiting for an answer.

If he tried to stop me again, I would fight him tooth and nail—literally—till he either let me help or he was unconscious. I'd prefer if he let me assist him, but I'd settle for the latter.

The grim look on his face didn't change, well unless you counted his frown deepening. With a nod, he said, "Let's go."

Chapter Twenty-Three

I have nerves of steel. I have nerves of steel. I have nerves of steel.

I repeated the mantra over and over in my brain. Despite my courage and wanting to save the boys, I was shaking in my shabby black Adidas shoes—not that I would admit that out loud. If Kanyon knew how nervous I was, he would send me away. That was the last thing I needed right now.

Before we started through the trees toward the cabin, Kanyon used his mind link to his pack to tell his enforcers and Blayde what was happening and where to go. I could only imagine how much anger Blayde was expressing, since Kanyon stood there, massaging his temples. Afterward, I asked him what Blayde had said, and Kanyon gave me a flat stare and answered, "how do you think he took the message?"

Not well, that was how.

We stopped at the edge of the perimeter. The cabin was a straight shot from us, but we were still in the coverage of the foliage.

Kanyon grabbed my shoulders and forced me to face him. This was the time for him to give me a pep talk. What awe-inspiring words would have for me?

"Don't die," Kanyon said.

My expression fell. *That was all he had for me?*

"Don't die? That's the best you can do?"

"Don't die...please. I really don't want to deal with Blayde's wrath if you die. Actually, if you die on my watch, it will be sending me to my death. So I'll repeat. Don't die."

I rolled my eyes. "I promise to not die if I can help it."

"Good. On my mark, we'll shoot out from the trees and to the side of the cabin. Don't stray from my shadow. Where I go, you go. Once in, we'll take down the hostiles and extract the boys."

I swallowed the lump in my throat and nodded. He glanced around, searching for any threats. Finding it clear, he let out a long, exaggerated breath. With his index and middle finger, he pointed to me, then to the cabin in some weird traffic controller fashion. I assumed that meant we were ready to move on his lead.

He deciphered my confused countenance and whispered, "We are going to head to the cabin. I'll mention to Blayde that you need tactile training. It's better to communicate with as little noise as possible in these situations."

I brought my hand up to my temple and saluted. He shook his head and looked down at the ground, trying to cover up the small smile that formed.

"All right, Winnie. Let's do this." *Before I lose all nerve completely.* I was just glad I kept that thought to myself.

We sprinted toward the target location. I didn't even have to tap into my Vampire speed to keep pace. Adrenaline flooded my body, and my heart sped up like a freight train as we came to the cabin. We pressed our bodies against the side of the wood, only a small distance from a window.

Kanyon took a quick peek to assess the situation. He wracked a hand over his face.

"This would be so much easier if you had training or shared the pack link."

"Bite me," I retorted.

I was trained... in awesomeness. Pinky and Blacky hung on my belt, and not to mention my wicked-cool abilities. I was a bona fide weapon. Blayde was my mate, and if this was happening to his pack, then this was my fight, too.

"I'll let Blayde know you said that." He smirked.

I snorted. Kanyon was becoming a brother I never had. Annoying and all.

His smile fell, and a serious expression settled in. "There are two guys and a group of kids. It looks like all the missing kids are in there. With only two hostiles, we can handle them. There could be more lurking in there that I couldn't see, so stay vigilant," he said.

I nodded, getting my head back into the right frame of mind. No more jokes. The circumstance was dire, and we needed to remain focused.

I pulled my chakrams from my belt, and their fire ignited. I followed a few steps behind Kanyon. We rounded the corner and reached the front door. He made a motion for me to halt, which I did without a complaint.

Kanyon's leg rose and slammed into the barrier, breaking it in. Apparently, the cabin didn't have good locks. That seemed far too easy.

Claws sprouted from Kanyon's hands, and he moved past the threshold. I rushed in after him with my chakrams raised. My eyes adjusted to the dark room to only be disappointed.

No one was there.

What the crap? We didn't sit that long outside. Where could they have gone?

I spun. Tables were filled with stacks of books and trinkets. There was only this one room with an old wood-burning stove in the corner.

"Where did they go?" Frustration leaked into my voice.

Kanyon didn't answer. His silence said it all. He didn't know.

"I don't sense any lingering magic, so they couldn't have done a transportation spell." He thumbed through the books on the table.

The air smelled musty and full of mildew. Only a shower would elevate the dampness on my skin.

I went from table to table, scanning for anything that stood out. There was one thing, in particular, I was looking for. The journal.

When I had come full circle, I was disheartened. It wasn't here. My hope dashed away.

"Everything that had been reported stolen is here," Kanyon said.

I reached for my necklace and rubbed the charm between my fingers. Most of the trinkets had been jewelry. I wondered if they had been scavenging for the Shifter crystal ornament or my necklace. That would be too big of a coincidence, wouldn't it?

I retreated backward, and the floor thumped. I stepped twice to the right and there wasn't a sound. I returned to the spot, and the floor creaked. I did it a few more times before I noticed Kanyon's questioning stare.

"If you are doing a dance, it's not good." He folded his arms across his chest.

"Ha. Ha. The floor sounds weird."

He moved toward me, and the floor thumped beneath him. He tilted his head and toed to the side, then back again.

He dropped to the floor, knocked on the floorboards, and pressed his ear against it.

And he thought I looked ridiculous.

He sat up and squeezed his fingers between the boards, prying it up. Then another. And another.

My mouth parted. Well, I didn't expect that.

The hole revealed concrete stairs leading under the cabin. A part of me wanted to scream "don't go down there," but I refrained. I was sure Kanyon wouldn't appreciate my joke.

"All right, remain here and wait for backup, and I'll go see where this leads," Kanyon said.

Ha! Like that was going to happen.

"Nope. We're going after those kids. They had to go this way." I gave Kanyon my best "don't mess with me" glare.

He sighed. "Fine. Stay close and don't—"

"Die. Yeah, yeah. I know."

Kanyon started down, and I followed, unhooking my chakrams from my belt. The light from my weapons lit up the creepy staircase. Fourteen stairs down, and we arrived at the bottom that opened into a tunnel.

This seemed like a scene in a scary movie. And the blonde girl always died first. Always.

Gripping Pinky and Blacky tighter, I pushed down my silly notions and trailed behind Kanyon down the eldritch tunnel.

Kanyon's nose pointed up, and he sniffed. "The kids definitely went this direction. It shouldn't be long until we catch up."

He'd spoken in hushed tones, and I was surprised that it didn't echo.

"Are we in an underground tunnel?" I lifted Pinky higher to light the path.

"Yes. There are tunnels underneath pack land. They were built during one of the magical renovations our town has had. We haven't updated them recently. They are supposed to be for if someone attacked us that there would be an easy escape route," Kanyon whispered.

"Are these the same underground tunnels Griff has the conspiracy theory about?" I asked.

"The one about mole people living in the tunnels?" His eyebrow quirked in amusement. "There are no mole people to my understanding, but yes, I think this is what he was referring to."

How much of the nonsense Griff spouted had a grain of truth to it? Could the mole people actually be these guys who were leading the children down here? Were mole people really a type of Shifter? So many questions about Griff's conspiracy theory that it made my mind dizzy.

I shook my head. I was starting to feel crazy. *Mole people, ha! As if.*

I stifled my chuckle and continued after Kanyon. An uneasy feeling twisted in my stomach. We had been walking through the tunnels without a hitch for a while. Stupidly, I hoped we were having good luck. Experience told me to expect the worst—that something was going to happen any second.

And it did.

Kanyon halted, and his arm jolted out. I crashed into the Shifter, and I stumbled backward. I scanned for anything that would cause his abruptness.

Nothing. I didn't find a reason.

I took a step forward to walk around him. We didn't have time to dilly dally. I grabbed onto my shirt, he jerked me back and barred me from going past him.

"Don't you feel that?" he muttered sharply.

My senses opened. There was a strong vibrating energy current right before us.

I nodded. "What is it?"

"No clue. I can feel the energy, but I can't see anything."

I attached my chakrams to my belt and searched to only find bupkes. I touched my top knot and freed a bobby pin. With a flick of my wrist, I hurled it in front of us, aiming as deep down the tunnel as I could manage.

Two feet. That was as far as the accessory had gotten. Something had stopped it. The bobby pin seemed to be blocked by an invisible wall.

I reached out to prod the invisible wall, but Kanyon grabbed my arm and yanked me back.

"Don't touch stuff you don't know if it will hurt you or not," he chastised.

"Yes, Master," I spat.

Kanyon shot me a look of disdain, and he held out his hand. "Give me one of those."

I pulled another from my hair and slapped it down against his palm. The sound echoed through the tunnel, earning me a glare.

"Sorry," I whispered sheepishly.

He rubbed the bobby pin between his fingers, inspecting it, and threw it into the invisible wall. Once again, it didn't go past it.

It fell, and Kanyon squatted to retrieve it. He studied the bobby pin in his hand. He tossed it again, this time nearer to the ground. Again, it hit the invisible wall and dropped.

He studied the bobby once more and stood. He extended it toward me, and I took it. I waited for him to tell me anything. Instead, he stared at me. I brought the small clip closer to my eyes and examined it. It was charred.

Not only had the bobby pin bounced off the invisible wall, but it also got burned. Gratitude filled me. If Kanyon hadn't stopped me, then my hand would've been burnt.

"Well?" he asked.

"The invisible wall charred my bobby pin." I rotated it in my fingers. "And slightly melted some of it." I was doubly grateful I hadn't touched it.

"And?"

And... I refused to inflate his ego and tell him that he was right.

"And it isn't going to hold my hair in place anymore." I grinned.

He gave me a half smile, and he shook his head. "It conducts electricity."

"Okay. So, how do we break the spell blocking us?" I transferred my weight from one foot to the other.

"I never said it was a spell. If it is, I've never seen one like this before. I also don't sense any magic coming from the barrier. It could be good old-fashioned technology."

"Then why can't we see the electrical current?" I asked.

He shrugged. "I'm not up to date with the latest devices. I have enforcers under me that I specialize in that category."

My chest tightened, and my body was jittery. The longer we stayed here, the higher the chance of us losing where those kids had gone. If we couldn't save them soon, I was scared we never would.

"So now what?"

"We need to find an off switch or wait for my enforcers to get here," he said casually, with no hint of urgency in his voice.

I brushed my hands over the concrete walls, trying to search for an object that could turn off the deadly current. I stood on my tiptoes, then hunching down at the bottom, I found nothing. I did the same to the other wall, and the result was the same.

Time was running out. My fear for the kids grew every minute. As my anxiety increased, my anger grew as well. I wouldn't let anything happen to those kids.

I took Blacky from my belt. I wrapped my hand around it, feeling the humming against the palm. Its fire ignited but stayed close to the blade.

"No!" Kanyon hissed.

I jammed Blacky into the invisible wall, sending sparks flying, and Blacky's fire expanded. I put pressure on Blacky and twisted it from side to side. If there was no off button, then I would create my own way through.

I funneled my emotions through Blacky, trusting the connection between us. The flames exploded and sent a wave of energy back. My feet slid against the concrete.

I gritted my teeth. I kept a grip on Blacky and pulled Pinky from my belt. I lifted Pinky and stabbed. Repeatedly.

I didn't aim for a spot in particular. I just kept putting all my anger and all my strength into destroying the blockade. I brought Blacky and Pinky behind my head and slammed them into the invisible wall. And all it took was that final hit.

Electricity exploded. The flames from my chakrams expanded, forming a protective barrier around me. The electricity bounced off the concrete walls, and pieces fell to the ground. I turned and looked at Kanyon, who was sprinting toward me.

My chakrams' flames died, and Kanyon barreled into me. He shoved me to the floor, covering my body with his. His arms lay over my head, and the rubble roared like thunder. Concrete descended on us in a cloud of smoke.

Chapter Twenty-Four

Rubble from the tunnels crushed us. Not only did I have concrete on top of me but also Kanyon's weight. And he was no stick figure.

After the destruction had settled, I self-evaluated by wiggling my fingers and toes. I squirmed under Kanyon and winced. Pain radiated from my left shoulder, and other than some minor cuts, nothing seemed broken. Luckily. Thank the Angels, I had enhanced healing.

"Winnie? You dead?" I tried to joke, even though I feared my carelessness might have gotten him killed.

He groaned, and instant relief washed over me.

"You can't get rid of me that easily," he mumbled.

"Can you stand, or are we stuck?"

"Maybe. I'll need to do a partial shift to get the concrete off."

I didn't say anything. I didn't know what to say. So, I lay there, unmoving.

I couldn't see him, but his fur brushed against my skin. So light and fluffy, a mane of the Angels, I swear. I had major hair envy. To my knowledge, Shifters didn't shampoo and condition their animal coats, but one day I'd find out their secret.

Kanyon huffed and growled. Slowly, but surely, the pressure on me lightened. His weight dissipated, and I quickly scrambled to move away. All the while, ignoring the sharp ache from my shoulder. With a final huff, the concrete smashed to the ground.

Standing, I looked at the Lycan in front of me. Blayde's was bigger. Scarier. But that didn't mean that if I hadn't known Kanyon was a giant teddy bear, I wouldn't be scared of him.

Instead of a half-dog half-man form that Blayde had, Kanyon was half-man half-bear. He had a round face in lieu of an elongated one. He had more fur than his older brother. Similar to Blayde, he had claws for his fingers.

Kanyon did a twirling motion, and I turned my back toward him. Once the crackling of bones stopped, I spun. Tattered clothes hung on Kanyon's body. I didn't know if it was from the wreckage or the shifting. Probably both.

Kanyon had taken the brunt of the falling debris. Blood and purple bruises colored his skin and, thankfully, already showed signs of healing. With what little skin wasn't engulfed in injuries, soot covered the rest. A twinge of guilt hit me. He'd got harmed protecting me. Everyone around me seemed to get hurt because of me.

"Don't give me that look," he scowled.

"What look?"

"The look of culpability. No matter what you think, you are important, not only to Hunters but, to every magical species. A Huntress must defeat the Dark Master, or his evil will continue to spread. Saving you gives us a fighting chance."

"I don't want anyone to get injured, or worse, because of me," I said in a small voice. It was hard to let people protect me when it meant they could die.

He paused for a moment. "Saving you benefits me personally. If I had let you get wounded, I would have to deal with the wrath of a seriously pissed-off wolf. I love my brother, but I have no intention of ever being the subject of his warpath when it concerns you." A teasing smile lit his face. His tone was joking, but we both understood what he'd said was true. Blayde was extremely protective of me—good thing I liked it, well, most of the time.

The pile of rubble behind him caught my eye. I groaned.

Greeeeaaaat. Just great.

It hadn't been a few pieces that broke and fell. It had caved in. The way we'd come was now blocked by a mountain of concrete from floor to ceiling.

I gestured to the debris and said, "You better use your mind link to tell Blayde and your enforcers about this. Either they will need to find a different route through or move the fragments of concrete."

Kanyon nodded. His eyes got a distant glossy look, and his brows knitted in concentration. Impatiently, I alternated my weight from leg to leg. A few minutes passed without Kanyon uttering a word. An uneasy knot formed in my stomach.

He let out an exaggerated exhale. "We must be out of range."

I snorted. He made it sound like their mind link was walkie-talkies or something.

Wait...He had been trying the entire time to talk to them?

"Shouldn't they have arrived at the cabin already?" I asked. Nerves tangled together.

"You would think. My guess is that Blayde got Agrona and Chantel, then met with the enforcers. It must have taken a lot of control to not leave the others and storm after you. I'm sure Agrona had to reason with him." He shrugged.

Even though his words sounded serene, his body was stiff and rigid. He was anything but calm. And that sent me into a panic.

What if Blayde, Chantel, Agrona, and the enforcers were captured? What if they were hurt? What if they were dealing with a colossal event up there?

I took a deep breath and closed my eyes. I focused on the mate bond. With my heart hammering, I thought only of him. Of the fondness, of the happiness, of the love we shared. Letting all other feelings go, I felt him. Or rather, his soul. He was alive and not injured. He was... angsty. I tried to send soothing, reassuring thoughts through our connection, but I had no idea if he received them. I didn't know much about the magic in our bond. Who knew what we were capable of? Maybe, just maybe, I could reach him like I had when he went on a run with other Shifters, when I had appeared to him.

But I didn't get to try.

Kanyon shook me, pulling me out of my concentration and thoughts of Blayde. His face was scrunched with concern.

"What just happened? Where did you go?" His hands were steady on my shoulders, forcing me to give him all of my attention.

"Thanks to you, I went nowhere. I was using my bond

to make sure Blayde was okay," I said. I gave him the Cliffs Notes on how I was able to see Blayde before and I was going to attempt it.

"Sorry." His voice was genuine, and even though it was only one word, I knew he was apologetic. "But at least we know he is safe."

"And real antsy." I smiled, and Kanyon's expression mirrored mine.

"I can only imagine the torment he is experiencing because he can't get to you fast enough." He laughed before adding, "It is nice to watch my brother's world be turned upside down because of you. You are good for him."

I rolled my eyes and nudged my hip into his. Yes, Kanyon was like the brother I never had...and sometimes the brother I never wanted.

We continued down the tunnels. Kanyon led the way, still tracking the kids by smell. Sporadically, we had a stop for him to dial in on their most recent scent. It appeared that the kids had been down here before, several times, in fact. And according to Kanyon, the creepy guys basically lived down here. Their spoor was everywhere.

Uneasiness settled in, and my stomach twisted. We had been walking for a while without anything stopping us. No guards. No traps. No invisible walls. No magic. Nothing. It seemed almost too easy. Maybe they figured nobody could get through their invisible wall. Good thing I wasn't like most people. Unfortunately, the comforting thought didn't ease my disquietude.

A few minutes later, Kanyon stopped and pressed up against the wall. I stared, holding back a laugh. I had no idea what he was doing, but whatever it was, it was idiotic. No one was around. Even if someone glanced down the hall, they would spot us regardless of this folly. Utterly stupid. And I opened my mouth to tell him so.

"Shhh." He flattened his hand over my lips.

I didn't like being treated this way, so I taught him a lesson. I stuck my tongue out and licked his palm, and I instantly regretted it. A lick full of concrete dust. *Yuck.*

Kanyon pulled away, and he scowled in disgust. "What was that for?" he hissed.

"Don't do that to me. Ever. Again." After a beat, I added, "Why are you against the wall? You're acting like an imbecile."

Kanyon scoffed. "First, focus on your hearing. Second, if someone comes barreling down the tunnel, I won't be such an easy target, unlike you."

I narrowed my eyes and shot him a glare. It took it a second to sink in before I realized his words were the truth. I was standing in the middle of the tunnel and would be a much easier target than him. I pressed myself against the wall, and Kanyon gave me a I-told-you-so look.

I rolled my eyes before I closed them and focused on my hearing. At first, I didn't hear anything besides Kanyon's breathing and the beat of his heart. Envisioning myself traveling down the tunnel, I picked up faint voices. Male voices. Saying what, I had no idea. It was too distant for me to understand. Nevertheless, I got Kanyon's point. We were getting close to them, and we needed to be careful.

I opened my eyes and rested the back of my head on the tunnel wall. Instinctively, my hand reached up and fiddled with my charm. My nervousness was overwhelming me, and my necklace had always brought me solace. It reminded me of my dad. And the peace and comfort he had given me. After a few seconds of me moving the crystal charm back and forth, my nerves calmed, and I knew I was doing the right thing.

I opened my mouth to urge Kanyon forward, but I noticed something on the adjacent wall. It was tucked in the crevice of where the ceiling met the wall. It moved down the tunnel from where we'd come and where we were going.

I shoved off of my spot and peered up. It was there as well, only this time I could see it better. It appeared to be rubber tubing. But why was it there?

"What's that?" I pointed to the object in question.

Kanyon turned, and his head tilted from side to side, him trying to figure it out. He ran back in the direction we had come, and I remained there, not knowing what I should do. Once I decided, I trailed after him.

He hadn't gone far by the time I caught back up to him, which I was glad for. He stopped underneath a manhole. The tubing seemed to be going up through it. There were metal bars spaced out on the concrete wall, forming a ladder up and out.

"Wait here." He climbed up the ladder and pushed the manhole covering up and to the side. While I stood there, waiting for something to happen, like a dolt.

A roar erupted from the surface, and a small gust of wind followed it. *Uh-oh.* Kanyon was in trouble.

Holding on to the metal bars, I went up a few before the bottom of Kanyon's shoes were coming down. I backed up and gave him space. He jumped off the ladder and smashed into the ground, not caring how loud.

What I noticed first were his eyes. They were pools of black, no sign of warmth anywhere. Fur was present on his arms, and he bristled. With his head canted down and his full attention on me, he moved with purpose.

Oh my gosh. What was wrong with him?

His muscles flexed, and his veins bulged. Whatever had happened to him wasn't good, I knew that for sure.

"Winnie...What's happening, big man?" I said uneasily.

His lip curled, and he snarled. The sound sent a shiver down my spine. Warning bells chimed in my brain. *Danger! Danger! Danger!*

Taking a few steps back, I lifted my hands in the air, showing him that I meant no harm. That I wasn't armed.

But it didn't matter.

He rushed toward me and pinned me against the wall. His forearm rammed into my jugular, holding me in place. Luckily, I was still able to breathe. A small tug on my belt spurred alarm, but I couldn't move to peek even if I wanted to.

In a blink, Blacky was pushed up against my throat. My breathing became rapid, and panic tightened in my chest. The only good thing I had going right now was that Kanyon couldn't use my chakram fire on me. Only I could do that.

Kanyon snarled and pressed Blacky closer, slicing a shallow cut. Tiny droplets of crimson trickled down, dancing along my skin.

No matter how much I wiggled, I couldn't break free of him. If I did manage, it would come at a great cost to either him or me. Most likely me. I couldn't bear the thought of the guilt that would weigh on Kanyon. I also couldn't fathom the anguish it would cause Blayde. It was a lose-lose situation.

I closed my eyes, preparing for the inevitable, but instead, Kanyon's touch brushed my neck. My eyes snapped open, and I watched Kanyon rub my blood between his fingers. Bringing it to his nose, he smelled it, cocked his head, and sniffed again. A drop of blood got on his face, and he used the back of his hand to wipe it. Haplessly, it smeared. His nose twitched, and he sneezed.

Moisture sprayed across my face, inciting a flinch. *Gross.* Unfortunately for me, my movement swiped against Blacky's blade, inflicting a moment of sharp pain. It reaffirmed that I needed to hold still, or I might cause my own death.

Kanyon shook his head a few times, as if trying to emancipate his mind. He focused on me, and slowly, the black cleared. I had never been so relieved to see his chocolatey brown irises.

His hand trembled, and he took a few quick steps back. Kanyon dropped Blacky, and the clang echoed in the tunnel. He brought his hands in front of him and looked at his palms. Blinking rapidly, he didn't utter a word.

I inched forward, only to have him flinch and retreat further.

"No. Don't. I don't know what came over me." There was so much guilt and sorrow dripping in his words.

"What happened up there?"

"There was something coming out of the tubes. I smelt it. It was as if all my strength had disappeared. I was so angry. Next thing I know, I have your chakram against your throat and your blood on my fingertips." His voice quivered. He didn't like being helpless.

"Do you know what the smell was?" I asked. His non-answer said it all. "We will figure it out. Are you okay?"

"Physically, I feel fine. Mentally... I'm not sure how I could hurt you. You're a sister to me. I'm so sorry." His head drooped.

Stepping toward him, I wrapped my arms around his waist and hugged him. I pressed my head against him and listened to his heartbeat slow. Eventually, he embraced me and pulled me closer.

After a moment, I withdrew. "You're the brother I never had. You wouldn't ever willingly harm me. I'm starting to think everything that has transpired lately is all connected. First, we find the kids. Second, we figure out what exactly is in those tubes. But no matter what happens, we are in this together."

Chapter Twenty-Five

A brother. My mate bond affected my life in ways I never could've predicted. I had gained a sibling. But now that I thought of it, Kanyon wasn't the only one I had obtained. Agrona and Chantel were my sisters—from other misters—and even Ricardo pestered me with brotherly affection. Kanyon was the first with an official title who would be my brother. Well, I guessed the technical term would be brother-in-law. When Blayde and I moved forward in our relationship, I would officially gain a real sibling.

The only thing that crushed this tender moment was the guilt and regret shining out of Kanyon's gaze. He hadn't been himself. His black irises had told me that. But now he was back to normal. Unfortunately, the psychological damage from hurting me wouldn't heal as quickly.

Before we set off down the concrete tunnel, we came to the conclusion that Kanyon had experienced an anger flare. And now more than ever, I was convinced that the thefts, kidnappings, and anger flares were all closely connected. I just hadn't figured out why.

With my chakrams hanging from my belt, I followed Kanyon down the tunnel. We didn't speak, and we stayed close to the wall. Eventually, the voices became louder, and we were led to a staircase that went out of a manhole. This time, instead of metal bars for a ladder, it was concrete stairs.

At the base of the stairs, Kanyon faced me, and his eyes gave me the once-over.

"Are you ready for this?" he asked.

I nodded.

"Are you sure? Because once we go through, there is no turning back."

He was trying to prepare me for the worst. To give me an out. To give me an opportunity to wait for backup. To give me the chance to change my mind. But it was possible that the kids didn't have that flexibility.

"Let's do this." I mustered up as much bravado as I could.

"All right. Stay frosty."

He cautiously started up the stairs, and I took up the rear. In any other circumstance, I would've teased him for saying "stay frosty." I had only ever heard that term used in bad cop movies. Now wasn't the right occasion for that.

Kanyon pushed the manhole lid to the side slowly, working to not produce a sound. He climbed out and offered me a hand at the top.

Once out, Kanyon dashed to find coverage, and I copied his movements. We hid behind a destroyed car. It was burned to the point that I couldn't discern the make or model.

In front of us was a building—what appeared to be an abandoned warehouse. Glass windows were long gone, and in their place was plywood. Weeds grew without a care in the cracks of the concrete and around the structure.

I scanned and noticed several abandoned vehicles that were also burnt. In the stretch between us and the ware-house, there were dummies that were holding large pieces of metal. Holding it like it was a shield. They, too, were charred to a crisp.

I had no idea what had occurred here, but it was obvious that they liked playing with fire.

"Look." Kanyon pointed to different security cameras.

Okay, so whoever was the ringleader didn't care about the physical building or the surroundings, but cared enough to install cameras. If that didn't scream illegal activity happening here, I didn't know what did.

"Stay here, and I'll go check it out," Kanyon whispered.

"As if," I snapped. "We are in this together."

With reluctance, Kanyon nodded. Moving toward the cameras, we hid behind different cars, inching our way to the warehouse. With each step, my pulse beat faster, threatening to climb up my throat.

By the time we arrived at the outside wall, the rhythmic throbbing of my arteries thumped so rapidly that I was sure the sound would give our position away.

We progressed forward with our backs against the wall. We didn't want to take the chance to have the cameras spot us and yet the probability was high. We reached a window that had a small corner bare of any boards. Kanyon squared his shoulders, mentally braced himself, and peeked.

"Ashley," Kanyon said her name as a curse. He stepped aside and gestured to let me take a glimpse.

The kids were sitting in some type of pentagram. Whines and sobs came from them. I couldn't imagine how scared they were. A man stood next to the pentagram with a wand in his hand, flipping through pages of a book—most likely a spell book. Others were standing around in a circle, forming a perimeter. I counted ten of them and noticed each of them carried a rifle. Wanna bet that they had silver bullets in them?

Then I saw her. Ashley. All in her blonde posh glory. Her foot impatiently tapped the floor, and she threw her arms up in the air. My attention drifted to the person she was arguing with, and my stomach dropped.

"Jordan," I hissed.

Kanyon groaned. Blayde must have filled him in about Jordan. Or was it known everywhere that Jordan was helping the Dark Master? Every time I talked or thought about Jordan, it was like taking a shredder to my heart. I still couldn't stomach my childhood best friend's betrayal.

"What's the plan, Winnie?" *Please, oh please, tell me that you have a plan.*

"We wait for backup. We are outnumbered, and our weapons are the knife in my boot and your chakrams. This is a battle we can't win by ourselves." He took another look inside.

Later, when I thought back on this moment, I'd figure out that this was where I went wrong. Instead of searching for potential threats, I peered over Kanyon's shoulder.

Rookie mistake.

Metal tapped me on my spine, and I stiffened. *Crap.*

"Hands up," a man said.

Kanyon let out an irritated sigh and turned, putting his palms in the air. I did the same.

Three men stood before us in GI Joe attire. All three aimed their guns at us. If they had regular bullets and didn't shoot for the heart or head, Kanyon would survive. But if they were silver, he was a goner. Me? I had no idea what my body would do if I was shot, and I preferred not to find out.

"Well, if it isn't the little Huntress. Jordan will love this," the man said.

The two behind him snickered.

"Follow us."

One of the men led the way while the other two brought up the rear. This was everything Kanyon was trying to avoid. I'd got him messed up in all of this. I was the one accountable.

They pushed open a door and shoved me in, knocking me to the floor. A man grabbed me by the arm and dragged me to Jordan's feet. He didn't even spare a second for me to get up. They wanted me on the floor, beneath Jordan. They wanted to show me my place.

Pushing myself up, I propped myself on my knees. Jordan squatted in front of me and forced eye contact. A grin spread across his face as if he was actually delighted I was here. As if this was his lucky break. Nerves swarmed within me. Even though this situation brought him joy, his menacing leer was a steak knife to the chest.

"Cedar, what a surprise. I had planned to capture you in a few days, but no matter. This works for me." Jordan lifted the back of his hand to my cheek and brushed it down my skin.

I wanted to finch, to spit in his face, to yell at him. But I didn't. I schooled my features and acted like his words and his touch meant nothing to me. That *he* meant nothing to me.

Jordan leaned in closer and inhaled. He closed his eyes for a brief moment before they snapped open. Anger, untamed fury, colored his blue eyes.

"You've claimed that *dog*," he said through clenched teeth. Turning his head, he spat over his shoulder.

"What?" Ashley wailed. She bent over and clutched the collar of my shirt. "You did *what* with my fiancé?"

She was inches from me. So close, in fact, that I could smell her breath. Minty. Of course, she would have fresh breath. She was physically flawless from head to toe.

"Don't act like you didn't hear him. He is my mate. *Mine*. He will never be yours." I glared, willfully wishing that she would go up in a combustion of flames.

She vibrated with fury. Her free hand shifted to claws, and she lifted it in the air. She brought it back and prepared to smite. But Jordan stopped her. He clutched her arm and flung her backward. She skidded across the floor like a skipping rock.

"You promised!" Ashley yelled as she got up. "You said he would be mine!"

Jordan's looming gaze never left me. "And he will."

"He won't be mine if she is still alive. She needs to die," Ashley snarled.

Kanyon responded with a protective growl. I reverted to pretending that neither of them meant anything to me, but on the inside, I was a ball of rage, ready to burst.

"You don't get to make that decision. She is mine. She is going to help the Dark Master." He smiled like the Cheshire cat, and a shiver ran down my spine.

But when I started to lose hope, a sensation brushed against my mind and my heart. Like a feather sweeping across my skin. I didn't know how I knew, but I knew.

Blayde was close.

He was coming for me. I only had to wait a bit longer.

"Boss, we have company," one of the men announced.

Jordan punched the floor, but the pain didn't register on

his face. "Your dog just won't leave you alone. Slap silver cuffs on him, and she'll come with me." Jordan straightened and took a few steps toward the door.

It was now or never.

I grabbed my chakrams off my belt, and flames curled around my fists. I stood and thrust Blacky into the man closest to me. It sliced his stomach, and he fell to the floor. Kanyon joined me and head-butted the man next to him.

Ashley jumped on me and knocked me to the floor. She placed her knees on my shoulders, stopping me from being able to use my arms. Her pointy claws wrenched back, poised to maim. She slashed my chest, and I cried out in agony.

She laughed. "You are going to perish, slowly and painfully."

Not going to happen.

Once more, she brought back her claws to strike me. This time, I tapped into my Shifter strength and raised my right arm which held Blacky. I swiped at her and slashed her wrist. She screamed, and I used the opportunity to push her completely off.

I scrambled to stand, not wanting to be caught on my back again. Ashley did the same. My grip on my weapons tightened, and their blue fire grew. It crawled its way up my hands and encompassed my forearms.

This was new.

I wondered if I could engulf my entire body in their fire. But that would be left for another day.

Limited space separated me from Ashley. Her free hand was pressed against the laceration on her wrist. Determination was written all over her face. She wouldn't allow a gushing cut to slow her down. Points for tenacity. Unfortunately for her, I would come out the victor.

We darted toward each other, both of us with the unbridled need to win. I dropped to my knees and slid against the floor. Concrete wasn't easy to slide on, but I needed a move she wouldn't see coming. I extended Pinky in my left hand and slashed Ashley's shins. Immediately, she crumbled.

A roar shook the building, and I glanced over my shoulder and noticed that the Sorcerer had placed Kanyon in some type of bubble barrier. The rest of the men formed a circle around it, ready to attack if he somehow escaped. From the look of it, it wouldn't be anytime soon. Helplessly, I watched him writhe in torment.

My attention snapped to Ashley. This had to end, so I could help Kanyon. I moved nearer to her, and she glared at me like I was the scum of the earth.

"What? Are you going to kill me now?" she mocked.

But she couldn't hide the fear in her eyes. She really did think I was going to end her life. Shoot, I even thought I'd kill her up until this moment.

No, I wasn't going to terminate her. If I did and Kanyon didn't make it out alive, then the Shifters might not believe me when I told them she was working with Jordan. No, I would let Blayde and the other Shifters deal with her.

I mentally checked to see if I could sense Blayde. Yes, he was closer. Kanyon and I only had to survive a little longer.

I stepped to the side of Ashley, so we were side by side. Her kneeling, and me standing. I lifted the arm closest to her. To her, it would appear that I was performing the crushing blow.

Expecting to see tears in her eyes led me to be mistaken. There was only hate and dread shining back at me.

Instead of executing the final assault, I used my elbow

to hit her head, knocking her unconscious. Once she flopped to the floor, I turned and rushed toward Kanyon.

"No!" Kanyon shrieked out in pain.

"Stop her," the Sorcerer yelled.

Three men sprinted in my direction, and me at them.

I dropped once again to my knees. My skin ripped against the concrete as I performed the same move I had on Ashley. It was starting to become one of my favorites. Too bad it felt like I had just gotten a million paper cuts.

With both arms extending out, I slashed two of the men's shins, and they fell. I was able to stand and dodge the third man. I was past him before he could even think of a countermove. I guessed not all of Jordan's men were smart.

I ran at the bubble barrier and extended both chakrams over my head. I smashed Blacky and Pinky into it—expecting the same thing to happen as the invisible wall. Instead, I bounced off it and flew in the air, and landed on my butt. *Ouch. Major ouch.*

I scrambled to rise, only to find myself surrounded. At least none of the men were around the barrier now.

"Tie her up," Jordan yelled.

Great. I had to not only get through these guys and free Kanyon, but I had to deal with Jordan. The odds were stacked against me. I just needed to hold on until Blayde got here.

"Run, Cedar, run!" Kanyon called out.

My eyes darted to him and found him thrashing on the floor. I should've listened to him. We should've waited for backup. Not only were the kids still crying, trapped in the pentagram, but Kanyon was being tortured. I had failed.

If I was going to go down, I was going to go down trying.

"Come and get it, boys," I taunted.

Some of the men snickered. They all pounced on me at once. Descending on me like a pack of hungry wolves. They overpowered me and forced me to the floor. Faster than I could react, my wrists and ankles were bound together by zip ties.

I lay unmoving, hogtied. Jordan knelt beside me and took my chakrams that had been knocked to the side. With his other hand, he reached into my pocket and slid out my wand.

"Don't worry, I'll return your weapons. They'll come in handy for what comes next. Bring her," he said.

A man lifted me by my armpits, and another picked up my legs. I kicked and bashed my head backward, and simultaneously the men dropped me.

I groaned. That wasn't my smartest idea. I rolled to my stomach and inch wormed my way toward Kanyon.

Jordan laughed. "Knock her out and put her in the trunk."

The last thing I saw was Kanyon lying flat with his gaze locked on me full of fear. Then everything went black.

Chapter Twenty-Six

Pain. Despair. Anguish. Confusion. Fury. Kanyon. *Oh gosh, Kanyon.*

Jordan had me knocked out, and Kanyon was left in the bubble barrier, being tortured. Guilt. All-encompassing guilt. This was all my fault. Jordan would pay for what he had done to Kanyon, to me, to the Shifters.

Afraid to open my eyes, I focused on Blayde. Faint hints of panic and rage swarmed me through our bond. He was alive and uninjured, but I couldn't sense where he was. I was starting to understand that meant he wasn't close to my location. My only hope was that he had gotten to his brother.

I opened my eyes to darkness. It took them a moment to adjust. I realized where I was. My throat and chest constricted. Alarm thumped with every beat of my heart.

I was in a trunk.

How long had I been in here? Minutes? Hours? I had no idea.

The car wasn't moving, and I couldn't smell any exhaust fumes. We were parked.

No longer wanting to be a damsel in distress, I brought my feet to the trunk lid and stomped. The sound wasn't quiet, and I was positive someone heard me. I had to be fast.

By my fifth kick, I gave it all I had. Instead of seeing the trunk fly free, all I did was make a massive dent. Escaping would be harder than I thought. I summoned some Shifter strength and kicked like my life depended on it—because it did.

The trunk popped open, and light flooded my vision. Was it already morning?

Nope.

A flashlight was pointed at me. "I'm so glad you decided to wake up Cedar," Jordan said.

No fleeing now.

Jordan pulled me out of the temporary confines and set me down on the ground. Not only had they put ties on my wrists and ankles, but also silver cuffs. He was being overly cautious. *Dang.*

We were in the middle of the forest. There was a cave a short walk from us. The car sat in the center of a small clearing with no clear roads or pathways out of here.

He stood in front of me. "You're going to help me."

"No."

"No? I'm not sure you would be happy with the consequences." Jordan's penetrating glare dared me to try him.

My knee-jerk reaction was to rebuff. I didn't want to cooperate in any way. Helping him helped the Dark Master, and that was something I refused to do.

But they had Kanyon. Plus, who knew what else he had up his sleeve? Thinking of the worst, he could hurt everyone in Blayde's pack... including Blayde and my girl squad.

"Ah. The fight has left your eyes. You are so predictable, Cedar. If only you were this easy to persuade all the time.

Things don't have to be this way. You can be my partner. My mate. I want nothing else but you ruling by my side." He took out a knife from his pocket and twirled it between his fingers.

"What do you want me for? To help you with what? Killing the pack? Taking over the world? Your manners?"

Not only was I stalling to see if there was any way out of this without hurting anyone, but I also wanted to know *why*. Why the anger flares? Why the thefts? Why the kidnappings? And how all of this traced back to the Dark Master. The more he spilled, the more I had a fighting chance.

Jordan laughed a full belly laugh. It was loud and without caution, cluing me in that no one was around to hear it. Or to come to my aid.

"It was all a part of the plan. The thefts started because I needed information about the crystal. It was a nice perk that I got the journal. I was hoping you'd leave the Hunter crystal lying around. But you never did." He bent down and held my charm in his hands. "It's mine now." His lips twitched, and he yanked my necklace off me.

No!

My heart dropped into the pit of my stomach. He had my necklace. I promised my father I'd never take it off, and now it was gone.

"The Dark Master will be pleased with what I have accomplished. I have the Hunter crystal, and you'll fetch the Shifter crystal. We have the journal and that will lead us to the dagger's location. The cherry on top of all of this is that I found a technique to disable the Shifters," he gloated.

The only silver lining was my suspicions were right. My necklace was important. The charm was the ornament the Angel had given the first Hunter. But why were the crystals significant? A particular detail pinged in my brain, claiming precedence.

"Disable the Shifters?" I repeated, confused.

"You still haven't figured it out, so disappointing. Let me spell it out for you. We had tubes with a special gas that ran in the tunnels. We controlled when the gas was released in areas of their town. The gas is composed of part wolfsbane and part potion. The wolfsbane weakened the Shifters so they wouldn't be able to fight against the effects of the potion, giving themselves to it. The concoction tapped into their biological urges, you may say. It forced them to be dominant and see everyone else as prey."

"They went savage."

"Exactly. If you wouldn't have stuck your nose in where it didn't belong, over the next few days we were going to try a new solution to make the effects permanent." His eyes danced with mischief.

Well, thank the Angels for that. At least one good thing had come from this.

"And why is the dagger so important that you had to ransack my room? It was stalkerish of you, Jordan." I tried to make my voice sound light. As if we were still friends.

"You don't know anything, do you?" He laughed.

I waited for him to tell me more.

"Fine, I'll give you this freebie, since I have the journal, and you won't be able to find it without it. With all five crystals back on the hilt of the dagger, it has the power to kill Angels and Demons."

It has the power to kill Angels and Demons.

Was that the Dark Master's endgame? To kill the Angels and Demons? I knew Jordan wouldn't divulge the Dark Master's plan. But I would store this information for later. I was just glad I'd got more pieces to the puzzle. It also sparked more urgency to discover the crystals before the Dark Master did.

My gaze darted to my necklace dangling from Jordan's fingers. I needed to regain possession of it along with the Shifter ornament. But how? That was the double jeopardy question.

"Now you are going to go retrieve the crystal for me." Jordan picked me up by the collar of my shirt and shoved me toward the mouth of the cave.

Every time I saw Jordan, the less he was like the boy I knew. He'd grown more hard, more sinister. Happiness no longer danced in his eyes. It was long gone. If he continued down this path, I didn't think there would be a way back.

He gave me a final shove, sending me into the dirt. My cheek landed against a jagged edge of a rock, producing a small cut. Luckily, it would only take a few minutes for it to heal.

Jordan unlocked the cuffs encircling my wrists and ankles. He stood and threw my chakrams on the ground in front of me.

I stumbled to pick them up even though ties remained in place. Gripping Blacky in my hand, I spun on my knees toward Jordan, hoping to strike.

But he was too fast.

He held a knife up against my throat and chuckled. "You are getting better, but you're still no match for me, Cedar. Get yourself out of the ties and head into the cave. Don't try any funny business—I won't hesitate to slaughter you."

I used Blacky to get the ties off. My joints ached, and a red ring had formed around them. I wanted to rub where the ties had been, but I didn't. I refused to show Jordan any sign of weakness.

Standing with my chakrams in each hand, I headed for the cave. My mouth was dry, and my throat tight. It felt like I was walking to my execution. I reached the entrance, and before I entered, Jordan yelled.

"Oh, by the way, there are some traps in there. If you can't figure it out, it will cost you your life. Hurry up now. Times a wastin'."

Greeeaat. Traps that will kill me. Super.

* * *

I stepped into the dark cave, and it took a second before my eyes adjusted. *Thank you, supernatural eyesight.*

The cave was cold, at least ten degrees colder than outside. It felt nice escaping from the summer heat.

As I continued moving forward, a faint sulfur smell hit me. The more I went into the cave, the stronger it became. Currently, it was tolerable. I just hoped I wouldn't run into the source of the stink.

When I'd been growing up, my father had taken me on camping trips. He'd taught me about the stars and how to live off the land if I needed to. On one particular trip, he took me to a hot spring that happened to be inside a cavern. The spot had warm streams, and I could still remember the calming sound of water trickling as I fell asleep. This cave, however, didn't have any water or streams. It was nothing like what I had visited in my childhood.

I wasn't sure how long I had been wandering before I came up to a giant door-gate-thingy. I had no clue what to call it. It sealed the pathway from every angle. It was made up of wood planks with metal hinges and bolts, holding them together. It looked like it would be a door, except there was no knob. So, it had to be a gate. On the cave wall, there were five levers. They were all at varying heights.

Then I saw it. My stomach threatened to empty. Crushed skeletons lay on the ground near the gate. Jordan wasn't lying when he'd said the traps were deadly.

"What have I gotten myself into?" I swallowed the fear that surged to the surface, and I turned away from the gate.

I sauntered over to the levers and studied the chains that connected each to the ceiling. The metal links were also attached to sandbags and to the gate in a pulley system.

I placed my hand on one of the levers. There weren't any signs or clues or writing on the wall to tell me what to do.

Here goes nothing.

I yanked the first lever down, and the gate rose in the air a few inches before slamming shut.

Huh. It must be magically spelled to rise into the cave like that. Whoever created this was smart and magical.

The next lever was hovering between up and down. I pulled it. The gate to rise and shut like an alligator chomping its mouth.

I moved the others, and none permitted the gate to ascend high enough for me to pass under.

"Now what?" I stared at the levers. How was I ever going to get through?

Messing around, I operated two levers at a time. Then three. Then four. Then finally all five.

After much trial and error, I figured out a combination that allowed the gate to stay open long enough so that I could sneak through.

I dragged the levers into position. Up, up, down, middle, down. The gate rose to the ceiling. And I counted as I dashed toward it.

One...

Five...

Ten...

I was almost there. Only a small space separated me from the other side.

Fifteen...

The gate slammed shut, and my forehead bashed into the wood. I fell on my butt and groaned. I rubbed my temples, and liquid touched my fingers. I retracted my hand. My fingertips were smeared with blood.

I sat on the ground in front of the obstacle and glared. I was beyond frustrated and exhausted. I didn't know how long I'd been in here or how long it has been since I'd been able to sleep. Or even took a calming hot shower. Man, I missed those.

"Suck it up, buttercup. After this, I'm eating a brownie as huge as my foot," I muttered to myself.

I put on my metaphorical big girl panties, I stood and headed for the perplexing handles and reset them.

I gripped the first lever with my right hand and let my head relax on the cave wall. My eyes begged for sleep. For a moment of rest. It would be so easy to curl up on the floor and take a nap. But I couldn't. Not here. Not now. I was by myself. I couldn't trust sleeping in a cavern full of traps and mysteries.

No. I would have to push past the emotional fatigue, the exhaustion, the brain burnout.

Out of nowhere, an idea struck me. I knew how to make it pass. I'd been so dumb.

With a deep breath, I shoved all thoughts of sleep away and focused on the task before me. I jerked the levers into position, and the gate rose. I counted again. I only had fifteen seconds.

With an exhale, I tapped into my Vampire speed.

One...

Five...

Nine...

A few more steps and I would be under the door.

Twelve...

I passed through and slid to a stop.

Fifteen...

Once again, the gate slammed closed. I itched to perform a victory dance, but I was caught off guard as the cave lit up with torches on the wall.

"Oh, come on!" I shouted, throwing my hands in the air.

Ugh. The second obstacle already stood in my way.

Chapter Twenty-Seven

One down and one already knocking at my door. Figuring out the levers had been mentally taxing. I had hoped for a small break or to at least walk slowly through the cave. But no. Fate wasn't kind.

In front of me were twenty feet of stones with different symbols on them. On the ground and on the wall. There weren't any on the ceiling that I could see.

On the wall to my right, there were symbols, letters, and numbers carved into the cave. There wasn't any pattern to the graphics. It looked like a mixture of languages. Which didn't make sense to me. I stared at it as if it would reveal its secrets.

To my surprise, the graphics shook and blurred. I stood there transfixed, afraid to take my eyes off of it. Then there it was. A clear message.

Beware of where you step. Follow the eye. Or one false step and you will meet your doom.

Except the eye remained a symbol. I looked down at the stones. Only some had the same hieroglyph.

"Don't go down the creepy tunnel, Cedar," I said in a singsong voice. If this was a movie, I would be yelling that at the T.V.

I took a chance and gently placed the ball of my foot on a stone with an eye on it. Nothing happened. *Thank the Angels.*

I found the next one. Only a hop away. I repeated this a few times before the eye stones became closer together. I was nervous about the change in pattern.

Then I saw it.

A pit in the cave floor. I followed the stones until I was close enough to peer into it.

I groaned. Things were never easy, were they?

A mist of blue and purple swirled in the hole. It flowed similarly to dry ice or how a potion boiled. Was the mist hiding the danger or was the mist the danger?

"How am I supposed to get across this?" There wasn't a single Tarzan vine for me to swing on.

I ripped the hem of my shirt, tore a piece off, and released it. As the fabric dipped into the mist, it disintegrated as if it were dropped into acid. The mist bubbled and spat. I jumped out of the splash zone.

Jumping backward was such an involuntary action. My subconscious protected me from the mist from touching my skin. My active brain, unfortunately, was too slow. I made an error.

My left foot touched a stone that had a snake on it. "Crap," I cursed.

A little puff of sound was my only clue that I needed to get to safety. I turned toward the gate, and a blast of fire sprayed from the walls.

As I sprinted, I didn't focus on stepping on the correct hieroglyphics. I ran without regard. Fire shot out, trying to scorch me, and it would've if it wasn't for my Vampire speed. I was only mere seconds faster than the flames.

Once safely off the pathway of doom, I collapsed to my knees and watched the fire shoot and spit. It blazed, and the heat from the tunnel pricked my skin. I wondered how long it would take before it would cease. There was nothing for me to do but wait. I didn't want to risk learning how fast I could heal from a burn.

As I observed the inferno, I wanted to use this chance to rest, but my mind refused. My thoughts kept turning to Kanyon and the fear in his eyes. I hoped that Blayde got there in time.

It was one of these times I wished I wore a watch. I didn't know how long I sat watching the fire rage, but it eventually died. I had sat there long enough to mentally and physically feel like I'd had a breather. But not enough that I felt like a brand-new woman.

I stood, ready to try once more. I touched my chakrams hanging on my belt for a small piece of comfort. I psyched myself up, stretched my head from side to side, and crossed my arms in front of me to get my blood pumping.

"I got this. I can do this. I was born for this. All I have to do is not die. Yeah, I can do that. Easy peasy...Man, I better get a truckload of brownies after this," I said, squishing the hornet's nest of nerves in my stomach.

I moved carefully, mindful of the placement of each step. My toe first followed by my heel, almost like a ballet dance. Smoothly and gracefully, I placed each foot on the right stone.

I approached the pit of acid mist. I studied the walls and found that some of the stones did, in fact, have an eye on them. Some were high, some halfway in the mist, and some in between.

I stared at the pit and tried to judge the distance. Could I jump it? I wasn't sure. In training, I never attempted to see how far I could jump. I knew I could jump high, but how far? I had no idea. The pit was as wide as a school bus. Was jumping worth the risk?

I headed back to the start, and then back to the pit. I counted how many steps were in between. I did it over and over and over again, learning it. Committing it to memory.

"One potato, two potatoes, three potatoes, four. I don't really want to go across this floor," I sang like a child jumping rope—it helped pass the time and it was amusing.

I stopped by the pit, and I entertained the idea of using my chakrams to get me to the other side. I would have to stab each eye stone to make it across. But my weapons weren't shaped like knives. I didn't even know if it was possible to spear the walls with them. Another thing to add to my list to expand my training—if I emerged victorious.

Each stretch down the tunnel, I increased my speed, trying to muster the courage to jump the pit. At a slow jog, I fixated my gaze on the ground. With a popping noise, the gurgling mist earned my regard.

That was when I made my mistake.

A puff emanated from the cave, and my eyes darted downward. I let out an annoyed *grr*. A part of my shoe was half on an eye stone and half on another. I only had mere seconds before the fire started. Should I retreat to the start and wait it out? Or did I take a risk and test my athletic ability?

"Now or never," I muttered.

I tapped into my Vampire speed and dashed toward the bubbling pit. I stopped caring about where to step and focused on clearing the abyss.

I ran as fast as I could. I pushed my legs harder than I ever had before and angled myself to the wall on my right.

I sprang off my feet and aimed for the middle. With my right foot, I shoved off the wall in the direction of the opposite side of the pit.

For a few seconds, it was as if I was flying. My adrenaline was pumping, overpowering any other emotion. I landed on the other edge of the pit. My balance faltered, and I slipped. I threw my weight forward and crashed down on the stones. I wanted to kiss them.

I had successfully breached the acid mist. And I wasn't dead...yet.

"I'm alive? I'm alive," I squealed with glee. I didn't think that would've worked.

Another puff sounded. "Oh, come on," I screamed.

I scrambled to my feet. I didn't have a second to lose.

I sprinted once again, apathetic to where I stepped. I didn't know how far these stones went, and hopefully, it wasn't that much further. If it was, I might end up being roasted barbeque.

Fire shot out, and the heat brushed my skin like a paintbrush. The hair on my arms and the back of my neck stood at attention. I advanced a smidge faster and pumped my arms diligently. But the blaze kept pace.

I imagined a cheetah in my mind's eye and combined it with my Vampire speed. I had never tried this before, but I was running out of options.

Luckily for me, it worked.

I moved faster with the grace of a cheetah. A small piece of joy broke free. It was exhilarating to be going this quickly. If I survived, I'd have Chantel hold a radar gun to see how fast I could run.

That was when I saw it. The end of the stones.

"Yes. Thank the Angels." I fought the urge to throw a fist pump.

I crossed the last stone and skidded against the dirt to a halt. I watched the fire scorch. It was wild, and I hadn't ever been more grateful for my unique magic than I had at this moment. If I couldn't have mixed my abilities, then I would've been burnt chicken.

My stomach growled. With a sigh, I dropped my head. I was physically and emotionally spent. And now I was also hungry.

How long have I been here?

I took a minute and leaned against the cave wall to rest. I closed my eyes. I focused on Blayde and our bond. So many negative emotions swarmed me. Fury. Rage. Fear. Anxiety. Pain. Sadness. Love.

Love.

I pictured Blayde in my mind. His amber-flaked blue eyes and his scruffy beard. His rich brown hair and how it most often looked wind-blown. Bulging biceps and his oh-so-shapely butt. And his smile. His teasing smile. His smirks. And the grin that had me going jelly in the knees. I couldn't forget about his laugh. I'd listen to it all day. It was one of my favorite sounds in the world.

Happiness bloomed in my chest, and euphoria settled over me. I loved him with every part of my soul.

Love. Love wasn't easy. It didn't make everything right. Love took work. Patience. Effort. Love gave you a slice of hope to cling to in your darkest hour. It lit the way and let you know that somehow, some way, that everything would be okay.

All I had to do was get the crystal, get out of the cave, stop Jordan, and find Blayde. *Ugh, if only it was that simple.*

With a new sense of resolve, I pushed off the wall and headed deeper into the cave.

* * *

The journey through the cave was making me antsy. I needed to recover the crystal. I had to keep it away from the Dark Master at all costs.

Out of the corner of my eye, I noticed something shiny. I walked closer. This could be a trap. I bent over and studied it.

It was gold. A gold coin, to be more exact.

I didn't touch it for fear it would set something off. So, instead, I moved along. But then I spotted another. And another. And...a golden chalice?

The more I walked, the more I saw. Jewelry. Chalices. Coins. Swords. Gems. Oh my!

My mind was spinning. If I didn't know any better, I would say this was someone's trove.

The pathway led me to a giant opening in the cave. The sulfur smell was strong, as if it originated from here. It was filled with gold and an assortment of treasures. If my eyes went any wider, they would pop out of their sockets. This part of the cave was bigger than a football stadium. The ceiling was round like a giant dome. It had to have been magically altered.

In the middle of the area was a rock formation. Rocks the size of my head, stacked on top of each other. The structure was at least as tall as me. At the apex was the crystal.

I edged closer and looked around. "It couldn't be this easy. Things are never this easy, at least not in this cave," I said.

I arrived at the rock structure, and I searched for something to stand on. I found a rock and rolling it over was no small feat. I balanced on it, and my gaze fell on the crystal. My necklace had a white crystal on it. This one was blue. It shone with brilliance, and the glimmer from the gold bounced off it. It was flawless.

All that was left was for me to remove it from its glass container. I wiggled my fingers. *Hmm*, I wondered if anything would happen once I extracted the lid.

"This must have been what Indiana Jones felt like," I mused. Too bad I didn't have a bag of sand to put in its place.

There weren't any characters carved into the stone, so I went for it.

I placed both hands on the sides of the glass, lifted the lid, and sat it on the ground. Without breathing, I removed the crystal.

I got off my impromptu step stool and ogled the ornament in my hand. It was bigger than the crystal on my necklace. *Huh*. I thought all of them would be the same size to fit on the dagger's hilt.

With a shrug, I slipped the object into my pocket and turned to leave the cave.

My heart dropped. The way I'd come was blocked. How was I so foolish in not checking my surroundings? I stared at the creature blocking my path. I gulped.

Now all I had to do was fight a dragon.

Chapter Twenty-Eight

A dragon. A freakin' dragon. I thought they didn't exist, but here one was, blocking my way out. I knew it wouldn't be this easy.

I froze in my spot. Were dragons similar to dinosaurs? If I didn't move, would it see me? My feet were stapled to the ground—I couldn't move if I wanted to. My heart beat erratically, with no pattern to it.

The red dragon before me was something out of a fairy tale. Big as a house with claws out of each of its four paws. Its wings were tucked close against its body. The dragon's scales reflected light off of them and were magnificent next to the riches. If I wasn't so terrified of the dragon right now, I would be in awe.

"Thief!" a deep booming male voice said.

It was so deafening that I covered my ears with my hands. The voice bounced off the walls in my skull.

"Thief," he repeated.

I realized the dragon hadn't spoken out loud. I had heard his words in my mind. If he had the power to do that, I was afraid to know what else he could do.

My gaze connected with the dragon's, and his eyes blazed gold. He stalked toward me, each step thunderous. Taking slow steps, I backed up, my attention never leaving the mythical creature.

My legs hit a mound of valuables. It knocked me off balance, and my knees buckled. I fell into a pile, and it cascaded around me.

The sight of me in the dragon's precious possessions made everything worse. The dragon rushed at me with smoke puffing from his snout, and he only stopped when he reached me. For the first time, I got to see how sharp his teeth were. Each was serrated sawtooth points. My stomach cramped. I was sorely underprepared.

You come to steal my treasure, his voice echoed again in my head.

There was no way to answer truthfully and not get myself further into trouble. I only came for the crystal, and it wasn't really his. It was the Angel's.

"I did not come to steal your treasure." I forced bravado into my tone. It wasn't much, but it was better than sounding like a mouse.

The dragon inched forward and brought his nose to me, sniffing. If I hadn't been dehydrated, I probably would've peed my pants in terror. Every inch of me trembled.

Liar, he hissed in my head. *I can smell it on you.*

And I can smell the sulfur on you. But I didn't allow the remark to leave my tongue.

"What I have isn't yours," I bravely declared. I closed my hands into tight fists to stop them from shaking.

Everything here is mine. I will deal with you, thief. The dragon spread out its wings and flapped until he was high above me.

A bad feeling formed a pit in my stomach, turning the taste in my mouth sour.

Smoke wafted from his nostrils, and his wings flapped a gust of air toward me. I became buried in the hill of gold.

I struggled against his strike, but I refused to die via a pile of treasure. I gritted my teeth and pushed my way out. Once free, I sprinted toward the exit.

I heard it before I felt it. The sound of fire blowing after me.

Oh crap. Oh crap. Crappity-crap-crap.

I glanced over my shoulder. The dragon was flying and shooting fire from his mouth at me—only I was too fast.

Heat pricked the back of my neck, searing the ends of my blonde locks. The dragon flew overhead and dropped to the ground, blocking me.

I wondered if I could mimic him and throw fire at him. I was able to use other magical creature's abilities, so why not his?

I gathered air in my lungs and blew like I was trying to blow a hundred candles out. No fire. No smoke. Nothing. And to top it off, the dragon's laughter echoed in my brain.

He launched a blast, and I drove to the side, getting out of the path of the fire.

All right, let's try this again.

Think hot. Think fire. Think red, anger, wild.

I gathered air in my chest again when a feather-like sensation brushed my mind. Blayde was nearby. I wanted to cry in relief.

He was close. He was coming for me. We would be reunited. A team. All I had to do was get out of this stupid cave.

I needed fire.

Without a second thought, I screamed. I screamed out

all my frustrations, my fury, my hatred. Fire erupted from my throat and traveled the distance between me and the dragon. While the dragon's fire was big and consuming, mine was little and not intimidating.

No damage was done to my opponent. Were dragons impermeable to fire? I was incredibly inane for even attempting it. Plus, I now had major heartburn.

You are a Fire Mage? he asked in my mind. His head cocked, waiting for my response.

"Nope. I haven't even met a Fire Mage."

Give me what you have stolen.

Hard pass. "No can do."

Then you will die.

What had Caroline taught me? Flip my hair, smile, and I'd command the room. *Worth a shot.*

I tossed my hair over my shoulder and grinned. "You will let me leave with the crystal," I said so sweetly that it would give him a toothache.

His eyes glazed over, and he froze.

I hadn't expected that to work. Color me pink, blue, and purple because I was surprised.

His wing brushed over his eyes, and he shook his head. *You use Siren magic? Magic does not affect dragons like it does others.* His tone was full of anger.

Siren magic? Before I had a chance to comprehend his words, he flew toward me with talons outstretched.

I reacted too slowly. His massive paw swiped at me, knocking me to the ground.

His paw rested on me, keeping me flat and unmoving. A single claw was inches from my jugular. One false move and it was game over.

He tapped his claws against the ground. His head tilted, he asked, *What are you if you aren't a Fire Mage or a Siren?*

"I'm a butt-kickin', name-takin' Huntress," I sassed.

A Huntress? he repeated.

"Yep. And I need the crystal to stop the Dark Master, or it's lights out for me."

Dark Master, the dragon mused.

Hearing his voice in my head was starting to feel normal. Almost.

"Yes. The Dark Master is hunting down all the crystals and the dagger. He currently has people outside the cave. If I don't get the crystals before him, who knows what would happen to the world as we know it? I'll find a way to kill the Dark Master."

The dragon brought his nostrils to my body and took in a large sniff, then withdrew slowly, inch by inch. I sucked in a breath, no longer feeling the fear of death.

In a swift motion, faster than I could blink, he transformed from a dragon to a Human. There were no bones cracking like Blayde and the other Shifters. Instead, a haze expelled from him.

I gagged and covered my nose with my dirty, sweat-stained shirt. It smelled strongly of sulfur, and it stung my eyes.

"Oh, my gosh, man! Put some clothes on!" I covered my face with my hand. That was the last thing I wanted to see.

"You may uncover your eyes, Huntress." His voice was smooth and sweet, like cream cheese frosting.

He was now wearing—what appeared to be—a red toga. I gave him the once over, assessing out the situation while he stood there amused.

He had no hair on the top of his head, but his red beard made up for it. It covered the line of sight to his neck and was in the shape of a square. His toga displayed his muscles, and he was ripped. His muscles had muscles, and I wasn't sure how that was possible.

The pungent odor cleared, and I pulled my shirt back into place. "Where did the sulfur smell come from?" I asked before I remembered my manners.

"Brimstone," he corrected with a twitch of his mouth.

"Same thing." I half smiled, still uneasy about the man in front of me.

He took a few steps and put his palm on my shoulder. I stiffened at his touch.

"You are much more than a Huntress. You will accomplish what you set out to do." He held out his free hand in a fist, then opened it to reveal a bracelet made out of twine with a crystal charm. It was identical in size and shape to the one on my necklace, except it was blue.

I stuffed my fingers into my pants pocket and pulled out the crystal I'd collected from the stone. My brows pinched together. Which was the real thing?

He nodded to my hand. "Decoy."

His hand slid off and plucked the decoy from me and proceeded to toss it over his shoulder. He transferred the crystal to me and closed my fist around it.

"Thank you, Mr. Dragon," I said.

"Arlo. My name is Arlo."

"Cedar Hastings." I pointed to myself, then shook my head. Why I did that, I had no idea. "So, how long have you been here for?"

"Many, many moons. I estimate more than a few thousand years," he said casually.

My jaw dropped. I hadn't expected that.

He continued, "I became the new protector after my mentor retired."

"Protector?" I asked, confused.

"The Angel gave the first Council Shifter this crystal and told him to protect it at all costs. He sought after my kind in protecting it. A wise dragon flew over to this land before the Humans had settled on it. Every five thousand years, a new protector is chosen to keep the crystal safe until the warrior who seeks it comes for it."

Dang. He thought I was that warrior. It couldn't be a coincidence that he'd used the same word as the prophecy.

The heavy weight of what my future held threatened to crush me. I didn't know how to be the savior everyone expected me to be. Instead of confessing my insecurities, I merely said, "Thank you."

He gently gripped my left bicep. His hold seared my skin, and I screamed in agony. A chuckle crossed his lips, and I stared at him in horror.

Dragons were officially my least favorite Shifter. Not that I would admit that out loud.

He removed his hand, and the pain disappeared. I shot him a glare. I had so many specific words I wanted to say to him, but I kept my mouth shut. I had enough self-preservation to recognize I shouldn't piss off the man who'd turned into a giant, red dragon.

"We are now connected. If you are ever in need of me, I will know and come to you. Farewell, Cedar Hastings." He bowed and laced his hands behind his back.

I looked at my arm, and a small dragon tattoo was where Arlo had burned me. I made a mental note to learn more about dragons and their weird magic.

I gave a farewell nod and turned to the exit. I stopped and faced Arlo once again. "Come with me. You don't need to be here if the crystal is gone."

His lips pursed. "Maybe one day. But today is not that day."

"Could you at least help me with the Dark Master's man outside?" I asked. It would be fun to scare Jordan to death.

Arlo nodded, and in a blink, he was in his dragon form. A sulfur—I mean brimstone—haze emitted from him. I coughed and waved in front of my nose.

Man, that smell happened every time. Just another reason why I preferred my wolf over a dragon.

Cedar Hastings, get on my back, he said in my head.

He dropped a wing to the ground, and I climbed up. Sitting on his back, I held on to his red scales.

His wings flapped, and we were in the air. He soared toward the tunnel of the cave.

We were too big. There was no way this hulking dragon would fit into the cave's tunnel. A scream at the tip of my tongue was halted. Arlo surprised me.

My eyes widened as Arlo shrank beneath me. He was no longer the size of a house. He was more comparable to a bear, but way, *way* longer in length.

Once I wasn't afraid that we would get stuck, I enjoyed the wind blowing past us. Arlo's speed was faster than anything I have ever experienced. If I had it my way, this would be the only way I traveled from now on. He blew by the acid mist, and I couldn't wait to be out of here.

Most of all, I couldn't wait to see the look on Jordan's face when I arrived riding a dragon.

Chapter Twenty-Nine

"Arlo," I said in a wave of panic. "Arlo!"

What was he doing? Was he trying to get me killed?

Arlo increased his speed and barreled toward the gate. He wasn't slowing. *Why wasn't he slowing down?*

"Arlo! The gate," I screamed. I clenched his scales.

Crazy dragon Shifter!

I shrieked, and Arlo matched my intensity with a roar. At the last second, the gate opened, and he sailed through effortlessly.

Once on the other side, Arlo tripled in magnitude. I tightened my hold on his red scales as he grew back to being the size of a house.

Arlo flew out of the cave and climbed higher in the sky. Down below, Jordan was there staring at us. His gawking only lasted a few seconds before he dashed to the car and pulled out a sword.

Hah! Like that would save him against a dragon.

Is that him? Arlo's words resounded in my head.

"Yep. That is the coward who works for the Dark

Master. Don't barbeque him too badly. I need to ask him some questions and get my necklace back."

I can do that, Cedar Hastings, Arlo spoke in my mind.

He roared, and I clamped my hands over my ears to lessen the sound.

By now, Arlo was high enough that I could see the tops of the trees. Jordan had positioned himself in the middle of the clearing. I could barely make out that he was standing in a battle pose. Poor schmuck didn't know what was coming for him.

Arlo's nostrils flared and huffed out smoke. I knew what was happening next. *Bring on the fire, baby!*

Arlo sucked in a breath, then released it, shooting a stream of flame from his mouth. Without warning, Arlo swan dived toward our adversary. I hardened my grip and muffled my screech.

Jordan raised his sword, ready to strike if Arlo got close. But Arlo had a plan.

Arlo backed off when we were a small distance from Jordan. In the air, Arlo circled his target. He blew a stream of fire and encased Jordan in a blazing ring.

As if on the same wavelength as me, Arlo set me down on the ground. I charged up to the barrier of heat and I read the apprehension on Jordan's face before he schooled his features.

"Nice entrance," Jordan said.

"Pretty cool, huh?" I smiled.

I wanted so badly to go back to the friendship we used to have. My head screamed that the Jordan I knew was long gone, but my heart—my stupid heart—had a glimmer of hope that a piece of my childhood friend was still in there.

Dropping the pleasantries, I said, "Hand my necklace over, and I'll let you live."

He responded by laughing. Had working with the Dark Master ruined his will to survive?

"You won't kill me. You don't have it in you," he barked.

He was right. I didn't have it in me to execute my childhood friend.

"I won't kill you. My dragon buddy here will." I thumbed in Arlo's direction.

Arlo helped by roaring so loud that the ground shook beneath me. I stumbled and shot Arlo a glare. Hopefully, he got the message not to roar that loud next time.

Jordan held my sanity chain in his fingers. "Is this what you want? Too bad I can't let you have it."

"Give it to me, and the dragon won't eat you," I bluffed.

I had no idea if dragons ate people, and with luck, I would never have to find out.

"No." Jordan tossed the crystal into the flames as if it were worthless.

I drove after it, not caring if I got torched. I needed the crystal. I needed my necklace back.

The fire burned my flesh, and I swallowed a scream. Reaching down, I picked up the crystal and the chain that had begun to melt. I tore my hand out of the inferno, and water welled up in my eyes.

My hand to mid-forearm was black. Boils already formed. I sent a prayer up to the Angels that my increased healing ability would take care of this, and I wouldn't require additional medical treatment.

I looked at the piece of jewelry, and fury erupted in me. It wasn't there. He had taken the crystal out of the metal that carried it. He had duped me. Tears of pain and frustration rolled down my cheeks.

Do you want me to eat him? I don't enjoy the taste of Humans, but I'll make an exception, Arlo's asked.

That caught me off guard. "What? No," I yelled to Arlo. I cleared my vision of any remaining sadness. I wouldn't show weakness in front of my opponent.

I wondered if my chakram fire would protect me from dragon fire. Taking a risk, I plucked my weapons off my belt and gripped each in one of my hands. I pictured their magic encasing me, and it only took a second before blue streaks danced up my arms and down every part of my body. It surrounded me from head to toe.

I stepped into the blazing ring, and Jordan's jaw was slack in shock. My chakrams had protected me, and I didn't feel a single inch of heat prickling my skin.

I took the final step into small entrapment. The circle was five by five feet. Barely any room to fight, but I wouldn't leave here without the crystal.

Jordan laughed and raised his weapon in the air. "You think you will win? Your tiny chakrams against my sword? It's cute that you think you even have a chance."

He was assuming I would meet him head-on. Good thing I wasn't planning on doing that. I had no intention of letting him get close enough to kill me.

While he was still chortling, I took the opportunity to attack. I aimed Blacky like a frisbee and threw it at his upper body, while Pinky traveled lower.

Jordan wailed, then his face masked in anger. Like boomerangs, my chakrams sailed back to me. I repeated the same strike, only this time I ran toward him.

I was sick of his games. His cruel smiles. Him thinking he would win.

Pinky and Blacky hit their marks, and I dropped to the ground. I extended my right leg and swept out his legs from under him.

Jordan fell, and his sword rolled out from his grip. My

chakrams returned to my hands, and I kicked his blade into the fire.

Finally, I had the advantage.

I jumped onto my combatant and slammed my knee into his spine, inducing him to groan. I put all my weight on him. I pressed my forearm into his shoulder blades and held him in place. My other hand brought Blacky to his neck.

There was no escaping now.

The feather-like sensation brushed against my mind. Blayde.

Blayde was close. Real close.

"Arlo, help with the fire, please," I called. I didn't watch what Arlo would do. I didn't want to take my attention off the grade-A jerk. I wouldn't let him weasel his way out.

"Jordan, where is it? Where is the crystal?" I hissed.

He responded by laughing, or at least making sounds that sounded like laughter, so I eased up on the pressure on his neck.

"Even if you get these two, there is no stopping the Dark Master. He will come for them," he coughed out.

"Where is the Dark Master? Where do I find him?"

"You don't. He will find you."

His head was to the side and the corners of his mouth turned up. All it did was boil my hatred.

"How do I kill him?" I knew getting him to actually tell me was a long shot, but I hoped for some type of clue.

"You can't. That's what is so amusing about the Huntress prophecy. You are supposed to kill him, but there is no way to." He laughed.

The rage inside me morphed into fury. Easing Blacky from Jordan, I raised my arm in the air. I wanted to hurt him. To make him pay for all the pain and anguish he'd caused.

My elbow went down and smashed into his skull, eliciting him to lose consciousness. I wanted to do more than that, but I didn't want to be like him.

Arlo was in the air, flapping his wings. The gust of wind aimed at us was powerful. My hair blew everywhere, and my shirt lifted, revealing my skin. I flattened on Jordan to ensure we didn't blow away, and even then, I wasn't positive we wouldn't.

People are coming, Arlo said in my head. He swooped down and landed over me. His four red legs surrounded me, creating a protective barrier.

Warmth pervaded my chest. I had just met him with a terrible first impression, and yet he saw me as someone worth protecting. A shadow of a smile graced my lips. I had gained an impressive ally.

Arlo stood over me, facing my left side. His tail fanned to cover the gap between his limbs, hiding me from onlookers. I could barely see around it, but what I could see filled me with joy.

Blayde raced toward us with a scowl. Anger contorted the lines on his face. He was ready for battle.

My gaze searched up and down him, noticing cuts and dried blood. Thankfully, nothing was broken—though I doubt a broken bone would've thwarted him.

Arlo gave a warning growl, and Blayde halted. Blayde sprouted claws from his fingers, and he held them out as if saying "bring it."

"Arlo, he is with me," I shouted.

Then Agrona barged out of the trees, followed by Kanyon carrying Chantel on his back. They stopped next to Blayde. They all had gashes and looked like they'd been through a meat grinder.

The red dragon roared, threatening to harm anyone who came close. A sweet gesture, really.

"Arlo! Stop! They are my friends! Stand down," I yelled.

Are you sure? his voice echoed in my brain.

"Yep. I promise."

He slowly retreated, never taking his focus off them. He hovered behind me, poised to attack if they even stared at me funny.

I smiled at them, still sitting on Jordan. Blayde ran at me at full force, while the others took cautious steps.

Blayde knelt before me and placed his hands on my shoulders, inspecting me for any injuries.

"You found me." My tone was soft and full of gratitude that he was in front of me. I watched as sadness, guilt, and outrage got replaced by relief in his eyes.

He enveloped me in a hug and lay his head on top of mine. "I will always find you, Princess."

"Can we help you with him?" Agrona asked.

Blayde and I reluctantly broke apart. He rose while I remained on the foe. I wasn't going to take any chances despite that he was unconscious.

"The crystal should be somewhere on him," I said, and Agrona switched spots with me.

"How I wished he was still awake for me to give him a piece of my mind," Agona hissed.

Kanyon searched Jordan and found the crystal in his jeans. He handed it to me before tying Jordan up.

Putting the crystal in my pocket, I watched Agrona and Kanyon place Jordan in the trunk of the car. Karma at its finest.

Blayde's fingers slipped into mine, and the ruckus from Chantel stole my attention.

"A dragon! Holy smokes! A dragon! I thought you guys were all extinct," Chantel squealed, jumping up and down. "Can I have a ride?"

"Hey, we are going to return to town. Are you okay with Chantel transporting you?" Agrona called.

I nodded. Agrona got in the passenger seat, and Kanyon started the engine. I watched them drive away.

"What's on your arm?" Blayde asked with a hint of panic, touching the spot Arlo had branded me.

The dragon tattoo was there in all its glory. I brought my burned hand to touch it and was amazed that it had mostly healed. There were no boils, no open burns, but lots of ash remained.

"Arlo gave it to me," I said.

Blayde's brows pinched, and I filled him in on the details.

"Introductions should be made."

Taking Blayde by his hand, I led him to where Chantel was standing.

"Arlo, this is my mate, Blayde, and my friend, Chantel. Blayde, Chantel, this is Arlo."

Arlo bowed his head. Chantel turned to me and said, "Do you think he will let me ride him?"

I shrugged. "Ask him, and he'll give you an answer."

Her face fell. "I'm not a dragon. I can't hear him when he is in this form."

Now it was my turn to be bewildered. I swung toward Arlo, seeking answers.

She says the truth. They cannot hear me, Arlo said in my mind.

"Then why can I?" I asked.

Blayde and Chantel wore matching confused expressions.

"You can hear him?" Chantel asked in awe.

You are more than a Huntress, Arlo paused, and after a moment he added, *I will give her a ride.*

I relayed to Chantel what was said, and she screamed in excitement. Blayde and I viewed in silence as Arlo ascended into the sky with Chantel on his back.

Blayde tugged me to him, and I slid my arms around his waist. Safe. Home. Right. He was everything I needed and so much more. I belonged with him. At his side. I could stay wrapped in his embrace forever.

"I could've lost you," Blayde whispered, hiding the cracking of his voice. Every word was laced with sadness.

I pulled back and looked him in the eyes. "You will never lose me."

His eyes held hesitation. And I didn't blame him after all this time I'd spent building walls between us. I had kept him at arm's length. I did this to us.

And now I was going to fix it.

Unwrapping from his waist, I placed my palms on his cheeks, forcing him to look me in the eye.

"Mate," I began, and the edges of his mouth turned up. "You complete me. I don't know why it took me this long to figure it out, but I can't have a future without you in it. I love you, Blayde. You are my forever."

Blayde's mouth met mine, and his hand pressed against the back of my neck, bringing me closer to him. His other hand entwined in my hair. I slid a hand down to his chest and clutched his shirt. I nibbled his bottom lip, and a low growl escaped him. He detangled from my blonde locks and hauled me to him so that no space lingered between our bodies.

Our kiss was full of passion, and we held nothing back. Feeling his emotions from the bond, I noticed a hint of fear of losing me that slowly melted away. In its place, love bloomed. He was mine, and I was his. He was my other half, and I refused to spend a day without him. Fate, for once, had done something right.

Remembering our location, I withdrew and sighed. Blayde rested his forehead against mine as we both slowed our breathing. With every kiss, it only got better.

"I love you. You are my everything. I didn't know what I was missing before you entered my life," Blayde said.

I beamed. Those three little words made my heart burst. Never in my wildest dreams did I think I would meet someone who was perfect for me. Who completed me.

"Now what?" I chuckled.

"The next step would be to complete the mate bond. Don't freak out, I won't push you. Completing the mate bond is like getting married, except it's more intense and more permanent. It will literally be forever, you and me. You aren't in any rush to decide... I don't want to force you into something you aren't ready for—" Blayde rambled.

I put my fingers to his lips, cutting off the crazy train. "All you have to do is ask."

I wanted eternity with him. I was all in, and I was never going to change my mind.

Blayde's arms encircled my hips and pulled me to him. He swung me around, and the pure joy on his face warmed me all over.

For once, I wasn't mad at Fate, because I was one lucky girl.

Chapter Thirty

Saying goodbye to Arlo was harder than I thought it would be. I had just met him, and he already felt a part of my friend gang. At some point, he shifted into his human form and greeted everyone. Before he left, he reassured me he would know when I needed him.

We ended up going back to the academy after a few days—where I got my brownie the size of my foot. Blayde and Kanyon had helped sort out the mess Jordan had created. Kanyon stayed with the Woodpine pack but promised to join us soon. I understood he had responsibilities, but we had gotten close, and it was weird to not have him with us.

Before we left, Hilt and Tammy had Blayde and I over for dinner. To say things were awkward at the beginning would be an understatement. In the end, the Alpha King softened and gave us his blessing—which was nice, but we would've completed the mate bond with or without it. I thought Tammy had been a big reason why the Alpha King came around, oh, and for the fact that I'd stopped Jordan.

Jordan. What a headache he was becoming. The Council wanted to put him in Darkmare Prison, but Blayde refused. His argument was that Jordan knew he would be sent there if caught, so he and the Dark Master would've formed a plan for him to escape. The Council eventually agreed. So, a jail cell was built at the academy.

It was strange being back at the academy again. Nothing had changed, but I had. I was no longer Defensive Huntress of the Year. I wasn't going to shy away from a fight that had no other course of action. I was going to prepare in every way possible. My life and freedom were depending on it.

Chantel received a call from Ricardo—which was long overdue. She was getting stomach pains from a high level of anxiety over not hearing from him. Ricardo would arrive tomorrow, and I would let him tell me as many jokes as he desired.

As for Councilman Ralph, I was still wary of him. Thankfully, Headmaster Hunter Grant was able to spin our impromptu trip as in-field education. The Alpha King even collaborated on the story—surprising, to say the least, but it was nice knowing he was an ally.

As for Blayde and I, we started talking about what we wanted for the mate bond ceremony. He was used to grand events that were celebrated for days, but in the end, we agreed that a small intimate gathering would be better—we would be able to limit the number of potential threats. For me, all I knew was that it didn't matter as long as it was him and me. I didn't care as long as it happened. I wanted to be bonded with him forever.

But I did know one thing for sure: I wouldn't allow my future to slip through my fingers. I wouldn't let the Dark

Master get his hands on the crystals or the dagger. I made it my mission to retrieve them first.

Nothing—*nothing*—was going to get in my way.

About the Author

Tiffani Skye is an urban fantasy romance author who is a Dr Pepper addict, a mom to three kids, and married to her best friend. When Tiffani was little, she wrote stories for the fun of it, but it wasn't until she became a mom that she realized this was her dream—to share her imagination with others to make them smile. Her hope is to provide you with an escape from your everyday worries and leave you happier than when you picked up the book.

 instagram.com/author_tiffaniskye